The Forgotten Gift

A first novel by J F Mitchell, Undiscovered Authors Regional Fiction Winner.

The Forgotten Gift

By
J F Mitchell

First edition published in Great Britain in 2007
by Discovered Authors

A Discovered Authors Diamond

ISBN13 978 -1-905108-48-0

Printed in the UK by BookForce

BookForce UK's policy is to use papers that are natural, renewable
and recyclable products and made from wood grown in sustainable
forests where ever possible

BookForce UK Ltd.
50 Albemarle Street
London W1S 4BD
www.bookforce.co.uk
www.discoveredauthors.co.uk

Acknowledgements

With thanks to those friends and family who listened patiently, encouraged wholeheartedly and criticised constructively.

Thank you too to Samuel and Quicksilver who turned up unexpectedly one day to tell me their story. I hope I got it right guys...

Love to you all, J.

Only when the last tree has died
And the last river has been poisoned
And the last fish has been caught
Will we realise that we cannot eat money.
19th Century Cree Indian

Loss

The young woman lay on her side facing the wall. The boy stood statue-like in the doorway, his eyes fixed on the slight figure in the bed. He stared, studying her profile, watching for movement, any telltale movement that could halt the panic creeping through his veins.

It felt like the length of winter before he heard the woman's faint exhalation and watched relieved as her form gently moved beneath the worn blankets. Slowly she turned to face him.

'My baby. You look so pale, sweetheart, come to me.'

Hesitating only for a moment whilst the fear passed by, its shadow rolling away over the hills for one more day, the boy ran to the bedside and threw himself into his mother's open arms.

'Oh now, honey, what's wrong? Were you worried?' she asked, feeling stifled shudders working through the body of the child as he broke down and began to sob. 'No, no, my darling, Mama's here, still here. Please, no tears. Come on now, let me see you.'

Gently taking his wet cheeks in her hands the woman lifted his face so that they looked into each other's eyes. She rubbed noses with him and made him smile through his tears. With delicate long fingers she trailed his blonde fringe across his forehead and over to one side. Her breath was warm and a little sour but he did not turn away. 'You have the most beautiful eyes I have ever seen. Did you know that?' she smiled.

'Of course,' the boy replied gently, 'I have my mother's eyes.'

That night Samuel allowed his mother to rock him gently to sleep, something his father, if he had still been around, would have said he was far too old for. He had lain in her cool slender arms, his face placed gently on her fragile chest, listening to the laboured beat of her tired heart.

Samuel had tried hard to keep awake, had hoped that his mother would fall asleep first so that he could tuck her in, make sure she was warm beneath the covers, but he had been so tired.

Mr Sanderson, his boss, had been particularly tough on him that day. He had pushed Samuel to work far harder than the other older boys. The large and unpleasant owner of the bakery had sent his youngest employee with the delivery of three huge boxes of loaves to the eatery at the far end of the village, all by himself. There were several other lads who could easily have done the job, probably in half the time it had taken Samuel, but whenever Mr Sanderson appeared with an order to fill, the others would suddenly spring into action, stop their chatting and find something convincingly industrious to do. Samuel had long since given up trying to stand up for himself on such occasions and had done as he was instructed.

Earlier that same night, just as Samuel was about to leave for home, Mr Sanderson's loud voice had stopped him.

'Where do you think you're going, boy?' he had scowled down at Samuel.

'Sir?'

'You fool! Get those scraps cleaned out!' Mr Sanderson had pushed his face close to Samuel's. 'And be quick about it, I've an important dinner to attend this evening.'

Samuel had noticed a smear of cream with a number of pastry flakes stuck in it that had congealed at the corner of the horrid man's mouth. His stomach churned as he tried not to grimace. Mr Sanderson's greed knew no bounds it seemed; even though his great gut already threatened to send his buttons careering off his trousers like bullets from a powerful gun, the awful man still found room to stuff any unsold cakes, buns and other delicacies into himself at the end of each business day.

'Sorry sir, right away.' Samuel replied, put his bag down again and moved off towards the large bread ovens.

Ever since Samuel had started work here it had been his job to clean out all the scraps and burnt crusts left behind in the bread ovens after each day's baking. He hated the time that it took, time that he would rather have spent at home looking after, and being with, his mother.

The ovens were red-hot all day, churning out load after load of sweet-smelling delicious bakes. It took a long time for the ovens to cool down enough for it to be safe for Samuel to begin cleaning them, which meant that he was the last worker to leave the bakery every day. He had tried suggesting that he clean them out each morning instead, offering to arrive earlier than everyone else and before the ovens were fired up, but Mr Sanderson had baulked at the suggestion.

'You expect *me* to get out of my bed earlier each morning just to let you in here to do your work!' he had shouted. 'You're just a lazy little good-for-nothing! You'll do it after hours or not at all. If you're not happy working the way I tell you to then you're quite welcome to leave!'

As Mr Sanderson's spittle had sprayed in his face, Samuel had made up his mind to keep any future ideas to himself.

Samuel had long ago learned to secrete the leftover odds and ends that he found inside the ovens by pushing them deeply into his pockets. He would take them home and share them with his mother to supplement their meagre diet. The scraps were invariably burnt and rather crunchy but they were free, and that was the best price for a poor boy.

It wasn't such a bad job really. But Samuel couldn't help but feel uncomfortably vulnerable as he delved into the deepest corners of the great ovens remembering, as he did so, what the bakery owner had done to him on his first day. He still had nightmares about it. As his idea of a 'joke', Mr Sanderson had sneaked up behind Samuel and closed the great metal door of the oven he was cleaning behind him, locking him inside. The

6

huge man had shouted to Samuel that he was going to cook himself a '*lazy-boy pie*' as he banged repeatedly with the heel of his hand against the door to further terrify him as he sat wide-eyed in the still-warm darkness within. Samuel had huddled near the door hugging his knees against his chest and imagined he could hear the fires being lit, could feel the metal box around him getting hotter and hotter. He had been too afraid to call out, too busy wondering what being baked to death would feel like and what would happen to his mother once he was gone. It was only a few minutes later when Mr Sanderson opened the door again and let him out, but it had felt like a lifetime to Samuel. The baker had stood there laughing with his great belly jiggling, as he pointed at Samuel's horrified expression.

'Look at you! Did you think I'd really do it?' he had bellowed, slapping his thighs, tears of laughter streaking his big red face. 'Well, you be sure never to cross me lad or perhaps I will... one day.'

Mr Sanderson had never done it again, but Samuel didn't trust the man. He had made it his habit to dangle a foot out of the oven door as he cleaned, to prevent his ever being tricked again.

The baker was fully aware that, with his mother too ill to work and his father nowhere to be seen, Samuel desperately needed to keep hold of his job. Mr Sanderson owned the only dwelling that Samuel and his mother could afford in Crossways; a tiny wooden hut near the edge of town, so their home was also at risk should Samuel ever displease his employer. The extortionate rent for their shack was taken out of Samuel's pay each week leaving barely enough to buy food for his mother and himself never mind having any left over to purchase medicine to ease his mother's pains. But there were no other jobs to be had and so every unreasonable demand that the awful man made of Samuel, he followed uncomplainingly. For the sake of his mother, Samuel had bitten his tongue and controlled his anger, each and every time.

Samuel felt exhausted. A deep and consuming tiredness seeped right down into his bones. Though he fought to stay conscious, to fix his eyes on his mother's drawn yet still beautiful face, he could not prevent his eyelids from drooping. As he listened to her gentle singing that always soothed away the day's troubles, the smile on his face began to relax and fade as he journeyed into dreams and a land full of good food and happier times.

When something woke him during the night, Samuel found himself beneath the covers and his mother quiet and still beside him. She had turned back onto her side and was facing the wall once more. Her slim body took up hardly any room in their small bed.

A gentle breeze flapped at the cover hung across the only frameless window in their home. The fire still danced behind the guard in the centre of the room. Samuel watched the tongues of flickering light travel up the walls and the thin trail of smoke make its way snakelike upwards, towards the opening in the roof. As he studied the patch of night sky that could be seen through the opening, Samuel saw his first shooting star. His mother had told him about them many times but he had never been lucky enough to see one for himself before. It winked in and out of his tiny field of vision almost before he realised what he was seeing. He screwed his eyes up tightly and wished on it, praying that no one else had seen it before him and used up its magic already.

The wish made, Samuel opened his eyes again and turned to his mother.

'Mama, are you awake? I saw a shooting star and made a wish! I wished for you always to be with me and for you to get better. Mama?' Samuel whispered to his mother's back. No sooner were the words out of his mouth than he realised that he had not wished well. He had used the word 'and' in his wish. If he had used the word 'and' that meant he had made two wishes, not one. He feared that he had wasted his first shooting star and felt annoyed with himself. But perhaps not, Mama would know, he would ask her.

'Mama?' Samuel tried again and reached out a hand from under the covers to place it on his mother's pale bare arm. She felt cool. Her arm was out of the blankets, that was all. He pulled them up over her, moving her hand gently out of the way. It slid off her hip where he had placed it and landed with a dull pat on the mattress. Mama was deeply asleep. That was good,

Samuel thought, she needed a lot of rest to get over her illness and she had not slept well for a very long time.

But Samuel knew that his mother was not really sleeping, and that her arm was not cold just from having been outside of the covers.

He had dreaded this moment for so long, had suffered nightmares, panicked about it, been sure that when it happened he would not know what to do, where to go, or who to turn to. But, as Samuel gently touched the long strands of sun-gold hair that lay draped over his mother's shoulder, the beautiful hair that had made all the women in the village jealous, as Samuel lay there singing quietly the lullaby his mother had sung to him every day since he was a babe, he felt calm inside and knew what he would do the next day.

But the next day could wait.

For the rest of that night he would stay with her, take care of her and treasure every moment before the sun would strike its fire along the horizon and end the last night of Samuel's childhood.

The dawn came too quickly, and with it the task that Samuel would be able to recall in full detail until his last breath.

It was the day of rest, the one day in the week when no one in the village worked. Today even Mr Sanderson would sit on his big fat rump in his fancy house and forget about his bakery, his profits and how he could squeeze more work for less pay out of his employees. It was the day that Samuel looked forward to more than any other, not just because he did not have to work or get up early but because it was the day that he and his mother would spend together. It was *their* day.

On cold days or during the winter months they would spend this day inside their tiny home playing games, making up stories and keeping warm in front of the fire. But it was now high summer and they had planned to spend this particular rest day in their special clearing in the woods. It was a perfect and peaceful place filled with wild flowers and flitting insects, where the tall velvet green arms of the trees reached and stretched for the sky encircling an azure patch of it just for the two of them.

Samuel lay for a moment longer imagining it; the warm sun beaming down on his mother's hair, watching her fingers work nimbly on a huge chain of multicoloured flowers. Sometimes, when she was feeling stronger, his mother would even dance for him. Barefoot through the long grass she would move like a shimmering butterfly, a crown of linked blooms adorning her hair and trailing all the way down to the small of her back. She always looked so happy there. It was as if the forest breathed fresh life into her, into both of them.

Samuel would still go to their clearing today, and he would be taking his mother with him, but there were some things that he had to do first.

Sifting through their few belongings, Samuel decided which he would take with him. There were some cooking implements;

a roasting fork, two meat skewers, a ladle and spoon, all of which he imagined he might need. The only food in the hut were the handful of crunchy burnt crusts he had salvaged from the ovens the night before, he placed them in the centre of a clean handkerchief and turned in the edges carefully, keeping all the morsels packed tightly in the middle. His clothes, few items as there were, he folded neatly so they took up as little room as possible in his deerskin bag, these were placed on top of the other items.

His mother's book lay on the uneven wooden table beside the bed. Samuel cast his eyes over her still form for a moment then turned back to the book. He longed to keep it but wondered if he should leave it with her instead. His mother had taught him how to read, how to write, and this book had played an important part in that teaching, he didn't want to leave it, or all the memories that it held, behind.

In Crossways it was no longer usual for children to be taught how to read and write. It had been decided that these skills were unimportant for the majority of the youngsters who grew up there. If you were born poor, and destined to work for the rest of your life using your hands rather than your brain, it seemed that you were considered not worth the effort or expense to teach. The school had closed its doors for the last time many years before. Now the normal way of things was for the local businesses to take on young boys and girls from a very early age in order to teach them a trade. The few families who still had a

12

desire to have their children taught, and who had the money to pay for it, employed a live-in tutor to attend to their offspring. The rest of the village's children, however, grew up ignorant of the joys of learning.

In a different place, and before Samuel had been born, his mother had been a teacher and her passion for it had never faded. She had seen to it that, even if her son was destined to work in a bakery for the rest of his days, he had the continued benefit of her teaching skills. She had shared her considerable knowledge with him and had helped to nurture in him the intense pleasure that she herself gained from being able to read and write.

Stroking the cover of her book Samuel remembered how the light had shone in his mother's eyes when she had taught him. How wonderful it had felt when she'd praised him the day he had first recited, then was able to form, the letters of the alphabet on the crisp white pages of her journal. Gently flicking through the book he looked at her neat and steady handwriting followed by his spidery scrawl as his younger self had attempted to copy out her words. They had worked together on it every night when he got back from work and also during their rest day, once a week, when nothing else forced its way in to interrupt them; building on and improving all he had learned before arriving in Crossways.

They had to be very sparing with space on the pages. Books, even ones made for writing in, ones that had blank pages for you to fill for yourself, were very expensive. A pen was also a luxury they could not afford; they had made do with a pencil. They kept their letters small, using every scrap of space on every page. When they had worn their first pencil down to a tiny stump, Samuel had wondered what they would do, but fate had stepped in and provided him with a replacement.

His mother had scolded him when he had admitted to her where the new pencil had come from but, although she had said it was as bad as stealing, she had omitted to tell Samuel to return it to where he had acquired it from. He knew that she had been secretly delighted that they didn't have to discontinue their studies. No one had any idea that Samuel was able to write so there had been no reason for Mr Sanderson to suspect that his youngest employee would have any use for his missing pencil. The day that Samuel had taken it from the bakery was still clear in his mind.

He had had to stifle his laughter on seeing Mr Sanderson on his hands and knees looking between the floorboards and under his counter in an attempt to find the illusive pencil. The man had so much money that he had a whole box of fancy paper sitting on the table in his room at the bakery and yet he had still scrambled around on the floor in search of the dropped pencil, which was by that time already secured in Samuel's pocket.

That same pencil now lay on the cover of his mother's writing book. He stared at it. No. He couldn't leave them

14

behind.

'I'm going to take your book with me, Mama. I'll take good care of it.' Samuel said softly.

He placed the book in between his clothes, tucking the fabric around all its corners so that they wouldn't get rubbed or damaged as the bag moved around. Hanging the straps over his shoulders and placing his water pouch across his chest, Samuel pulled his small fishing rod from under the bed and went to the door.

'I'll not be long Mama, I'll be back for you very soon.'

The other huts nearby were all quiet. It was rare to see anyone else around much before the time when the sun rose to its highest point, on the day of rest. Working folk were just too tired and most had nothing much to get up for in any case. Samuel still had a good few hours before he would have to be out of sight but he would need to be quiet.

Stopping only to collect the spade propped against the side of their hut, Samuel made his way towards the edge of the woods. Before the closely knitted trees swallowed him up, he cast a look back towards his home. For a moment, he saw his mother waving to him from the open window as she did every morning when he left for work. Lifting a slender ivory hand to her lips she sent him a kiss through the air and smiled as he caught it in his hand.

And then she was gone.

Her image lingered for a moment in his mind like the ghost

of something dazzlingly bright stared at for too long, but eventually she faded away. Reluctantly he turned his back on their hut and walked silently into the forest.

He took little time over the decision of where he would place his mother. There was really only one spot that would be good enough for her. A massive, healthy, and thickly-trunked tree at the far side of the clearing had always been her favourite. A tumble of blue and white flowers growing around the foot of the great tree nodded slowly in the morning air as Samuel made his way towards them. It looked as if they were agreeing, very solemnly, with his choice.

Concentrating deeply, Samuel walked back and forth in the dappled shade cast by the thick, widely spread branches above him. Getting down on his knees he ran his open palms over the earth at his feet until he found it; a safe area under the soil where the roots of the ancient tree did not venture. He could sense this space beneath the ground and knew that his mother would be welcomed there.

The digging would have been hard work even for one twice Samuel's age but something inside him took over and as the ground opened up to his spade Samuel never wavered for a moment in the task. Before returning to collect his mother he travelled a little further into the forest to wash in the stream there. He wanted to be clean for her; he didn't want to get any mud on her clean pale skin.

He wrapped her carefully in a large blanket that she had

embroidered herself, with the images of trees and forest animals, and gently raised her up from the bed and into his arms. She had been so very slim, so fragile and barely taller than he was himself. She felt so light; nothing compared to the heavy crates of loaves that he hauled around all day at the bakery. The enormity of what he was doing almost broke through his resolve, but he fought against it. He had this last thing to do for his mother and he refused to fail her; he had to be strong.

Walking carefully, stepping over twigs and exposed plant and tree roots, Samuel made his way back through the trees to their special clearing. On the way he paused only once to gather his strength before reaching the place he had prepared.

He laid her, ever so gently, on the ground and opened the blanket a little so that he could see her face. She looked so peaceful. The lines around her eyes that had lately grown deeper as her pain had increased had now smoothed out and were gone. The dancing air teased past Samuel and played with a strand of his mother's bright hair.

'These are for you Mama.' Samuel said, placing a small bunch of the blue and white flowers on her chest. He leaned in close and kissed her cool forehead.

'I shall miss you always, Mama. I love you.'

After it was over and Samuel had washed the grave-soil from his body and clothes, he decided that there was one more thing he wanted to do before he turned his back on the village, hopefully forever.

His mother would not have approved but Samuel pushed that knowledge aside as soon as the image of Mr Sanderson passed through his mind.

Samuel remembered all too clearly the look of disgust on Mr Sanderson's face when he had asked him for an advance on his wages to buy medicine for his mother. The way he had shouted at him in front of the other bakery workers when he had asked to take a day off to care for her when she was going through a particularly bad time and needed him at home. The man's expression of contempt when he had caught Samuel crying one day over the hopelessness of their situation. Samuel felt all the misery and sadness over losing his mother redirect into blood-boiling anger and he had chosen where to direct that anger. There was only one way to hurt Mr Sanderson and make him feel just the slightest sliver of the pain Samuel now carried. Only one place that Mr Sanderson felt anything at all: his business, his precious bakery.

Samuel moved like a cat through the dozen or so other wooden huts, which dotted the side of the track that led into the village. He passed the rotting hulk of the school building, now in such disrepair that it was home to only rats and birds. The desks and chairs had long since been stolen and broken up for firewood, the blackboard covered with moss and ivy. His mother had never taught at that school, it had been closed already when they had arrived in the village, but still it had saddened her every time she saw the terrible waste of it.

As he stealthily continued, Samuel passed by the homes of the richer folks, then the eatery, the clothes shop, the cobblers and the bar, as he moved up the main street. Then Samuel spotted Quicksilver, the butcher's dog. He was up ahead on the front porch of Mr Cardell's shop, and the sight of him brought Samuel to a sudden stop.

Quicksilver was a massive dog. He was huge and powerfully built with a vibrant silver coat and large silver eyes to match. All the children in the village were afraid of him, and many of the adults were too. Their fear was mostly because of the dog's unusual appearance and size but mainly it was due to his bark. Samuel had heard it only the once but that had been enough; Quicksilver's bark was immense.

The great silver dog was asleep, one back leg periodically jerking back and forth causing his claws to scratch at the wooden boards of the shop's veranda; he was dreaming. Samuel thought hard. He wasn't afraid of Quicksilver, but he *was* afraid that if the dog awoke suddenly, a bark might alert the whole village to his presence.

Samuel composed himself, then closed his eyes.

With his mind he recreated the image of the street that lay before him and everything in it. In his mind, Samuel crossed that dusty street, walked quietly up the three steps onto the veranda and sat down by the dog's side. Gently he lifted

Quicksilver's huge and heavy silver head onto his lap. With his voice no more than a breezy whisper Samuel spoke to the dog.

'Quicksilver, hear me. It's Samuel. I'm your friend. I need you to wake up now but I want you to keep ever so quiet for me. I'm across the road from you. There's nothing for you to worry or bark about. All I want you to do is open your eyes and see me, stay where you are and keep quiet. I don't want to wake everyone up. Do you understand?'

Samuel heard a guttural rolling sound vibrate through the dog's throat and felt the rumble of it against his thigh. The sound was barely audible, even in his mind, but at once Samuel knew that the enormous animal had heard and understood him.

Samuel opened his eyes to look at the real street. Across the road Quicksilver was awake and had raised his head to look intently at him. Samuel nodded, once, and Quicksilver lowered his head to rest it again on his huge silver paws. He didn't make a sound as Samuel passed him by and made his way towards the bakery.

As Samuel lit the pile of dry rags he had stacked in the very centre of the bakery floor he imagined Mr Sanderson's face looking down on his beloved business from his bedroom window in his huge, comfortable home; the home that was paid for by the work of the poorly paid employees whom he treated so badly. The mouth-watering aromas of baking bread, scones and pies would today be replaced by the expensive reek of his bakery

20

going up in flames.

It would take a while for the fire to really catch hold. But the weather had been very dry lately and Samuel knew how to get a good fire going, he had needed to learn that skill to keep his tiny home warm during the cold nights and bitter winters. Mr Sanderson had a maid who lived in his home and took care of such things for him. Samuel wondered if Mr Sanderson had ever really done anything for himself. It would be a while before the first ghostly fingers of smoke would travel on the breeze to the nearest house to the bakery: Mr Sanderson's. But by the time the big man roused his lazy bones Samuel hoped that it would be too late to save the building.

'Good riddance!' Samuel muttered as he left by the back door with half a dozen brand new pencils stuffed into his trouser pocket.

Quicksilver's nose was twitching, his head bobbing slightly as he smelled the air. Samuel looked into the dog's eyes as he walked quickly by.

'It's all right boy, nothing for you to worry yourself about,' Samuel whispered to him as he passed.

There was no one whom Samuel would miss in the village, no one except for Quicksilver.

'Goodbye boy,' Samuel said quietly before quickening his pace to a softly-footed jog.

There had been some snuffling noises from one of the huts as he passed by and for a moment Samuel had stopped, listening carefully, but nothing had come of it, no one emerged, it had just been a sleeper turning over in bed. He finally made it all the way back to the forest clearing without seeing anyone.

On reaching the clearing again Samuel collected his belongings and stood for a few minutes, thinking. With his bag on his back, water pouch slung across his chest and his fishing rod in his hand there was nothing more to hold him back. The village and everything he had known for the last five years lay behind him; in front of him lay trees and more trees, stretching on tall and wide, covering the land for... he had no idea how far.

He had heard stories of those brave enough, or stupid enough, to have ventured into the forest. Tales of men who had seen terrible things; giants and flesh-eating monsters, creatures that could disguise themselves as trees then devour you whilst you slept in their branches. But Samuel was not one easily led by the yarns spun by bored workers after they had downed a few mugs full of Bearclaw at the end of a difficult week.

Samuel figured that what lay ahead of him could be no worse than what was behind. Besides, once Mr Sanderson figured out who had destroyed his livelihood he would surely have a taste for vengeance. It was likely that he would send out a group of boys and men to hunt Samuel down along the only other way out of that dead place; the road over the hills. It wouldn't cross Mr Sanderson's mind that a thirteen year old boy would instead choose to travel into the dense forest, alone.

A gentle breeze rustled the leaves on the trees, set the ferns to dancing and brought the scents of the forest to him.

Come on. Come in. The great forest seemed to say to him, and Samuel heard her call.

'Until we meet again, Mama.' Samuel said quietly and nodded towards his mother's unmarked resting place as he walked across the clearing and disappeared between the trees.

2

Beginnings

When Samuel and his mother Lily had come to the shabby and unfriendly village of Crossways five years before, it had been out of necessity rather than choice. They had travelled for many days along the dusty trail that had led them over the hills and away from their home with his father.

Samuel's mother had been forced into marrying by her parents. She had been by far the most beautiful girl in her home town of Genesis and much desired by all the single men there. Many of the married men of Genesis also longed for her to be theirs but Samuel's mother had never shown interest in any of them. She had been a brilliant student at her school and by the time she had finished the last year there, she exceeded even the teachers in knowledge.

Due to her obvious intelligence and, if the truth were known, even more to do with the way in which Lily's beauty and grace impressed the young man who interviewed her for the post, she had been accepted to take up the position as chief librarian at the town library once her schooling days were over.

Over the last few days before he finally retired, her aged

snowy-haired predecessor had shown Lily around the well-stocked shelves. The old librarian, Mr Hardy, had shuffled around explaining his filing systems and pointing out books of particular rarity and value. Lily sensed that the whole time the odd little man spoke to her, all he was thinking about was how wonderful it was going to be to leave all this behind and be able to read continuously, without any interruptions from wretched customers.

Both her age, and the fact that she came from one of the lowliest families in town, would usually have been barriers against Lily being offered such a post in the very grand Genesis Library but she proved herself more than able to fill Mr Hardy's shoes.

The building was a joy to work in; it was the most impressive and beautiful of all in Main Street. Its thick whitewashed walls kept the place cool during the summer months and held in the heat when winter howled outside. Lily loved being there, sorting out books, putting them into categories and reading whenever she could.

Before the new librarian came to work there the library was only rarely visited by the wealthier folk of the town. But soon after the word went round that there was a 'change of scenery' within the great white walls, and a scene worth taking the time to gaze at, the number of town men who suddenly took to the joys of reading was quite surprising. When Lily carefully filed their returned books on the library shelves, she had no way of knowing that many of them had never even been opened during their time away from the building.

It was not long before Mr Cuthbert, son of the town's mayor, had started to appear at the great doors of the library on a regular basis. Lily was never vain about her looks, in fact it was true to say that she was not even aware of the effect that her beauty, gentle ways and graceful movements had on the men of the town. So, when Mr Samuel Cuthbert began to show an interest in her she had at first thought him merely friendly and an avid reader like herself. But, after his fifth visit in as many days, Lily came to realise that his interest lay more with the librarian than with the books on the shelves.

She had been flattered; he was quite handsome and seemed pleasant enough, but it was not in her mind to be courted and marriage was a thing that she, unlike most of the other girls in town of her age who paraded themselves like prize cattle, had never spent any time considering. It seemed to Lily that a great deal of effort was wasted over the art of attracting a husband. To her it was all a mystery and she was happy for it to remain just that.

She had her books, her love of the countryside and its animals. What more did she need? Nothing felt so good to Lily as sitting beneath a big old tree with an open book in her lap. With her back to the warm trunk, the wild and free woodland creatures scampering all around and with the sounds of the town far away, she felt totally at peace. What use had she for marriage? Most girls seemed to get married just to have someone to look after them and buy them things. She neither wanted nor needed that.

Although Lily's wage at the library was very poor compared to those who had held the job before her, the pittance that she took home to her parents each week was still enough to feed and clothe them all. Indeed, it was more than anyone else in their neighbourhood was bringing in. But Lily's father squandered it.

Bitter at not being able to work for his own money, after an accident with a new threshing machine had left him with one arm and a taste for Bearclaw, Lily's father managed to drink most of her earnings before her mother had a chance to fill their larder with it.

So, when Mr Cuthbert had called on Lily's parents, arriving on his chestnut mare in their grubby little lane, immaculately suited and oozing charm, Lily's father could hardly believe his luck. Lily had returned from her day at the library to find the stunning horse pawing the ground restlessly outside her home. She had gone to the creature and calmed it, with her face close to the horse's she had hummed a quiet tune and looked into its huge brown eyes. The great horse was settled and at peace when Lily had ducked under the tarpaulin, that served as a front door to her shabby home, and found Mr Samuel Cuthbert (Junior), son of the mayor of Genesis, seated inside.

He had looked so out of place there, sitting between her mother and father, his crisp white shirt brilliant against the grime that clung to her parents' scruffy clothes. She gave the young man a polite curtsey, her eyes flitting from one parent to the other looking for an explanation. The explanation that she found there chilled her heart. Surely it couldn't be true? But she saw that it was.

She had been *sold*.

For a lump sum, enough to pull her parents out of the filthy existence they lived in and into a sweet little cottage closer to the centre of town, she had been promised in marriage to Mr Cuthbert.

She had managed to hold her tongue whilst the mayor's son had continued to sit there chatting amiably with her parents. She had even managed not to pull her hand away when Samuel Cuthbert had taken hold of it, brought it to his lips and kissed her skin. Lily had stood there dumbstruck, as the young man had disappeared through the tarpaulin. She had heard the scrabbling hooves of the mare struggling to find purchase on the muddy track as Mr Samuel Cuthbert had driven her into a gallop to celebrate his acquisition. She had felt the horse's pain as sharp heels where thrust into her ribs, taking her breath away, as she was forced to her rider's will. Lily had stood there motionless, taking it all in, until the sound of the horse's hooves were swallowed by closer more domestic and familiar noises. Only then did she turn to stare at her parents.

'How *could* you?' she had asked them in a whisper.

'What d'you mean girl, you like him don't you?' her mother

had looked quizzically into her daughter's face. 'He's a fine looking fellow isn't he?' she winked at Lily.

Lily's skin crawled, 'A fine looking fellow? Does that really matter to you mother or are you more interested in how much money he has? Or should I say, how much money *you're* going to get?' Lily asked bitterly.

'Don't you take that tone with us, young Miss! It's a better match than you could ever have hoped for. He's the mayor's son!' Her father was on his feet now, standing before her, his face pushed close to hers. The stale smell of Bearclaw hung around him like a foul cloud.

Lily took a step back from him, 'I don't love that man and I won't marry him. You had no right to promise me to him. No right at all.' she said it firmly but quietly.

'You'll do exactly as you are told to, you little witch!' her father exploded at her and before she had time to react he had lifted his one good hand and struck her hard across the face.

'Oh! Not her face! Don't spoil her face you fool!' Lily's mother shouted.

Lily had reeled from the blow but had forced herself to keep upright. Turning from her father she had walked outside with the imprint of his hand burning scarlet on her pale cheek.

With no one to turn to for help, and nowhere to go, Lily had eventually been worn down to her parents will. The preparations for the wedding and the wedding itself had passed

29

her by in a blur. Her wedding night had been an experience that she had not taken part in; she had hovered outside of herself and just let her new husband do what he wanted. She felt no more important to him than his horse; she was there to fulfil a purpose; to look good in his company and do as she was told which, for the sake of peace, she mostly did without complaint.

Her parents never did move from their filthy home. They received the money promised them by her new husband, more in fact, but her father had found better ways to spend it than investing in new property and Lily's mother had done nothing to stop him frittering it all away.

Lily threw herself into her work at the library; the only joy she had left, but that wasn't to last for long. Her new husband became more and more aware of how much attention his pretty young wife attracted from all the other men in town and soon he insisted that she give it up.

'It's not as if we need the money!' he had shouted at Lily when she had broken down on hearing his demand.

Try as she did, there was no way she could make him understand how much being around all those books meant to her.

'Look, if you'll stop wailing on about it, I'll allow you to teach a little at the school instead,' he had offered.

Lily had looked up at him, her face blotchy, eyes puffy from crying. It had been the only compromise her husband had offered so Lily had seized on it before he had time to change his mind.

Teaching children had been something that she had never before considered. But as she shared all the things from the books she'd read, and heard the children discussing them amongst themselves, it gave her life a new focus and purpose. To see how some of the youngsters took it all in and thrived on it, just as she had done, filled her with joy.

So long as she was around whenever her husband wanted or needed her, he had no complaint with her new position and, in that area of her life at least, she found contentment. However, things were soon to change dramatically for her when, returning from a visit to the doctor's, she had relayed the news that she was carrying a child. Messrs Samuel Cuthbert – Senior and Junior – had been delighted with the announcement.

'At last! Better be a boy,' her husband had said. As if that was all that mattered to him.

Samuel's birth had been a difficult one. Lily had been confined to her bed for several weeks before his arrival and for many months afterwards. Her health was never to be the same again. Both her husband and father-in-law had been ecstatic with the 'outcome'.

'He's a healthy looking chap! Wonderful, a new Cuthbert to continue the line. The future mayor!' her husband's father had said when he had first been introduced to his new grandson. 'Well done lad, very well done!' he had bellowed and slapped

31

Lily's husband on the back as if *he* had done all the hard work.

Lily couldn't help feeling that her husband and his father saw her beautiful baby boy more as an object that they could take possession of and mould as they saw fit, rather than as a unique and wonderful new person. Though neither man wanted to hold the child; it seemed to be her job alone to care and show him affection.

'Never mind little one, I have more than enough love and cuddles for you,' Lily had whispered into Samuel's soft blonde curls as he lay snoozing against her chest.

Word was sent to Lily's parents about the baby's arrival but neither of them chose to come and meet the child.

Lily had not returned to teaching at the school, her health did not offer itself to the task and in any case her husband believed that she should commit all her time to their young son. This was something she did gladly and with all her heart. But, when young Samuel was old enough to attend school his father had insisted that his mother teach him at home instead. Lily had tried to explain that it would be good for Samuel to mix with other children of his own age but her husband wouldn't hear of it. He did not want his son wasting time making playmates, or on any studies that he himself thought frivolous. Lily's gentle persuasions on the matter only angered him. The conversation was closed.

Young Samuel was a complete wonder to his mother. Every

day she felt blessed to have him.

When Samuel's father wasn't too busy he would call his wife and young son to him at the end of the day to find out how Samuel was progressing. But he never played any games with the boy or took him up onto his knee for a story and there were never any hugs or displays of emotion, all of which saddened Lily. All he seemed interested in was how clever the boy was and how well he was coming along in his studies. Lily would try to tell her husband what Samuel had done that day; whether he had been playing outside in the nearby fields, painting pictures or looking at books with her, but her husband waved her words away impatiently. It soon became more and more obvious that the only thing his father was interested in was knowing how quickly his son would be ready to start learning about the 'family business'.

Lily's father-in-law had passed away from a heart attack when Samuel was just three years old and her husband had then taken over the position of mayor of the town. The position of mayor had passed down through the Cuthbert family for many generations and now it was becoming clear to Lily that whatever her young son's potential, whatever his strengths and interests, all he would ever be allowed to do would be to become the next mayor of Genesis. It seemed that his father, and his grandfather, had mapped out Samuel's life, even before he had been born.

Every creative and loving thing that the boy did was just so much wasted time according to his father. Time when he could have been learning about paperwork or being taught the importance of making as much money as possible out of any given situation. Lily didn't know what to do, the idea of her beautiful, bright son being forced to live his life in a way that she knew wouldn't suit him made her feel sick to her stomach. She could visualise how miserable Samuel would be stuck in a stuffy office all day, shut away from the sunlight and fresh air, but she had no influence over her husband's decisions; he had made that quite clear over their years of marriage.

The turning point came on the day that Samuel turned eight years old. His father appeared home early with his son's birthday present. A young stallion, his jet-black coat gleaming in the sun, stood towering over Samuel Junior. Lily ran her hand over the horse's side and could sense that, although he was young and still half-wild, he had a good and gentle heart. But, as she watched her husband lift their young child onto the horse's back, not giving him a saddle to sit on, reins to hold, not waiting until he had even been given proper lessons, something began to kindle in her soul.

Standing with her eyes closed Lily had reached out with her mind to the young stallion.

'It's all right, no harm will come to you. Be gentle with my little son, be calm.'

The horse heard her and gently snorted and shifted beneath the wide-eyed boy on his back. Samuel leaned carefully over the horse's neck.

'Isn't he beautiful Mama?' he had smiled down to her.

And then it happened. When Lily next connected her mind with the horse to reassure and calm it once more, she sensed another person in the unheard conversation, a young and very familiar voice:

'Good horsey, I won't hurt you. Good, beautiful horsey.'

It was her son's voice in her head. He was using his mind to talk to the horse too. The gift that she had always had, that she had thought was hers alone, she knew now was shared by her son. The love she felt for him tumbled through her like adrenalin as she opened her eyes again and looked up into Samuel's beaming face.

'Mama!' he said aloud. He had also sensed his mother's connection with the horse and seemed delighted by it.

'Sit up properly, boy! You can't ride a horse like that. Come on, dig your heels in and get him moving.' The voice of Samuel's father pierced the special moment between mother and son.

'He'll move in a moment, Daddy. He's not quite ready.'

Mr Cuthbert's brow furrowed in confusion, 'What the devil do you mean? The horse does what you tell it to do, not what it wants, or when it wants. Do as you're told, boy, dig in.'

Samuel had looked down at his mother then.

'Don't look at her! I'm your father, do as I tell you!' his father shouted in annoyance.

Samuel considered for a moment whilst stroking the horse's

strong neck, running his hands over the tightly knotted muscles in the stallion's shoulders.

'No Daddy.' Samuel looked into his father's eyes and spoke gently, 'I'll just wait until he's ready.'

Lily's look of admiration at her son's compassion turned to horror as her husband lifted his hand high above his head. His face contorted with anger at being defied as he brought his broad hand down with all his force on the horse's rump. The sound of contact as his open hand hit the horse was startling enough, like a gun going off at close-quarters, but the almost human scream that came from the young stallion as it took off across the meadow was terrifying.

Samuel had held on bravely for the whole length of the field, his body bucking around on the animal's back as the horse's hooves tore at the ground throwing up great clumps of grass and earth in its wake. Samuel's small legs gripped tightly to the sides of the powerful beast, his hands wound deeply in its glossy mane, as it careered towards the fence that bordered the field. But even with both his mother and himself calling with their minds to calm the bolting horse, it could not be slowed.

The fence was high, too high for the horse to make it over. Samuel could see what was going to happen. He strained to steer the head of the pounding stallion, now covered with thick streaks of sweat, over to the left. He tried to get it to turn, if only he could get it to run itself out in a circle, just to keep running until it had escaped its fear, but it was no use.

Terrified, the inexperienced horse thundered on, the fence loomed closer and Samuel had no choice. He loosened his grip on the horse's mane and threw himself clear. By the time his mother and father had run across the field to where Samuel lay, the horse's screams of pain were mere whimpers and snorts.

The brave horse had so nearly made it over.

He lay on the ground speared by two of the wooden fenceposts. They pierced his strong sleek belly that now spewed-forth thick dark-red blood.

Samuel's mother ran over to where Samuel lay covered in mud and grass. His father marched on past his son and went instead to look at the horse.

Lily ran her hands carefully over her son's body, 'Thank goodness, oh thank goodness! Are you all right my darling? How do you feel? Are you in pain?' Samuel shook his head, accepted her fierce hug and buried his face into her shoulder.

'Bloody animal! I'll have that man's job, so I will!' Samuel's father ranted and pulled at his hair. 'He told me it was broken, he told me it was a Goddamned bargain! Just wait until I see him, I'll be getting my money back in triple, I can tell you!'

Lily stared incredulously at her husband's back. He had not even cast their son a glance to check that he was unhurt.

'Your son is fine,' she said to him bitterly, through gritted teeth. 'He hasn't broken anything. Not even his *neck*!' she shouted.

'What?' at last he turned to look at his wife and son, 'Of

course he's fine, he's a Cuthbert,' then turning back to the horse, 'but what am I going to do with this mess?'

Samuel gently pulled his mother's arms from around him and got to his feet. He walked over to the young horse whose sides were shuddering with the effort to keep breathing.

'Come away from it Samuel. You'll get covered in blood,' his father called.

Samuel gave him a scathing look and crouched down by the horse's head. He placed his small grubby hands gently on the stallion's neck and closed his eyes.

'I'm so sorry. I know you're suffering my beautiful one. I'll help you.' Samuel thought this to the horse, speaking to it again using his mind.

He laid his brow against the brow of the horse for a moment and the young stallion's breathing seemed to quieten, just a little. Samuel then got to his feet and strode over to his father. Samuel Cuthbert Senior flinched, stunned by the speed of the boy's hand as he snatched the revolver from the holster on his father's hip.

'What the hell are you going to do with that?' he demanded of his young son, making a move towards him, then he stopped dead in his tracks as the boy stared at him with loathing in his eyes.

For a moment neither Lily, her husband nor their son spoke. The sun beat down relentlessly on the scene.

Young Samuel raised and pointed the gun at his father.

A streak of the horse's blood stained his forehead and the hand that held the gun was slick with it.

Unable to move, Lily, who was still on her knees at the place where Samuel had come to rest, looked on in horror.

A pathetic whinny of anguish from the stallion shattered the tension and Samuel turned his back on his father and went over to the horse.

'You come back here with that right now, boy, do you hear me?' his father shouted at him, his composure now regained.

Samuel ignored him.

'I'm sorry. Go well,' Samuel said as he aimed the gun at the horse, and pulled the trigger.

It had been later that very night when Lily had stolen silently into Samuel's bedroom and sat in the glow of the candle that she had set on his bedside table.

She looked down on him and brushed her fingers gently across his soft cheek, 'Darling?' she whispered.

'I'm not asleep, Mama, I was waiting for you.' Samuel opened his eyes and smiled up at her.

He pushed back his covers to reveal that he was fully dressed in his most casual clothes. Clothes that he was never allowed to wear in front of his father. Clothes that he loved more than any of the finery that his father paraded him around in because he knew that when his mother laid these clothes out for him to wear it meant that a day of fun, games and togetherness was on the agenda. Those special days had been filled with time spent making up stories for each other, of playing hide-and-go-seek in the small nearby wood, of listening to his mother tell him about the wonderful dreams that she had of being like a wild and free animal darting between the trunks of massive trees and being befriended by fabulous creatures. Days he would always remember and treasure.

'These will be best for the journey, won't they Mama?' Samuel asked, gesturing at his clothes.

Lily had looked down at Samuel and nodded. As her eyes became more accustomed to the dim room she saw his packed bag at the foot of his bed and knew that he had guessed what she was thinking about doing.

'Are you sure baby? What if...' Lily's words had been silenced by Samuel's small fingers being placed gently over her mouth.

'We will be together Mama, that's all that matters,' he had said simply.

Lily had nodded and embraced her son.

That night Samuel and his mother left quietly through the front door of their beautiful and comfortable home. Behind them they left a husband and father sound asleep in his bed, completely oblivious that his most prized possessions were stealing themselves away from him.

It was late the next afternoon before Mayor Samuel Cuthbert finally admitted the truth to himself. Sitting alone in his study surrounded by important papers he realised that his wife and son had not simply gone out for the day without informing him of their intentions but had instead run off and left him. By that time Lily and Samuel were many, many miles away.

They had taken the mayor's chestnut mare, Spirit, along with them. Lily had gleefully torn up the skirt material of her wedding dress and secured the strips around the horse's great hooves to muffle his footfalls and so aid their silent escape through the sleeping town of Genesis. As they had passed by the library in the main street Lily had looked at it one last time and wished it a silent goodbye. Seated behind Samuel on the mare's broad back Lily had wound her arms tightly around her son's shoulders and squeezed.

'You're the best thing to come out of this town, Samuel, the best thing that ever happened to me,' she had whispered in his ear.

Samuel had held onto her arms, feeling how slim and delicate they were.

They travelled all that night without stopping. The horse had moved swiftly on over the sparsely wooded hills and into the open land beyond. They did not stop until later the next day when the sun was high and the heat too much for his mother to bear any longer.

Samuel gently guided Spirit to a standstill and helped his

mother down from the horse's back. He settled a blanket for her to rest on in the shade of a small crop of trees by the edge of a trickle of a stream.

'You're sure you can do this, Mama? You look exhausted.' Samuel had asked her but Lily had taken his face in her hands and kissed away his fears.

'Any life together, just you and me, will be better than what we had back there,' she had answered.

They travelled that way for many days, finding it easier to travel by night out of the glare of the sun. It seemed safer that way too in case the mayor had sent anyone out to look for his wayward family.

Samuel would slip into the villages along their way to buy supplies of food with the small amount of money that they had taken with them. He kept his head down, spoke only to the shopkeepers and always made sure that he wasn't followed back to the place where he had left his mother resting.

It soon became clear to Samuel that his mother was weakening. He saw past the brave face Lily put on for him. The travelling was taking too much out of her. They needed to find a base, a home; someplace they could settle down and start to live their new life together.

The day they crested Swallow Hill and looked down on the ramshackle village of Crossways, Samuel decided that they could travel no further. He left his mother with a little food and some water in the shady mouth of a crevice cut into the rocks and released Spirit so that she could roam free and graze.

'Wish me luck, Mama,' Samuel said and kissed his mother's brow.

'This is all wrong, my sweet, you're much too young. Perhaps we should go back? I shouldn't have taken you away.'

Samuel had looked deeply into her eyes and spoken with a calm strength that surpassed his age, 'No Mama. I am going into that village and I will find a place for us to stay. Don't worry Mama. Trust me.'

'Oh my love, I trust you, I trust you, of course I do, but...' she said, her eyes filling with tears.

Samuel silenced her by placing his hand gently across her mouth and raising his eyebrows at her. She made a little grunt of frustration but then a smile had spread behind his fingers and she had shaken her head in resignation.

She took his hand away and kissed his fingers. 'All right little man. I'll wait here like a good Mama.'

Samuel had walked down the hill and into the village alone. After asking around the shopkeepers, and those people going about their business in the main street of Crossways, Samuel learned that there was only one man in town with a possible vacancy for one as young as him.

When he returned to his mother, the globe of the sun was just beginning to flatten out on the bottom as it dipped behind the great mass of trees that spread all the way to the horizon on the far side of the town.

'Come on, Mama, time to go home.'

Samuel had helped his mother to her feet. Her strength was a little better for having spent the day resting in the shade.

'Can you walk to the village Mama? How do you feel?'

'I can make it, sweetheart, with your help.'

They both knew that turning up in the village astride a well-bred horse would raise unwanted queries. They would end up having to sell Spirit to pay their way and neither of them wanted to be forced into doing that. There was only one thing to be done.

Noticing the boy's return, Spirit ambled over towards him and his mother. The gentle horse nuzzled Samuel's neck with her soft muzzle and playfully snorted her hot breath over his face.

'Hello, my big beauty,' Samuel said, hugging the horse around the neck with one arm and reaching for his mother with the other. They stood holding onto Spirit's strong neck together with their eyes shut and their minds gently searching.

'Thank you for all you've done for us girl,' Samuel told the horse with his mind. 'You're free now. Go well and be happy.'

'We'll miss you, girl,' his mother added before stepping back with Samuel and holding him close to her.

The dipping sun burnished the coat of the great horse turning it a brilliant rich red. It was such a vibrant colour that they could actually feel the warmth exuding from her strongly defined flanks. Spirit whinnied quietly and tossed her head up and down. She thoughtfully eyed Samuel and his mother then cast a glance towards the distant hills where there was a small group of wild horses. Some gambled around after one another whilst others lazed in the dying sun.

'That's right girl, off you go.' Samuel nodded.

Spirit pawed the dry ground at her feet with a restless hoof and gave one last snort before turning herself around. She galloped down the dusty hillside heading in the direction of the other horses, whinnying as she went.

As they made their slow progress towards the hut that was to be their new home, Samuel told his mother of how he had secured a job at the village bakery. To save his mother worrying he missed out some of the things that had happened that day. He didn't tell her how Mr Sanderson, the owner of the bakery had threatened to throw him out of the job the first time he was late for work. Neither had he told her that, as he was the youngest employee that Mr Sanderson had, he had offered Samuel a very mean wage.

'Take it or leave it," Mr Sanderson had spoken to him through a mouthful of bun, crumbs and raisins cascading down his chin and scattering over his wide wooden desk. 'It makes no odds to me boy,' he had said.

Samuel led his mother passed the staring faces of the other inhabitants of Mr Sanderson's little huts to the one that was to be theirs.

'I'm sorry it's so small, Mama, it's all I could manage. It goes with the job.' Samuel held open the door for her.

'It's just perfect, sweetheart.' His mother had kissed him on the cheek. 'We'll make it nice and cosy, a place of our very own.'

Samuel knew that, on that first meeting, Mr Sanderson had seen him as a desperate boy, hardly more than an infant and one whom he could exploit and then throw away once he was finished with him. But time would show that Mr Sanderson had not reckoned on Samuel's inner strength and his determination not to fail his mother. Over all the coming years that Samuel was to work in the bakery he was never once late and had put in double the amount of work of any of the other boys employed there.

Samuel had also proved himself to be very useful in cleaning out the huge bakery ovens due to him being smaller and more nimble than the other employees and this particular talent was something that the baker wasn't too anxious to lose by letting the boy go, but that didn't mean he had to make his life easy. Samuel had put up with the comments and jokes made at his expense but things took a turn for the worse for Samuel after his mother rejected Mr Sanderson's romantic approaches.

The first time the bakery owner had seen Samuel's mother he had been immediately obsessed with her beauty. Everything about her intrigued him and he could simply not get her out of his mind. At first he had tried to woo her, his own wife had been dead for the past five years and the thought of filling her place with this exotic creature made his mouth water and his ill-treated heart race.

He had begun his pursuit of the lovely Lily by sending her small gifts of bread and cakes but she had returned them to him unopened always thanking him for his kindness but saying that she could not accept them. Next he had tried flowers, then a beautifully embroidered lady's hat, and after that, a box of the finest cocoa. His last and desperate attempt to make her love him, or at least give in to him, was to offer her a little house in the town to live in rather than the tiny wooden hut that her son's job at the bakery secured. Nothing had worked. Lily had politely refused all his advances. She had never given Mr Sanderson any more than a pleasant smile and an appropriate greeting on passing him in the street. His anger at her rejection had caused him to become more and more disagreeable towards her son but Samuel had been proud of his mother and had borne all the hardships that came his way, right to the very end, to the day she died. That was all in the past now.

From here on there were no more time-schedules, no work to get up for, no mother to care for, no one to look out for except himself. Nothing was going to be the same, not ever again.

3

The Forest

Samuel began to follow the course of the stream that ran close by their special clearing and deep into the woods. In the past he had been lucky enough to catch a few small fish in it. The flash of their scales beneath the surface danced and tantalized like hidden treasure. He remembered how he had triumphantly brought home his small catches to his mother, unwrapping the silver and slate coloured delights and displaying them proudly before her, like precious jewels.

Samuel thought that even if his fishing skills, or luck, had deserted him, the stream would at the very least provide him with a constant source of fresh drinking water on the journey.

Samuel knew a little about the stars. He could recognise a few constellations and find the North Star without too much trouble on a clear night. He also had a fair idea of how to track his direction from the arc of the sun across the sky, but he was in no hurry to get anywhere. Besides, going in a direct and definite direction would not aid his survival if he ran out of food and water. As he had no idea of where his travelling would take him, no clue of what lay within the bounds of the woods, never mind what he might find should he ever make it through and out the other side, there was nothing further to sway Samuel's decision on which route to pursue. What he did know was that the stream only ran through Crossways in one place so he could be sure that following its meandering through the great trees would not bring him full circle, back to the place he longed to escape. That was the only thing that really mattered to him now.

The deeper he went, the more alive the woods around him became. Nesting birds sang and chattered nervously in the branches above and flitted here and there eyeing him suspiciously, ready to protect their vulnerable youngsters newly hatched from their shells should Samuel make any sign of being a danger to them. Flying bugs buzzed and clicked around his head. One landed on the sleeve of his course shirt and rested there a few moments rubbing its multi-coloured back legs together lazily. When it eventually flew off Samuel watched until it was out of sight, its fragile wings lifting it up into the canopy of leaves high above. Other insects were less attractive to look at. Some of them were completely foreign to him with alarmingly large bulging eyes, their segmented bodies supporting viciously long and sharp stingers that seemed out of proportion to their size.

Even though Samuel had seen no creature bigger than a rabbit so far, he knew that they were there, hidden from his view by the thick greenery. Every now and then he would sense their presence or hear a snapping branch accompanied by large and heavy movements that were only slightly muffled by the thick carpet of growth on the forest floor. But those larger forest animals kept their distance and remained cloaked by the gloom the density of the trees afforded them. Occasionally Samuel would stop walking and stand with his eyes closed, sending out a message with his mind to any creature nearby that might hear him.

'I am just passing through your forest, I mean you no harm.'

It was difficult to know if any of the unseen creatures were picking up his message of goodwill, he had never tried to use his mind to speak in this way before. He had only ever communicated with one specific animal at a time but he hoped that these forest dwellers would understand and know that he was no threat, and better still, not see him as an easy option for their supper.

The going was good underfoot and the air was fresh and cool in the shade of the trees. Sometimes the stream would be right by Samuel's side and he could make his way quite comfortably along its bank but other times the ground became broken up and rough, with outcrops of rocks and boulders which, for safety's sake, forced Samuel to walk further away from the water, deeper into the trees. Once the ground levelled out again Samuel was glad to be able to rejoin the gentle babble of its flow and watch the light glinting on the water as it tumbled over rocks and broken branches caught in its path.

Shafts of sunlight pushed their way through the canopy of leaves above and beamed their brilliance into the dimness below, bringing with them the energy and heat needed to bring life to the vegetation on the forest floor. Blankets of thick springy moss covered rocks and fallen trees, casting odd shadows here and there. Some looked like twisted faces or hunched old men asleep with their heads tucked away under hoods of fine green velvet.

Although Samuel's stomach had not yet begun to complain or grumble for food, he realised that his body needed something if it was to carry on until he found a place to stay for the night. As he approached a large flattish rock that was being warmed by a single dazzling beam of sunshine it seemed like an invitation to stop. He seated himself cross-legged on the rock and felt almost content to be there, munching away on the crusts of bread from his bag and slurping cool water from his water pouch.

It was as he was looking upwards, studying the numbers of differently shaped leaves on the trees and noticing their various shades of green, that he noticed how quiet the woods around him had become. As he watched the dancing motes spangling down in the sunlight towards the forest floor he became aware that the only nearby sound he could make out was the trickle of the stream.

From his position on the rock, Samuel allowed his senses to radiate out around him. Almost immediately, he felt his muscles contract as he became aware that something large was nearby, and it was watching him.

Quickly he sent his mind-message once again: 'I'm just passing through, I mean no harm.' But he didn't wait to see if the creature hidden in the trees had received it or had understood him.

The fact that every other living creature nearby had seen the need to keep silent was enough to warn Samuel that whatever the unseen entity was, it was not to be taken lightly.

He slid down off the rock and tidied his belongings away, keeping his senses alert, eyeing the undergrowth for any movement that could indicate an imminent attack. Backing slowly towards the water, trying his best to show himself as submissive and unthreatening, Samuel managed to leave the small clearing without incident. Thankfully, whatever was there didn't seem anxious to follow him to the stream. Samuel had planned to top up his pouch with water before moving on but now decided against it. It would be better to put a little distance between himself and whatever was lurking in the trees.

The stream was now growing wider and deeper, looking less like a stream and more like a river. After travelling along its bank for only another forty paces or so the sounds of the birds and the smaller creatures returned and grew louder. The hairs on the back of Samuel's neck, which had been standing on end, began to relax as he sensed that the danger was now passed. It seemed that whatever it was that had been watching him had lost interest, for now at least.

It had been a long and tiring day but still the daylight hours passed by quickly as Samuel continued on his way through the woods. As the sun dipped back down towards the earth and the light began to lose its intensity, Samuel decided that it was time to find a place to settle for the night. He had become quite accustomed to sleeping outside when he and his mother had travelled from Genesis, but that had been a long time ago and never in a forest as thick as this one.

I can do this, of course I can.

Picking out a good strong tree nearby, that he hoped would offer him shelter should the breeze pick up during the night, Samuel set about gathering sticks to build a fire. With his hands and the use of a thick piece of wood, he created a dip in the ground near to the base of the tree. He had tried this before and discovered that sleeping in such a hollow helped to retain his body heat far better than lying more exposed on the flat earth.

He daydreamed a little as he worked at it, wondering if his mother was fit enough to sleep outside, should he try to build her some kind of shelter instead? Perhaps the fresh air would do her good so long as it wasn't too cold a night? Then the realisation hit him like a fist; she was gone. It was second nature for him to consider her, a habit that would take a long time to break and one that would cause him heartache over and over again. That was to be the first of many times that Samuel would go through the same awful feeling of losing his mother all over again.

Pausing in his work Samuel realised how easy it would be to give in to his grief and simply sit down to wait for death to take him too. Just give up. What was he struggling to go on for anyway? But his mother's face swam into his mind and Samuel knew he couldn't do it. His mother had always told him how strong he was inside, how proud she was of how he took care of himself and of her. How could he sully her memory by giving up? He couldn't. He wouldn't.

Rising to his feet Samuel set about breathing life into the fire before making his way down to the water. Focusing on fulfilling his immediate needs Samuel cursed himself for not starting the job of catching his supper sooner. The light faded further and further and his stomach began to growl with hunger, a hunger increased by the physical effort of walking all day long after the great sadness and work of the morning before it.

Now, so much deeper into the forest, the river seemed more alive. It was clearer, cleaner and flowing faster. Water-smoothed pebbles skirted the edge where the brown water met the muddy bank. Further out there were jagged scatterings of rocks, and small boulders that had the river twisting into little whirlpools of white froth around them as it raced by.

Taking care not to cut his bare feet, Samuel ventured out

into the flow and stood up to his thighs in the water. Catching his face on overhanging branches he steadied himself and planted his feet a good distance apart from one another in order to anchor himself against the pull of the current. The challenge seemed immense; could he possibly catch something here? It seemed so different to the stream he had fished in before; it was difficult to believe that it was the same waterway. He could see that the river held far more fish here and silently wished that this abundance would help to increase his chances of landing his supper before too long. But with every fish that refused to take the feathered lure at the end of his bobbing line Samuel's hunger grew along with his frustration.

By the time he actually caught the fish it was almost dark. The now blooming light from his fire was dancing high, seeping bright colours into the purpling sky above it. Samuel had been so intent on the task, so immersed in the act of willing the fat little fish to take a nice big bite on his hook, that he did not hear the watcher as it broke cover of the trees and approached him through the water.

Samuel stood there in the river, the water sloshing and tugging at his trousers, his freezing feet a pale white smudge beneath the surface. As the fish took the lure, Samuel struck, yanking back the rod sharply in order to drive home the hook. Reeling in quickly, the feel of the fish straining and bucking at the other end of the line sending his mouth watering at the thought of how good it would taste cooked over his fire, Samuel fought to bring his supper out of the water.

'Yes!' he cried with a mixture of delight, exhaustion and relief. But his cry was quickly silenced as something that felt like a mallet, but a mallet with fur and long sharp claws, thumped him across the back of the head and sent him down like a felled tree.

The shock of the freezing water on his face revived him as he crashed full frontal into the river. As he surfaced, the back of his head felt heavy and wrong somehow. Pain thundered down his neck and into his shoulders. The realisation that whatever had struck him was now behind and looming over him, possibly ready to strike again at any moment, forced its way through his pain as he struggled to turn over in the water. There was a large rock jutting out of the river not too far away from him. It was further out where the water was deeper, and the current stronger. Perhaps if he could get himself over to it and grab on he could get out of his attacker's reach. Desperately he tried to get a look at his assailant but before he could do anything Samuel was suddenly deafened by an unearthly noise.

The booming was all around him; it was so loud that he feared, in his concussed state, that the trees themselves would be uprooted by the sound and come tumbling down on top of him, crushing his body and forcing him under the surface of the river.

Samuel wondered for a fleeting moment if this huge vicious creature, with a cry that could only come from Hell itself, would devour him or just pummel him to death. He hoped with all his terrified heart that it was not the kind of beast that ate its prey whilst it was still alive.

Reaching out behind him as he scuttled backwards in the cold water he caught hold of the rock and wiped his wet hair out of his eyes. As Samuel's vision cleared a little he was able to make out not one but two shadowy figures that towered over him as he lay there prone and vulnerable in the river. The larger of the two was a few paces away, the smaller, though still huge and terrifying in the eerie gloom, had placed itself between Samuel and the other.

It occurred to Samuel through the haze of his terror that he might be being fought over. Perhaps human flesh was a delicacy worth battling for out here in the woods. Should he just let go of the rock and let the current take him away? But what if his head smacked into another boulder on his way and he drowned?

Sluggishly, his twisting bruised mind tried to turn over his options as the terrible sound came again. The awful ear-splitting noise was coming from the creature nearest to him, the smaller of the two giants. So loud and fierce was the sound that he feared his head might actually explode with the pressure of it. It seemed that the larger creature did not appreciate it either; it appeared to be moving off.

The dark shadow of the retreating figure stumbled, obviously unsettled and disorientated by the raucous din. As it backed away it was briefly caught in the glow of the fire enabling Samuel to finally make out what it was. The massive, thickly coated bear walked on its hind legs for a little way before bouncing down on to all fours and bounding off into the forest.

The noise ceased immediately and Samuel's aching head pounded in the silence. He lay gasping and wincing in pain from the blow he had received and the punishing onslaught of sound. The animal nearby turned and came towards him through the gloom. Samuel closed his eyes and prayed that it would be quick.

'Please Mama, watch over me and let it be quick!' he murmured quietly as he braced himself for what was to come.

He waited for the claws, the teeth, the pain and suffering of being torn apart by a wild and hungry animal. Now he wished he had let go of the rock earlier and taken his chances in the river.

But, the sensation that came next was so surprising that Samuel was paralysed, not knowing how to react. His face was being thoroughly licked all over by a huge hot tongue. Was this mystery animal merely having a taste before beginning to eat him? Clouds of steamy breath continued to be blown into Samuel's face but no pain followed the incessant grooming.

Opening one eye Samuel looked into the eyes of the great beast that was washing his face. He looked into the eyes of the creature that had saved him from the mighty jaws of the bear; he stared into its big, wide, silver eyes.

'Quicksilver?' Samuel managed to whisper before the blackness took him and slid him gratefully into unconsciousness.

When Samuel came around later he felt both thirsty and hungry but the most overpowering of all his discomforts was the pain in his head. It appeared to be early morning judging by the faint light. Gingerly he slid a hand round to where the pain seemed to emanate from and tentatively felt his scalp for damage. His hair was matted together and stuck to his head, congealed blood he suspected. The edges of two nasty gashes angrily made their presence known as he ran his fingers carefully along their length.

The pain in his head was immense, like a large stone had been pushed inside it. Every time he made the slightest movement it felt like this stone was thumping off the inside of his skull. His senses told him that it would be best to try to sleep through the pain, so he drifted back into a slumber again only vaguely wondering why it was that he was not still lying in the water.

In his dream Samuel's wounded head no longer caused him any pain. He found himself sitting peacefully in a patch of sunshine looking at a tree whose broad trunk was covered with a thick veil of glossy leaves. As he watched, the leaves began to shimmer and move slightly as if caught in a breeze but all else around him was very still.

There was gentle laugh nearby, the voice was deep... a man's? It seemed to be coming from the tree itself. As he looked more closely Samuel suddenly made out a pair of vivid green eyes staring back at him from the foliage that coated the trunk.

'Who are you? What do you want with me?' Samuel asked, his voice sounding shaky even to his own ears.

The man laughed again, not unkindly, and this time stepped forward from the tree revealing that he had not been hiding behind the leaves but was in fact *made* of them. At least, that was the impression that Samuel had. The tall man was covered in greenery. Apart from his eyes, nose and mouth there was only a man-shape to be made out beneath the lush sinuous leaves.

'You are Samuel, son of Lily?' the man asked. His question seemed full of knowledge, not really a question at all but a statement, still Samuel felt compelled to answer.

'Yes, I don't mean any harm, I...'

That laugh again.

'You've nothing to fear from me, Samuel. I am a friend to all those who treat the forest with love and respect.' His green eyes shone as he spoke. 'You are welcome here, Samuel, you have been expected. But take better care of yourself, one day the forest will need you.'

'Need me? *Me?*' asked Samuel.

The tall green man didn't say anything more but gave Samuel a gracious bow, his eyes twinkling mischievously behind the living foliage of his face. Turning his leafy back to the bewildered boy, the Man In Green danced off into the forest singing a cheerful tune as he skipped away between the trunks.

When next Samuel came around it seemed that he had dozed for a whole day and he felt a good deal better for it. The memory of his strange dream was still with him but his thirst was now something fierce and desperate, quickly blotting out everything else.

He opened his eyes and carefully lifted his head to look around. Surely it was too much to hope for that his water pouch would be anywhere nearby. He saw that he was lying in his sleeping dugout. Had he dragged himself back up here after the bear had attacked him the night before? Samuel noticed that the fire was out but he didn't feel cold, why was that? Shards of memories came back slowly... the bear, the noise, the water, the silver moon... no, there had been *two* silver moons. No, that wasn't right either, they hadn't been moons they had been *eyes*, silver eyes...

'Quicksilver!' Samuel said aloud and was answered by a low grumbling growl that came from behind and partially underneath him. The huge silver dog had wedged himself into the dugout and pulled the boy in on top of him. It was the heat coming from Quicksilver's body that was keeping Samuel warm.

'It *was* you, boy! You *are* here.' Samuel carefully reached an arm behind him and stroked the dog's sleek coat.

'Thank you, boy, I wouldn't have made it without you.' Samuel winced as the lump of stone inside his head shifted and pain ran all over the inside of his skull. 'I know now why they call that awful drink 'Bearclaw': I think this is how it feels the next morning after you've had too many of them.'

Samuel felt Quicksilver shift around, the muscles in his powerful body moving and straining as the massive animal stretched for something on the ground somewhere out of Samuel's vision. The water pouch plopped gently onto Samuel's chest.

'Thanks, boy.' After a good long draw on the remainder of his water, Samuel settled back into the warmth of Quicksilver's body and drifted off into a healing sleep feeling both safe and protected this time.

The next morning he felt much better; the pain in his head was still there but bearable now. Quicksilver was not nearby but Samuel felt sure that the dog would be back soon. Whilst he waited for his new companion, he set about getting the fire going. His limbs were shaky; he badly needed something to eat. The fishing rod lay nearby, snapped into three pieces.

'Well, what now I wonder? I guess I'll just have to learn to catch fish by hand.' Samuel mused as he surveyed the damage incurred by the bear's actions.

It occurred to Samuel that not only had Quicksilver saved

62

him from the bear but he must also have dragged him up from the water and rescued his rod too. And what a tracker that dog must be, he thought, to have found him out in the woods so far from Crossways... but why was he here?

Perhaps Quicksilver had had enough of the old village too; maybe he had itchy paws and wanted to see some of the world. It would be a far cry from the life he had known as a butcher's dog. Now he would have to learn how to survive in the woods on whatever small animals he could catch. Samuel wondered if Quicksilver had any hunting instincts. That question was answered almost immediately as Quicksilver bounded into their small camp with a large thrashing fish clamped between his jaws. He dropped it at Samuel's feet and bounded around barking like a puppy, his immense paws shaking the forest floor beneath them. His barks of excitement were nowhere near as deafening or terrible as his barks of anger but the power in them was still too much for Samuel.

'No boy! Please, quiet... my poor head.' Samuel pleaded, throwing his hands to his ears.

The dog came to Samuel's side with his big silky ears flat against his head, a look of apology on his big wonderful face.

'Aren't you just the cleverest dog in the whole world?' Samuel said quietly, pointing to the gasping fish on the ground. Quicksilver answered with a throaty roll, his ears pricking up again.

'Raw or cooked?' Samuel enquired after he had gutted and

prepared the fish, pushing his half of it onto a branch-skewer and resting it to cook in the rekindled fire.

Quicksilver suddenly sat down heavily on his backside, licking drool from his chops. His massive silver tail swept back and forth powerfully, clearing a large area of the ground of all its vegetation.

'Okay boy, I get you. Raw it is. Here it comes.' Samuel grinned.

Quicksilver looked as happy with his self-caught breakfast as he would have been with any steak or mound of sausages served to him by the butcher back in Crossways.

Later Samuel leaned back with a hand on his stomach, 'That was delicious, Quicksilver. I really needed that. I guess its time to get moving on, old friend, what are your plans? Are you going back home?'

The dog watched Samuel and listened with his huge silver head tilted to one side.

He made a scratchy low growl. *No.*

'Or were you thinking of coming along with me?' Samuel asked.

Quicksilver's tail began to swing again and he gave a gentle breathy 'whooff'.

'Well,' Samuel began, 'I'd love for you to come along boy, but I can't give you anything but my friendship. You're the one who saved my life and filled my stomach, I don't really have anything I can offer you.'

Quicksilver got to his feet and strode over to Samuel. The huge dog looked into the boy's eyes. They stared into each other for a long time feeling like two parts of the same being. The sun shone down and warmed the two companions as they assessed one another.

Quicksilver broke the silence with a soft snort and placed his huge heavy head lightly on the young boy's shoulder. Samuel flung his arms around the animal's muscular neck and hugged him.

'All right boy,' he agreed. 'We go together.'

Samuel reluctantly released his hold on the dog and set about getting ready to leave. They filled in the sleeping hollow, stamped out and buried the fire, and Samuel gathered his remaining belongings together before continuing along the route of the river.

Samuel salvaged the line from the rod in case it might come in useful but he decided that the rod itself was not to be saved. Even if he mended it, the rod would never again be trustworthy to hold fast with a struggling fish on the end of its line. He would have to rely on his new companion to provide fresh fish to eat in the future or else figure out a new way in which to catch them.

It was so good not to be alone any more, Samuel thought to himself as he walked along with Quicksilver by his side. The huge silver dog had belonged to Mr Cardell, the village butcher back in Crossways. Mr Cardell had treated him well; had fed him on good cuts of meat and fresh thick milk. He had never been unkind to him so far as Samuel knew. In fact, Quicksilver had eaten a great deal better than many of the human inhabitants of Crossways and he'd had a more comfortable existence than most. In return for this, Mr Cardell had enjoyed the reputation of being the owner of the most impressive watchdog in Crossways.

Samuel had always had a soft spot for the dog. His mother had too. Whenever they were out together in the main street they would make a point of stopping to visit him. Quicksilver seemed to enjoy their company greatly, lying on his back with his massive silver belly exposed for a good scratching. He behaved like a wildly overgrown puppy whenever Samuel and his mother appeared and they had felt a strong bond with the outlandish animal. Mr Cardell found the dog's behaviour rather embarrassing on these rare occasions however; it was not becoming of a fierce and terrifying guard-dog to behave in such an unashamedly abandoned way. But he was easily won over by Lily's smiles and let it go without comment.

Samuel had never thought of Quicksilver as a lazy dog, just a spoilt one. It had not occurred to him that Quicksilver would not only be able to handle a life in the wild, full of trekking and hunting, but that he would actually thrive on it. But there was the magnificent proof by his side, day after day, as they

66

travelled through the forest. The dog's sinuous muscles moved those powerful legs on relentlessly.

Samuel, although getting fitter and stronger, found the going a bit more taxing. But even though his huge friend seemed anxious to keep moving, to take in everything around him in the forest, he was always patient with Samuel whenever he needed to stop for a few moments to rest. During Samuel's rest-breaks Quicksilver hardly ever took the opportunity to relax for himself. The great dog's energy appeared almost boundless, he didn't seem to feel the need or desire for much rest. During those times he would instead pad around quietly, sniffing the air, nosing through the undergrowth and listening to the sounds of the woods. He behaved as if this new life was the most natural thing in the world to him.

Sometimes Quicksilver would leave Samuel sitting in the shade whilst he went foraging nearby for small creatures for their next meal. Samuel loved to sit watching as Quicksilver lapped up huge mouthfuls of water from the river, seeing the droplets sparkling and dripping like jewels from his magnificent glossy coat and powerful chin.

One day when they were making their way through a glade, the sun dazzling and warm on the tops of their heads, Quicksilver suddenly sent Samuel sprawling in the ferns with a powerful thump of his flank.

Getting to his feet and brushing himself down, Samuel rubbed what was going to be a bruised hip and gave Quicksilver an indignant look.

'What exactly was that for?'

Quicksilver gruffed in response and stared into Samuel's eyes.

'What is it, boy?' Samuel asked.

Quicksilver gruffed once more and nosed carefully through the ferns and bracken just in front of them. Coming slowly to his side Samuel peered into the shrubs trying to see what the dog had found. He expected to find a snake or some other dangerous animal. What he did see was certainly dangerous but it was not one borne of nature.

How long it had lain there was anyone's guess. Grass, weeds and leaves all but hid it from view; its great rusted jaws lay open wide awaiting an unsuspecting creature to feed it. Samuel reached out his fingers to feel the metal but Quicksilver took the boy's hand in his mouth, careful not to pierce his skin with his sharp teeth, and pulled him away.

'All right, boy, I'll not touch it.' Samuel took the hint.

The dog turned away and moved off in search of something, returning a moment later with a branch the same thickness as Samuel's forearm. After one look into the boy's eyes, a look that seemed to Samuel to say '*watch this*', Quicksilver tossed the branch so that it landed in the centre of the metal jaws. The sound of the great trap clanging shut sent all the birds in the nearby trees squawking in a flurry of wings up into the blue sky above. A few feathers seesawed their way down to the forest floor.

The rust hadn't hindered the effect of the trap. Samuel had never seen such a thing before. The branch was mangled, torn in two places, exposing splinters and the fleshy pale pulp inside. For a horrible moment Samuel visualised his own body lying there in the trap, torn and bloody. Rubbing his aching hip where Quicksilver had struck him he realised how lucky he was to have come away from this new lesson with only light bruising. How long could he have survived out here in the forest if he had been horribly injured in that thing? Samuel shuddered at the thought of it.

He swallowed dryly, 'Thank you Quicksilver.' The dog gruffed contentedly as Samuel scratched behind one of his great silky ears. 'Thanks a lot.'

As the days turned to weeks Samuel too became more and more at home in this new life of travelling through the great forest, yet something inside him believed that he could be content anywhere so long as Quicksilver was by his side.

At first Samuel had experienced a lot of trouble from the insect-life in the forest. During the day he could see them coming and bat most of them away but each night, as he slept, Samuel would be bitten all over every exposed piece of his skin. In the mornings he awoke to a fresh crop of angry and itchy red spots. In desperation he tried rubbing a thin layer of river-mud over his face and hands before going to bed. This helped to deter them somewhat but the mud would crack once dry and make him itch. Also there was the need to spend a long time in the cold river the next day scrubbing at the brown smears to remove them from his skin.

Trial and error found that setting up their camp further from the river each night helped avoid most of the insects. They seemed to congregate by the water at nightfall and Samuel came to understand that he had been providing the hungry bugs with an irresistible night-time snack by sleeping so close to the river. Insect bites were few and far between now and Samuel's nightly 'mud' ritual was no longer necessary. Perhaps his blood had been a tasty and unusual meal when he was new to the forest but now that he was part of it; eating and drinking only things that the forest provided, his blood was no more interesting than any other forest creature to the insect's palate. Whatever the reason, he was delighted that they had now chosen to leave him mostly alone.

After many failed attempts at making shelters Samuel grew more knowledgeable about how best to set up a camp for the night. Soon he came up with a way of spotting just the right size and age of sapling trees, their immature trunks flexible enough to allow themselves to be bound together with twine. Carefully he could manipulate and hold them in place that way so that they offered overhead coverage at night and could be released, completely unharmed by the experience, when it came time to move on. Large ferns could be quite easily and quickly woven together to create small screens which could be tied to the trunks of the young trees. These simple screens helped to keep in their body heat and some of the warmth exuding from their nearby fire.

With his new diet of meat, fish, fruit and forest vegetables coupled with his now constant intake of fresh clean air and river water, Samuel found his body beginning to change. He felt stronger, healthier and able to endure longer and harder treks without feeling so weary.

On one of their many nights spent peacefully below the stars Samuel and Quicksilver witnessed a frightening, yet wonderful sight in the sky. At first Samuel had thought he was seeing another shooting star, like the one he had seen the night his mother had passed away, but as he watched, it was joined by many, many more. Soon the sky blazed with them.

Streaks of silvery glitter followed each pinprick of light as it hurtled down towards the earth. The sky lit up with the tiny fireballs that began their journey at the highest point of the night sky; silver on purple-black. Samuel had held his breath and pressed his body close to Quicksilver as he waited for the balls of fire to crash into the trees and set them ablaze. But as they stared at the awesome sight, the flaming lights gently faded away to nothing high above them.

When it was eventually over, the pair had sat quietly together wondering what they had seen, what it meant. Samuel had heard stories of falling stars before, star-showers they called them. Some people thought of them as a foretelling of bad times ahead; a poor harvest or of some kind of destruction, sometimes even as a prophet of death. Samuel remembered his mother had once told him that there were people in the world that only ever saw the bad in things, ones that never let their minds soar above the ordinary to imagine the possible good or see past superstition to the real beauty that stared them right in the face. She had never seen more than a shooting star in her lifetime but had told Samuel that it was her belief that the star-showers were nature's celebration of life, something to be marvelled at and enjoyed, not feared.

Lying side-by-side, the sky above now returned to its previous purple-black, the familiar stars shining down on them, Samuel stroked one of Quicksilver's silky ears and smiled. He preferred to take his mother's point of view. What they had seen had only been frightening because they hadn't expected it or understood what was happening, but his mother was right; it had been beautiful.

Quicksilver was endlessly inventive and clever. On returning from one of his explorations down by the river one day, he brought Samuel an invaluable aid to preparing their meals; a large flattish rock with a very sharp edge. It proved to be the perfect implement for cutting up everything from slippery fish to the hardest of plant roots. Together boy and dog were finding their way and learning as they went along, though often it was clear to Samuel that Quicksilver's instincts were far sharper than his own, something he was extremely grateful for.

'You're some dog, Quicksilver.' Samuel said one day as he sat resting with his back against a sun-warmed rock eating the root of a creamy-tasting plant that his friend had dug up for him. Looking up at his four-legged companion, Samuel saw that the dog's ears were pricked and alert, his whole body poised for movement. The silky soft pink-lined ears twitched and Samuel could tell that Quicksilver was hearing things that he himself had no hope of picking up.

'What is it boy?' Samuel whispered, reaching his hand up to gently stroke one of Quicksilver's legs, thick as the trunk of a young tree. A grumble began in the dog's throat. Soon it grew to a growl and Quicksilver's muzzle pursed, sending the long hairs that sprouted there bristling.

'Is it the bear?' Samuel asked nervously, trying to use his own senses to connect with what Quicksilver was feeling, but he had to throw his hands over his ears as Quicksilver began to bellow his awful bark and suddenly burst into action, disappearing into the trees. Samuel scrambled to his feet and took off in the same direction.

Even as the great dog ran further away from him, the sound of his bark was barely any easier on Samuel's pounding eardrums. The bark stopped for a moment and Samuel skidded to a standstill not wanting to go off on the wrong bearing. As he stood there panting, his ribcage heaving, something strange caught his eye. Close to where he stood there were odd markings on the forest floor; a path of dark indentations evenly spaced out on the ground, each a little longer and wider than his foot. They wound their way through the trees on a route diagonal to his own. He got the feeling that whatever had made them had been moving towards and past the place where he now stood, travelling away from something deeper in the forest. Still listening for sounds from his companion, Samuel walked over to one of the markings and hunkered down to take a closer look. Were these the markings of some kind of animal? Around each indentation the vegetation was slightly blackened. Burnt, Samuel realised.

Quicksilver's bark came again and snatched him from his thoughts. Closing his eyes Samuel frantically tried to connect with the dog's mind in an attempt to find out what he was chasing. But within a few heartbeats, Quicksilver's barking suddenly stopped once more.

Samuel felt sick as he struggled to reach his friend with his searching mind. For a horrible few moments his concentration was interrupted by unwanted images of the huge silver dog being trapped or injured, and one truly cruel vision in which his dear friend had been killed outright. Ever since the bear had attacked him, Samuel had feared that it might return one day. His imagination ran wild now as he worried that Quicksilver had been lured away into the dense trees by this same bear in order that it could take revenge on him, despatching his great friend with wickedly sharp claws. Samuel's healing wounds throbbed beneath their long crusted scabs at the thought of Quicksilver's powerful flesh being torn by the same brute force that could so easily have claimed his own life.

He forced his mind harder, deeper, thrusting through the space and vegetation that separated him from his goal. Making his skill work more fiercely than he ever had before, pushing it to a higher level than he had known was possible.

Then it happened.

Samuel connected with Quicksilver. This connection was stronger than ever before, it actually felt like he had *become* Quicksilver, was actually inside the dog's skin, breathing through his doggy mouth, seeing out of his big silver eyes. A smile crept over Samuel's own lips as he sensed that Quicksilver was unharmed and up ahead of him, just a short sprint away through the forest. Without stopping to consider the danger he was putting himself into, Samuel trusted himself to this new sensation and began to run through the undergrowth, darting quickly through the trees towards where he felt his friend was waiting for him.

As Samuel ran he felt the connection between himself and the dog like a taut rope that he could pull himself along. As he broke into the clearing behind Quicksilver's seated figure, the dog did not even bother to turn his head to check that it was him. He didn't need to look to confirm that it was his friend Samuel because their connection had been so strong and powerful that it was as if Quicksilver had travelled along with Samuel through the trees; both of them, in both places, at the same time.

The experience was both thrilling and a little frightening for Samuel but Quicksilver behaved as if it was all quite normal. Samuel walked over to his friend and reached out a hand to stroke his shining coat.

'What's this then?' Samuel asked quietly, directing his gaze to match the dog's.

Quicksilver gave a gentle groan.

About halfway across the clearing there was an odd green shape. At first glance it could have been a moss-covered rock or a grassy mound but it seemed out of place somehow and the only one in the clearing. It moved slightly as the companions stared at it and Samuel saw that the greenery was more like a blanket or a strange garment of clothing.

A garment of clothing? But covering who... or what?

'Hello?' Samuel ventured.

The green cloak-like covering shifted under the sunlight that beat down upon it. Samuel looked at Quicksilver, the dog stared back at him.

'We don't mean you any harm. If you're worried about Quicksilver here, he won't hurt you. Look.' Samuel put an arm about the dog's neck and continued to stare at the odd shape feeling a little stupid now at the prospect that he may well be addressing a weird forest plant of some kind.

There was a shiver, then a bigger movement, next a small pale face popped out from beneath the greenery. It was a young boy, his face worried and afraid.

Samuel did well to keep the surprise out of his voice, 'Really, it's all right. There's no need to run away. You can come and meet him if you like.'

Samuel and Quicksilver watched the boy slowly stand up. He had been cowering in terror beneath a green cloak of what looked like grass; its hood was up over the boy's head. Samuel grinned broadly to encourage him on. The young boy smiled back uncertainly and looked back over his shoulder in the opposite direction.

Samuel worried that the youngster was about to bolt off into the trees.

'What's your name?' Samuel tried.

'A... Ash,' the boy replied, looking back at Samuel. 'But... I'm not supposed to talk to strangers,' he added. Though he began to edge a little closer to Samuel and Quicksilver.

The strange boy's trousers and tunic were made from patches of animal skin sewn together and draped over these was the strange green cloak. Secured at the neck by a leather thong the cloak was long, hanging down to the boy's calves, its hood casting shadows over his face. An odd-looking necklace hung around his neck; it looked like a thin strip of leather adorned with dark uneven beads of some kind.

'Well, that's good advice, Ash. Do you meet many strangers

out here? How did you get here, are you lost? Where are you from?' Samuel asked, trying to sound as unthreatening as possible.

The boy sniggered. 'No, I'm not lost. I live here; *this* is where I'm from. You're the first strangers I ever met but... you aren't really all *that* strange.' The boy pointed to Quicksilver. 'I've got a friend just like him, only she hasn't got such an ear-splitting yowl.' He was calmer now, his smile more relaxed and easy, 'I wasn't going to hang around to see what was making *that* noise, I thought my ears might explode.'

It was Samuel's turn to snigger. 'Yes, pretty powerful isn't it?' Samuel knitted his brow in confusion, 'How do you mean, you *live* here?'

The boy was very close to them now. He seemed completely recovered from his earlier shock at the power of Quicksilver's bark and he reached out a hand to scratch the great dog under his chin. Samuel watched as Quicksilver stretched his neck back and closed his eyes in pleasure at the boy's touch. One massive silver back leg began to scratch at the grass as Ash found the dog's favourite place to be itched. The two boys laughed as he whined with pleasure at the unexpected attention.

'I didn't know he liked that,' said Samuel.

'Oh, just a lucky guess.' Ash grinned back. He had a mischievous look in his eyes and Samuel had a strange feeling that the boy knew something that he wasn't letting on.

'My name's Samuel,' he said, offering his hand to Ash, but the boy just looked at it and smiled.

'Greetings, Samuel.' Ash replied and stuck out his hand in front of him in a similar way. It seemed he had never been taught how to shake hands.

Samuel took the lad's hand in his and shook it gently up and down.

'This is how we say hello where I'm from.' Samuel explained.

'Oh, I see,' Ash giggled, 'It's a bit strange. We do it like this...' Without further warning Ash closed his eyes and Samuel heard the words 'Greetings Samuel,' once again, but this time they were not spoken out loud by the boy, Samuel had heard them inside his head. Taken aback, he stood staring at Ash in surprise.

A breeze worked over them as they stood there. A sudden gust puffed up inside Ash's hood lifting it up then off the youngster's head to settle it lightly on his back. Samuel continued to stare at the boy, this time at his hair; it was startlingly bright even lighter than his own, even more vivid than his mother's had been.

'Yes,' Ash said, noticing Samuel's expression, 'like your hair, isn't it?' Ash giggled as Samuel nodded stupidly. 'I don't think that you two are strangers at all, not really.' Ash added.

Samuel didn't have the chance to ask for an explanation before a slim woman, dressed in a similar fashion to Ash, a tumble of golden hair trailing out behind her, ran into the clearing from the far side, calling out as she ran;

'Ash! Ash! Where are you, you naughty boy? Are you blocking me out again? I've told you about that before you should never...' she stopped abruptly on seeing the gathered trio.

'Ah, that's Mama, I'm in big trouble now. And you're going to help me out of it. Come on.' Ash said as he pulled his hood back onto his head and began to walk towards the small pretty woman waiting by the opposite tree line. She was standing very still, her mouth slightly open, her eyebrows tucked up somewhere under her fringe.

'Hello Mama, these are my new friends; Samuel and Quicksilver. I think they should come home with us, don't you?' Again Samuel noticed the boy's knowing look this time directed at his mother.

The woman stared at Samuel as he said hello. Quicksilver introduced himself in his own way; tenderly licking the palm of the woman's open right hand.

'Yes, of course. Where did... but... how...?' She seemed mesmerised. Her eyes were wide and were searching Samuel's face as if he were the most surprising thing she had ever encountered.

'Well bless the Man In Green!' she finally said quietly.

Samuel instantly remembered the figure from his dream, the man made of leaves who had spoken to him.

'The Man In Green?' he asked her.

She continued to gaze at Samuel, 'Yes, the Man In Green. You know; the living spirit of the forest?' Ash's mother seemed puzzled that Samuel didn't know this already.

Samuel shook his head, 'Sorry.'

'He breathes life into everything and knows all that happens here,' she explained and carried on staring at Samuel with fascination.

Ash gave his mother a gentle prod in her side. 'It's rude to stare Mama!' Ash sniggered.

His mother lowered her eyes to her son and shook her head a little as if to clear it.

'Yes, of course. Excuse me,' she said directing her apology to Samuel, 'It's just such a surprise... a wonderful surprise. I'm Heather, mother of the elusive Ash,' she introduced herself.

Ash giggled.

'And there's no need for you to look so proud of yourself you cheeky boy.' Heather said to her son, 'how many times have I told you not to travel so far away from home? I've been worried something awful about you all morning. You were supposed to be helping me gather berries!'

'But Mama,' Ash looked coyly at her, his boyish charms obviously well practiced and effective. 'It was meant to be.' He put his hands out, palms up to the sky, 'If I hadn't come this far I would never have found them,' he added.

'Hmm, is that so?' Heather ruffled her son's hair and taking a hold of his shoulders turned him around to face the trees. 'Get along with you, rascal! Lead the way home,' she said and patted her foot playfully across her son's backside to get him moving.

Samuel could see love in her eyes, a mother's love, and he warmed to her but was also pained by the memory of his own mother and all that he had lost along with her.

'You'll have to excuse my son, he's still young and rather headstrong,' the young woman looked at Samuel. 'But perhaps that's not such a bad thing in these times,' she added this last, under her breath and almost to herself as they moved along after Ash.

They walked through the trees in single file, Quicksilver bringing up the rear. The branches and trunks became more densely packed the further they went and as they wound their way through the forest Samuel told Heather and Ash how he and Quicksilver had come to be there. He hadn't felt up to telling of what had happened to his mother, that wound was still too raw to expose, but he told them of the bear's attack and how Quicksilver had come to his rescue and saved his life. Heather seemed to sense not to push too hard with her questions. She let a comfortable silence fall between them, but Ash was very impressed by the story of the bear and insisted on stopping their trek to have a good look at Samuel's scars before continuing on their way.

A good few miles further into the forest the party of four came to the side of a hillock that sloped upwards from the forest floor to around the height of Samuel's old wooden hut. Only one side of the hillock was visible through the thickly knitted trees, ferns and winding vines. The slope in front of them was covered with a scattering of fist-sized boulders, a common enough sight within the deeper forest where the ground was often more rugged and uneven. Samuel couldn't see why Ash had chosen to stop here particularly.

'Here we are now.' Heather said. 'Samuel, if you could stand over there beside Ash.'

Without any further explanation or warning, Ash's mother stood before the boulders and closed her eyes. Samuel looked to Ash for a clue on what they were waiting for or what was going to happen but the boy only grinned and nodded towards his mother, indicating that Samuel should watch her.

Samuel began to hear faint sounds and incoherent words blossoming inside his mind. It took a few moments for him to realise that Ash's mother was the source of these sounds; sounds which she was making with her own mind. She was talking, persuading, connecting with someone or something. Was it an animal? Another person?

As Samuel glanced around in search of what or who Ash's mother was channelling her strength towards he heard another noise, but this one he heard with his ears. A grinding, crunching sound that grew in volume. He watched amazed as the collection of boulders before them began to twitch and shuffle against one another. For a moment Samuel expected a large creature to push its way out from under the heavy pile of rocks.

Perhaps some huge kind of tunnelling animal that he had never known existed was about to emerge into their midst at the beckon of this young woman? But as he watched, the boulders began to move purposefully; not to fall according to gravity, but to change their position and rearrange themselves. It was as if unseen hands were working tirelessly to bring structure to their jumbled assortment. Samuel could only stare in wonder as the last few stones moved into place to create a beautifully crafted stone archway, and beyond that he could see a dim tunnel.

Quicksilver nuzzled Samuel's shoulder and licked his face. His big powerful tail beat back and forth in a frenzy of excitement and he whined impatiently at Samuel's reluctance to step forward through the archway and into the tunnel.

'You know it's okay, boy, don't you?' Ash said, patting Quicksilver's side. 'You'll get used to this sort of thing around here,' he added to Samuel with a smile.

Quicksilver looked to Samuel to see what he would have him do, leaving the decision to his human friend. The dog's expressive silver eyes stared into Samuel's own and he seemed to be pleading with the boy to follow his instincts that these people could be trusted, that this place was safe.

Ash's mother turned around. 'This will all seem very strange to you I expect, but we are your friends, Samuel. You've nothing to fear here, and a lot to learn from us I think.' She raised a hand and gently stroked Samuel's cheek. No other person, other than his own mother, had ever touched him with kindness

84

before. The unexpected tenderness of the touch surprised him and he felt his cheeks redden but he held her gaze and nodded.

'All right, Quicksilver,' Samuel patted the dog's neck, 'we'll go with them.'

Quicksilver's ears pricked up and he gave Samuel a grateful lick on the forehead that made his fringe stick straight up. Samuel could sense that Quicksilver would not have gone forward without him but, for a reason that he didn't understand yet, it was also obvious that the massive silver dog desperately wanted to go through. Once more, the young boy silently thanked whatever force had brought the two of them together.

Samuel had expected the tunnel to be a passageway leading to a cave or perhaps going underground to some kind of lair where Ash and his mother sheltered. But, after only a dozen or so paces, the tunnel walls began to open out and up ahead Samuel could see daylight.

'Not far now,' came Heather's reassuring voice from the darkness behind him. She had needed to perform a similar ritual to close up the entrance before they had begun their journey through the tunnel.

Nothing could have prepared Samuel for what he was about to see when he left the tunnel and stepped into bright sunshine and birdsong. He found himself in a large cliff-rimmed area with a small village nestling within its protection. Samuel jumped a little as Ash placed a hand gently on his arm.

'Welcome home,' the boy whispered to him.

Samuel looked down at the younger boy's beaming smile.

Home? What does he mean?

The area that they had entered was teeming with life. Animals, birds and people all mingled as they went about their business. So much activity, after having spent so much time alone with Quicksilver, felt rather overwhelming to Samuel, he felt his legs wobble a little. Reaching out to hold onto the only familiar thing nearby, Samuel fastened himself to the dog's great side and pulled his silver companion along with him as he backed up against a rock wall in order to steady himself.

Everywhere he looked the people of this strange village had bright yellow-golden hair; so like his mother's, so like his own. It was eerie. Back in the village of Crossways, in Genesis, and all the places that he and his mother had passed through on their long journey in between, Samuel had never come across anyone else that looked quite like this; quite like *him*. He had always thought of his mother and himself as being different from other folk on the inside, but it had been their hair that had made them stand out as different on the outside too. He had seen people with very light brown, blonde, or sun-kissed bright hair, but he had never come across anyone with the same brilliant hue as theirs. But here in this extraordinary place everyone seemed to be that way from the youngest to the eldest inhabitant.

As the people of the village began to notice the newcomers that had entered the encampment they started pointing and waving in their direction. One old woman put a hand to her mouth and stood there with tears in her eyes just staring in what looked like a combination of disbelief and shock. Soon they began to move closer, to crowd around Samuel and his dog, closing in on them. Sensing Samuel's discomfort at the situation Quicksilver began a low growl deep in his throat to warn the others not to come too close.

Samuel tightened his grip on Quicksilver's flank and looked for Heather in the crowd but she had disappeared, Ash too. Everyone looked friendly enough, smiling faces pushed in on them from every direction but it was simply too much; stifling. Samuel found it difficult to catch his breath.

The voices of the gathered crowd grew louder as they gabbled between themselves and directed questions at Samuel. With a jolt he realised that they were not just using their voices to speak to him but also their minds. Their questions tumbled and crashed over one another like a battering waterfall which bore down on his already exhausted brain as they all tried to connect with him at once, their excitement palpable.

Suddenly the sun's heat seemed to intensify, Samuel's head swam with it and as his vision blurred he felt his legs turning to liquid beneath him. He lost his grip on Quicksilver, who reacted quickly by trying to nuzzle Samuel's neck in an effort to revive him but that seemed to have little effect. Realising that the boy was in real trouble, Quicksilver forced his great head under the lad's arm to support him. Samuel wavered and staggered.

As the light began to dim and fade away, Samuel was aware of a hush falling over the gathered crowd as they moved aside to let someone through. Raising his gaze as much as he could, Samuel set eyes on a very tall man who stood gazing down at him. At the man's side was a massive silver dog, a dog that seemed in every way to be Quicksilver's double.

'Welcome,' the tall man spoke, his voice deep and coming from somewhere far-off, 'I've been expecting you.'

Samuel tried so hard to stay upright but even with Quicksilver's help he could no longer fight the darkness that was claiming him. He gave in, plunged towards a black calm and collapsed into the arms of the stranger before him.

4

The Forest People

When Samuel came around some considerable time later, he found himself lying on a thin mattress on the floor, his body snug beneath a soft cover made of animal skins. He was warm, and other than a throbbing headache, felt relatively comfortable. A fire was gently crackling away in the centre of the floor, thin tendrils of white smoke tracking upwards towards a hole in the roof of the tepee-like structure he found himself in.

Freeing one arm from under the cover he reached a hand out behind him where he felt the reassuring warmth of Quicksilver's body. The dog made a move to get up and come closer to him.

'No boy, you stay there. I'm fine.' Samuel said gently and closed his eyes again. Quicksilver hesitated for a moment then resettled himself back down and continued his vigil over his young companion.

'He's a very faithful friend, I see. No doubt he's as good to you as his sister Blithe is to me.'

Samuel's eyes snapped open again. The voice was mercifully

not inside his head. Looking around the small room Samuel saw the tall man who had caught him when he fainted earlier. The man was sitting cross-legged on the far side of the fire arranging a number of colourful segments of dried and fresh fruits and roots on an earthenware plate. He smiled over at Samuel, his eyes twinkling with firelight.

'His sister?' Samuel managed, his mouth was dry and his head pounded as he attempted to get up.

The man got to his feet and came over to Samuel's side. He placed the plate of food and a large drinking bowl full of water on the ground beside them.

'Let me help you,' the man said, as he took Samuel's arm and helped him to sit upright. He held the drink to the boy's lips and supported him around the shoulders so that he could take hold of the bowl. Samuel drank deeply, cool fresh water dribbling from the corners of his mouth and down his shirtfront.

'Thank you.' Samuel gasped once he'd had his fill. He wiped his wet face with the back of a sleeve. 'Excuse me.'

'No apology needed. I'm sure you're both thirsty and hungry after your experience.' Taking the water from Samuel he gestured to the plate. 'Do you feel strong enough to eat?' he asked.

Samuel accepted it gratefully. Some of the items on the plate he knew, others were new to him. He made his way around them savouring each one as he went, holding their individual flavours in his mouth for a moment before swallowing them. When he was finished, he thanked the man who took the empty plate from his hands.

'Good?' he asked.

'Very, thank you.' Samuel put a hand to his pulsing brow.

'I think my friends were a little too eager to make your acquaintance Samuel. I can sense you've suffered for it.' The man leant towards Samuel, stretching out his large strong hands towards his temples. 'Will you let me ease the pain in your mind?' he asked.

Samuel backed away slightly.

'Please, trust me.' The man's voice was kind yet held a persuasive power in its gentle depth.

Samuel held still this time and allowed him to place his large hands on either side of his head.

'Ash tells me you call your companion Quicksilver?'

Samuel nodded.

'Well, shall I tell you a story about Quicksilver whilst I do this? The story of how he came to be lost to us when he was just a pup.'

Samuel looked into the large man's eyes in surprise. 'Yes, please.'

'It was a very difficult time for his sister Blithe. She was inconsolable for many sunrises, we all were, but we were especially worried about her. I was afraid that she would fall ill and give up on life altogether. She didn't eat properly for weeks afterwards; I think she blamed herself somehow.' The man's

91

hands moved gently around Samuel's head as he spoke. 'The two of them were out practising their hunting skills one day when Quicksilver, he was named differently when he was with us back then but we shouldn't confuse him by changing that now, he got overexcited and bounded off. He was always more flighty than Blithe, so inquisitive and headstrong. He loved being in the forest so much; there was just no stopping him. When he did not return, and we couldn't find him in the forest, we feared that he'd been killed or perhaps that a hunter or trapper had got hold of him. I guess he must have been caught and sold to an outsider.'

'An outsider?' Samuel asked.

'Yes, an outsider is someone who lives outside of the forest, in the villages beyond. I'm so glad to see he's well. Even back then he was a large dog, only a few months old but still bigger than any fully-grown dog that would ever have been seen by the outsiders before. I imagine he will have fetched a good price. Anyway, that's in the past now, we're all delighted that he's found his way back to us.'

As he had been listening Samuel had been aware of a gentle tingle making its way through the man's hands into his temples and deep inside his head. The ache began to ease and diminish as the healing sensation passed all the way through him, until the pain was gone altogether. The man released his hold on Samuel's head and patted him on the shoulders.

'There, that's better?'

Samuel nodded his astonished agreement.

'Here am I rambling on and I haven't even introduced myself. My name is Bruin. What do you say we take things slowly from here on, Samuel?'

Samuel took hold of the offered hand and shook it. It seemed that Bruin at least was familiar with this custom even if young Ash wasn't.

'I don't mean to be rude but are you quite sure that Quicksilver was your dog? Couldn't there be some mistake? He's been the butcher's dog in the village I lived in for as long as I can recall.' Samuel explained, afraid that, as kind as this man seemed, if he had a claim on Quicksilver that he would lose his good friend. That was something he couldn't bear to think about.

Bruin smiled. 'Oh there's no mistake there Samuel, he's definitely Blithe's brother.'

Samuel's gaze drifted over to Quicksilver. Dog and boy exchanged a look.

Bruin caught on to Samuel's thoughts. 'You've nothing to worry yourself about. Things don't work in the same way here as they do in the world you've been used to. Quicksilver is Blithe's brother and Blithe is my companion but neither one has ever been 'my dog'.' Seeing Samuel's confusion, Bruin continued. 'We are all equals in this place. Blithe chooses to stay with me and Quicksilver is as free to make his own choice in companions. Which I can see he has already done and, if I

93

might say so, he has made a good match.'

Quicksilver gave a *huff* of agreement, his great long tongue lolling out of his mouth. Bruin and Samuel exchanged a grin.

'You belong here too Samuel. You've also found your way home,' said Bruin.

'Me? Oh no, I'm not from here. And I certainly wasn't trying to find this place; I didn't even know it existed. I was born in the town of Genesis, that's miles away from the forest. My father is the mayor of that town and my mother...' Samuel's voice trailed off as thoughts of her flooded into his mind.

Bruin allowed a short silence to stretch between them before he spoke. 'Yes Samuel, I knew your mother and I share your loss.'

Samuel looked up at Bruin with surprise.

'She was incredibly strong. I've never heard of one of our own surviving for so long outside of the protection of the forest. She must have loved you very much to have kept going on for so many years.' Bruin placed a comforting hand on Samuel's shoulder.

What does he mean? How could he possibly have known Mama?

Samuel felt tears spring into his eyes but he continued to stare at Bruin hoping that the tears would stay put and not embarrass him by tracking down his cheeks.

'But how...?' was all Samuel managed to say out loud.

Bruin looked sadly at him, 'Lily was hardly more than a

baby when she was stolen from us. Only three years old. She loved the woods, and the animals, as we all do. But she had a special connection with life in the forest, a very strong one for such a young child. No one had the faintest idea that she'd discovered how to open the archway and get out into the woods all by herself. But then, she was a quick learner in everything she did.' Bruin paused and smiled to himself. 'Ever since she got her first look at the forest animals there was no stopping her curiosity.

'I've always imagined her running barefoot through the trees on that day when she sneaked away from us. I bet she was off chasing and playing with the forest creatures and just went too far. As soon as we found out that she was outside the forest village our elders left to search for her. They found her tracks and followed them all the way to the town of Crossways, but they were too late. Two of our people went into the village to ask if anyone had seen her but it was no good, she was already gone. We had to assume that someone travelling through had discovered her and taken her with them. We tried desperately to connect with her, you understand?' Bruin touched a finger to his own temple, Samuel nodded. 'Those of our people who were strongest in the gift tried to locate her, hoping to guide her back to us, but she must have been too far away by then for them to reach her.'

Samuel's head reeled. Had his mother not remembered that she had started her life here in the forest? That the people who brought her up and had eventually pushed her into marriage weren't her true parents? Samuel remembered the magical stories his mother used to tell him about the dreams that she had of being so close to nature and the animals. But if what this man was telling him was true, they hadn't just been dreams; they had been her *memories*. Distant memories of her life *here*.

'But *I* don't belong here. I was born outside of the forest, I'm... what did you call them... an 'outsider'. So how can you say that I've found my way home? How can I belong here?'

'Where is it that you feel you *do* belong Samuel?' Bruin asked gently.

Samuel considered. He had never felt that he fitted in anywhere. In his mother's company, when he was with Quicksilver; those were the only times he had really felt at 'home'.

'I don't know.' Samuel replied.

'I know this must be hard, Samuel, but think about it. Didn't you ever feel different from other children?'

Samuel nodded. Of course he had, always.

'Did you and your mother have ways that were considered strange by others?' asked Bruin.

'Well, yes. But I just thought Mama was special and that I had picked things up from her.' Samuel answered.

'She certainly was special Samuel, as you are. It seems that having an outsider for a father has not dampened the skills that have been passed to you by your mother, the powers that were passed down to her from our ancestors. That's how it has always been with our people. I can help you to understand your skills and to teach you how to master them. I can show you that you *do* belong here. With us.' Bruin patted Samuel on the shoulder. 'But that's enough for now. Please, rest. Time for learning will come soon enough. You and Quicksilver have earned yourselves some peace and comfort. You're both safe here, and most welcome. When you feel ready and strong enough to start work on your gift you can let me know. Until then, take your time.'

Samuel settled back down beneath his cover and watched Bruin walk to the door of the tepee. Quicksilver shuffled over towards Samuel and encircled the boy protectively with his body.

As he pushed aside the fabric doorway Bruin looked back over his shoulder and smiled at the great silver dog and the boy nestled within his four gigantic paws.

'Sleep well. Nephew.' he said, and then he was gone.

Samuel slept very deeply and his dream was so real and vivid that he could actually smell the flowers in his mother's long golden hair as she danced around their special clearing. Her face glowed, her eyes bright and happy.

'Oh Samuel, you're such a clever one. You've found your home. Be happy my darling, I love you.' She swayed and spun nimbly around. Her laughter like the tinkle of crystal bells as she glided through the tall grass and ferns. Samuel had never seen her looking so healthy and full of life.

He could have stayed and watched her forever. Perhaps he would have done just that if it had been up to him, but a strange sensation moved through his limbs and he felt himself being pulled strongly and steadily backwards, away from his mother. She was still smiling, blowing him kisses and waving goodbye as he flew noiselessly backwards through the trees away from her dancing figure.

'No! I want to stay with her. Mama? Mama!' Samuel tried to grab passing branches, to dig his fingers into the earth and tangled undergrowth that slipped by beneath him to stop his retreat, but he couldn't catch hold of anything. In his hands everything just melted away, nothing had any real substance. The light of the clearing began to fade as he left it further and further behind.

'Mama!'

Samuel sat up, his arms outstretched in front of him reaching desperately into the empty air.

He was back in the tepee.

As Samuel opened his eyes and looked around he saw Quicksilver standing in front of him. The big dog had his head tilted to one side, his tail tucked between his back legs.

'It's all right, boy,' Samuel stood and hugged his friend. 'It was just a dream.'

'Dreams can be powerful things, Samuel. Don't dismiss

them.' Bruin's voice startled Samuel. 'They hold truths that our conscious minds rarely perceive. I heard you cry out, I hope you don't mind my entering your tepee?'

Samuel shook his head.

'You're all right?' Bruin asked.

'Yes, thank you.'

Bruin smiled down at Samuel. 'Then let's begin.'

That first day Samuel and Quicksilver were shown all around the settlement and introduced to those who lived within the protection of its boundary walls. The main area was taken over by rings of tepees, which were arranged in a number of decreasing circles around a central open space. In this area, Bruin explained, the people of the forest village would hold their meetings, gatherings and where, on special occasions, feasts were held around a large fire.

Leaving the tepees behind, Bruin led Samuel towards a number of small timber buildings, which stood separately from the main area.

'These two are our nurseries.' Bruin opened the door of one and allowed Samuel to look in. Samuel cast his eyes over the neat rows of young plants which grew in the many pots and troughs laid out on the earth floor of the room.

'These are mostly sapling trees which will be replanted in the forest to replace the ones we cut down for firewood and for making other items we need,' Bruin explained. 'We make it our responsibility to ensure that the forest is replenished and harmed as little as possible by our existence here. Sadly that's not something that the outsiders do, or even understand.' Bruin shook his head as he closed the door again. 'That's why the forest is slowly being eaten away by their misuse of it. They take what they want and never think to the future.'

Samuel had seen much during his time in Crossways to know that there was truth in what Bruin said. Even in the five years that he had lived in the village of the outsiders he had noticed how wantonly the people who lived there cut into the tree line of the forest, pushing it back further and further. Harsh open land littered with tree stumps, splinters and rubbish now scarred the edge of the forest where once proud tall trunks had reached majestically skyward.

'These are our... well, you can see for yourself.' Bruin grinned and opened the door of one of three small huts.

Samuel looked inside. 'Ah, I see,' he laughed. 'What a luxury! I haven't seen one of those in a long time. We never had one in our tiny home in Crossways.'

The small hut had a deep hole cut into the ground in the centre of the slatted floor. A pile of thick soft leaves lay against one wall within reach of the hole and in one corner stood a large wooden bucket filled with fragrant pine needles. Surprisingly, for its function, the room smelled of nothing but fresh pine.

'Once you've... used it... you throw a handful of the needles down the hole.'

Samuel grinned and nodded that he understood.

'And over here,' Bruin gestured and led the way, 'we have our washing area.'

Bruin demonstrated how to use the hand-pump, which brought fresh clean water up from deep beneath the ground. 'If a quick freshen-up is all you need then most of us just stand in this area for that. But if you want a little more privacy, for a more thorough wash, we have these now.' Bruin proudly demonstrated how the village's new shower system worked.

A full bucket of water could be hooked onto a rope that could then be hoisted above one of three stalls. Each stall had four sides made from tightly woven reeds offering the occupant total secrecy. 'This is what we use to wash ourselves.' Bruin pulled open the door of one stall and handed Samuel a spongy lump from inside. 'It foams up in the water and gives off a nice smell. Just wet it, rub it all over then pull on this,' he said, pointing to the dangling rope which would tip the bucket that swung precariously overhead, 'and there you go, clean and fresh.'

Samuel agreed that the system was ingenious but wondered just how pleasant it could be to have a bucket-load of freezing cold water suddenly drenching you as you stood shivering below.

'Of course there's always the river if you want a long bathe but this is handy after a day of hard work; quick and close to home.'

They carried on their way and although Samuel felt slightly embarrassed by what had happened the day before, and worried how people might react to him, he soon found he had nothing to be anxious about. Everyone they met offered their apologies for their overbearing greetings the day before and welcomed him warmly to their village.

Bruin introduced him to Bluebell, the oldest living member of the forest clan. Her face was pinched and wizened like an old weather-beaten fruit. Her fingers were twisted and bent from long years spent doing what she loved above all else; making clothes for the forest folk. By way of a 'hello' she grunted at Samuel and gestured for him to slowly walk around her.

Bruin hid a smile behind his hand as Samuel did as he was told. The old woman remained seated on the ground and peered up at him as he wandered around her in a slow circle. An aged and grumpy-looking weasel sat by the old woman's side and bared its teeth at Samuel as he moved around. Both the woman and her well-worn companion had the palest grey eyes Samuel had ever seen. Eventually the woman grunted again and waved him away, dismissing him as if he had done something unacceptable or insulting. She got up stiffly and hobbled back inside her tepee, her weasel scuttling along at her heel.

'Did I offend her?' Samuel asked as they walked off.

'No, no. Bluebell is a woman of few words. But she has many other skills, as you'll see soon enough.'

As they wandered around from one dwelling to another Samuel came to see how the forest people, as he had come to think of them, looked after each other. If one was too old to gather food or to cook it, his neighbour would share what he had with him. If a woman had need of someone to watch over her young children whilst she went about an errand, another would happily lend a hand. Samuel had never seen this behaviour before, though he had longed for it during the most difficult times he and his mother had gone through. The forest people were more like one huge family than a village full of different households.

Many of them had animals, not pets or livestock, but more like friends, similar to the relationship that he had with Quicksilver. Their animal companions were not restricted to dogs, far from it; they shared their homes and their lives with wild cats, birds, rabbits and small deer, amongst many others.

Ash appeared and greeted Samuel warmly with an exuberant handshake. The young lad introduced him to Sorrel, one of his friends, whose animal companion was a snake the length of Quicksilver's tail. The reptile hung about Sorrel's neck, its body coiled around his arms like thick and intricately decorated bracelets. Samuel had watched amused as the young boy chattered away amiably to his companion as he wandered around the encampment, weighed down by the heavy snake.

Bruin had explained that animals within the village did not trouble each other. Even the fox and the rabbit tolerated one another's presence without so much as a hungry or worried look.

There was an unspoken law that within the boundaries of the forest village no hunting was permitted. Outside, in the deep of the woods, was another matter; there the animals were free to follow their natural instincts.

'Your existence here seems perfect,' Samuel said to Bruin when they were back in his tepee. 'Everyone gets along and looks after each other. It's such a shame that it's not like this everywhere. If only the people that live in the villages outside of the forest could learn to live peacefully like you do.'

Bruin was brewing them a delicious tea concocted of wild flowers and berries. The aroma permeated the air inside the tent bringing the scents of nature indoors, lifting their spirits.

'The outsiders aren't like us, Samuel. They're too greedy, too blind to see value in the things that we do. They can never learn to live in harmony because it's against their nature. Our existence here is far richer, better, but living in the forest also carries its own dangers. Over the years we've lost friends, and family members, out in the woods. Those losses are felt by all of us here. Our senses are heightened far above those of the people who live outside the forest.

'When one of the outsiders suffers the loss of someone they love or care for they feel the merest shadow of what we feel. They call it grief and grief can be a deeply felt thing that leaves an ache in the heart for a long, long time. But we feel it even more strongly because of our connection to each other. That's why it's so wonderful that you and Quicksilver have found your way here. You've given us all renewed strength and hope.'

'But can't the outsiders, as you call them, be *taught* how to

104

live better? To be more like your people? Couldn't you teach them?' Samuel asked.

Bruin sighed. 'You've lived your whole life around those people, you should know better than any of us how selfish they are. There is much you don't know or understand, Samuel. In the past our people have tried to help the outsiders to a less destructive way of life but they are deaf to our words.' Bruin opened up a small package he had brought with him. 'Here, try some of this.' he said, changing the subject.

Samuel settled himself more comfortably in front of the fire and accepted the strip of dried meat that Bruin held out to him. It tasted smoky, salty and delicious; the tang of it nipping his tongue was a wonderful contrast to the smooth fragrant tea.

'Let's hope those two don't smell this or we'll get no peace to eat it!' said Bruin.

Quicksilver and Blithe lay asleep beside them. Their limbs a silver jumble, so entwined that Samuel could not easily tell where one dog ended and the other began.

'They're getting on really well aren't they?' Samuel nodded towards the sleeping dogs.

'Yes, animals are far purer than us humans; their instincts are so precious. If two human children were separated at such a young age they would never know each other if they met again as adults. But animals, they have something rooted inside them far more deeply than we do.' Bruin smiled affectionately at them.

'Are you... am I... human? I mean, am I half-human and half something else?' Samuel asked.

'Oh no, we're all human, Samuel. It's just that when humans chose to live outside the woods they forgot their true ways, their skills and how to use their minds fully. Sometimes you may come across a person who lives outside the forest but has discovered a little of the skills hidden deep inside themselves. Perhaps they have a persuasive way with animals, or have a deeply intuitive way of understanding another person's feelings, or they may just choose to live a simple life near to the forest feeling somehow drawn to be there. But those people are often laughed at and ridiculed for their ways.

'Most outsiders don't like anything unusual, it frightens them, makes them feel uncomfortable. Soon they start to use words like "witch" or "wicked" or even "freak". Those ignorant ones believe that folk who are different have something wrong with them and often they cast them out or try to force them to conform to their way of thinking to fit in. It's best to avoid all outsiders, Samuel, they're only interested in making the most money or having the most precious possessions and they don't care what they have to do to get those things.'

Samuel thought of his mother and of how many people in Crossways had avoided her in the street or openly laughed at her simple and gentle ways - the men who only wanted her for her looks and the women who had sneered at her beauty afraid that she would take their husbands away from them. They had

106

been jealous of her, but Bruin was right, they had also been afraid of her, because she was different, because she was special. Perhaps Bruin was right; it was better to leave the outsiders to themselves and live separate to them.

'If you're my uncle, my mother's brother, are there others of our family? Don't I have grandparents?' Samuel asked.

Bruin stiffened and turned his face away.

Samuel's question hung in the air and he wondered if he had misspoken, then Bruin answered.

'You did have, but they're gone now.' He threw the dregs of his tea into the fire sending it hissing. A small cloud of smoke puffed upwards. Blithe groaned in her sleep and shifted position on the sandy floor.

'What happened to them?' Samuel ventured gently, sensing there was something painful here.

His uncle shook his head sadly. 'It was long ago, before your mother was taken away. It's something that I will tell you about in good time, Samuel, but not yet, now isn't the right moment for such talk, believe me.'

Samuel was desperate to hear more but he wasn't prepared to push Bruin on the matter. It was obvious that this particular subject was closed, for now.

'But,' Bruin looked up, his face brighter now, 'I would be glad to hear more about your past, Samuel, of where you were raised and, if you feel up to it, all you can tell me about your mother?' Bruin's eyes were gentle and expectant and Samuel saw something of his mother in them. He hesitated only a moment before he began.

Samuel and Bruin were not disturbed as Samuel told his story. His uncle listened intently, interrupting only a few times to ask for more details, pushing his nephew to bring his mother Lily alive again with his words. Samuel had feared that to talk about her would be unbearably painful but as he described all the things he had loved most about her; the sound of her voice, her kindness and patience, the way her hair flowed when she danced, it was as if she was there in the room with them. He even found himself telling Bruin of all the things that she used to do that had annoyed him; making sure he had combed his hair every morning, bidding him to be polite to everyone – even those people who wouldn't pass the time of day with them. The way she always insisted on helping to carry the heavy water bucket to their hut when she really should have been resting.

When he came to tell of how his mother had died, of how and where he had come to put her to rest, Samuel had to stop several times to collect himself. Bruin sat silently during these pauses, giving Samuel space and time. But it felt good to share the burden of those memories with his uncle.

'It sounds as if you chose a worthy place for her.' Bruin said quietly. 'Will you show it to me one day, Samuel? I would like to see it.'

Samuel nodded.

After wondering if it was the right thing to do, Samuel decided to tell Bruin what else he had done before leaving Crossways. His face reddened a little with the shame of his actions. But Bruin's laughter boomed out as he heard of how Samuel had burned down Mr Sanderson's bakery.

'Oh lad, such a temper. How you remind me of myself! Don't let me interrupt, I beg you. Do carry on.'

Samuel told him of how he had come to the decision to enter the forest and later recounted the story of his encounter with the bear. Bruin's face darkened with concern and he asked to see Samuel's wounds.

'That's not a mistake you can afford to make again, lad.' Bruin said solemnly. 'I'll teach you to read the woods and the tracks of the animals that live there. You were very lucky that Quicksilver showed up when he did. It's more likely that the bear was after your fish, but we've lost people to bears before, Samuel. You need to keep your senses clear and your eyes wide open.'

Bruin listened to how his nephew and Quicksilver had survived in the forest as they had made their way by the course of the river. Finally Samuel ended with how he and Quicksilver had met up with Ash and his mother.

'And the rest you know,' he said at last.

Bruin sat nodding, considering all that he had been told. He absent-mindedly stroked his sleeve as he thought.

'Oh, I almost forgot! I've a gift for you Samuel. Give me a

moment.' Bruin said and stepped outside. He returned moments later and handed his nephew a bundle. 'All ready, just for you.'

'For me?' Samuel asked in wonder as he accepted his uncle's offering.

It was a newly made set of clothes. The bundle consisted of a pair of deerskin trousers and a tunic with deep pockets in the front and, most precious of all, his very own cloak. They were identical to the clothing that all the other villagers wore. Samuel grinned as he suddenly realised the true meaning of his strange encounter with Bluebell earlier in the day. The old woman had been quite literally sizing him up. Without a measuring tape, without even laying a hand on him, only using her own two eyes, she had assessed his dimensions perfectly and set about making him his forest outfit straight away.

His new clothes were far more suited to life in the forest than his own threadbare fabric clothes. Besides, his old clothes were getting too small for him now anyway. Due to a lack of money, he had been forced to make them last. His new trousers and tunic were made of patches of treated deerskin sewn together with animal sinews; the fine stitches so precise and neat that they were barely visible. Bruin briefly explained the process the skin was put through to make them not only tough and hardwearing but also light and delicate against the skin. On Bruin's instruction Samuel reluctantly tried to tear a corner of the hide between his fingers but he was unable to do so.

Their ingenious design kept you cool when the sun was high

and conserved your body heat on cold nights. Samuel was delighted with them, especially his cloak. Ash's cloak was the first one that Samuel had seen and he had admired it greatly but hadn't been able to examine it up close. Now he had one of his very own and it was a magnificent and intricate thing.

'How did she manage to make all these in such a short time?' Samuel asked in awe as he ran his fingers over the tightly woven grasses that made up his cloak.

'I told you she was skilled! You can barely see that woman's fingers moving once she gets started, they're just a blur!' Bruin grinned.

'They're all wonderful. But my cloak... it's so...' Samuel couldn't find the words.

Bruin laughed softly. 'Beautiful isn't it? It's made from especially tall blades of strong grass that we gather only for this purpose. Bluebell weaves them together very tightly, it's a marvel to me how she manages it with those bent old fingers of hers but she's never produced a bad one yet. She's teaching a few of the young ones how to do it but no one can make them quite like her. If they're made with skilled hands they last a long time and keep both the wind out and the snow off your back in winter. In the greener seasons they're invaluable to us when hunting or for hiding from predators or outsiders in the woods.'

Samuel watched as his uncle took his cloak from his hand to demonstrate.

'May I?' he asked.

'Of course.' Samuel answered, though he was reluctant to give it up, even for a moment.

'Imagine that you've been caught in an open area, a small clearing, and you need someplace to hide quickly?'

Samuel nodded.

'The nearest trees are too far away to get to fast enough, there's no boulder or anything else large enough to crouch behind. What would you do?' Bruin asked.

Samuel thought, then shrugged.

Bruin flapped out the cloak to its full size and, nimbly throwing himself to the ground, tossed the cloak into the air above him so that it came down and settled over his body, covering him completely from view. Suddenly he was transformed into a moss-covered boulder or a small grassy mound right there before him. Samuel remembered how Ash had used his cloak in this way and how it had confused both himself and Quicksilver.

Samuel laughed in delight. 'It's wonderful!'

Bruin stood up again and handed the cloak to him with a nod. 'All yours.'

'Thank you, very much. I'll thank Bluebell, perhaps I could make her a gift?'

Bruin smiled. 'That's a nice thought but I shouldn't bother, she's not the sort that would appreciate a fuss.' Bruin patted his tunic pocket then reached inside. 'Oh, and before I forget,' he pulled out a string-like object and handed it over to Samuel.

'A necklace? I've noticed that everyone wears them here. What are these beads made from?' Samuel brought the oddly shaped beads closer to his face to examine them more closely. A faint earthy odour exuded from them.

'They're not beads, they are dried pieces of fungus which grow on a particular type of tree in the forest. If you're ever unwell or injured you should chew on one of them, it helps. For safety we carry them with us always. Forming them into a necklace makes them easy to carry and quickly accessible.' Bruin tied the leather strip in a knot at the back of Samuel's neck. 'The taste is rather bitter and unpleasant but the effect is swift.'

'Thanks.' Samuel could hardly wait to try on his new clothes too but carefully laid them aside for later on.

'Samuel, you mentioned a book earlier. May I look at it?' Bruin asked, gesturing towards Samuel's discarded bag that lay by his bed.

Samuel had not looked in his deerskin bag since he had arrived in the forest village. He hoped that his mother's writing book had not suffered any damage. Unpacking the contents he laid out the remnants of his previous life neatly on the ground and carefully unwrapped his mother's book. He was relieved to see that it was unharmed. He handed the book over to his uncle.

Bruin took it in his hands reverently. The large man closed

his eyes for a moment and held the book gently against his chest. When he next looked up, Samuel was surprised to see tears standing in his uncle's eyes.

'Forgive me, Samuel, there's so much of your mother here.' Bruin patted his open hand on the book's cover. 'It just took me by surprise. May I?'

Samuel nodded. 'Please.'

Samuel watched as Bruin leafed through the book, touching certain words, following the shape of letters with his large fingers. Every now and then he would stop to ask Samuel more about his mother and the time that they had spent together. Bruin and the forest people didn't have the skills of writing or reading so Samuel sat by his uncle's side and briefly explained some of the words and symbols as he moved through the book. Bruin gave gentle delighted laughs to see his young nephew's scrawl copying the cool steady hand of his mother. When Bruin had finished, he carefully closed the book and returned it to Samuel.

'You did well to take it with you. Your mother wanted you to have it. I can feel her love for you on every page.'

'Thank you.' Samuel replaced the book carefully in his bag.

'Now!' Bruin raised his voice and clapped his hands together. 'Let's celebrate the present and look to the future! We'd all like to welcome you and Quicksilver back home properly. If you feel up to it, we'd like to have a feast tonight in your honour. There'll be plenty to eat, some music perhaps, and a chance to get to know everyone a little better. What do you say? Would you like that?'

'Yes, very much.' Samuel replied with enthusiasm. He could make some new friends and have the chance to try out his new clothes; it would be fun.

'Good!' Bruin nodded. 'That's settled then. I'll go and let the others know that they can go ahead with the preparations.'

Samuel took the opportunity to take a short nap after his uncle left. When he awoke, the patch of sky, which he could see through the opening in the roof of his tepee, had dimmed to the shade of early evening. The burble of amiable chatter and gentle laughter floated in from all around. Women were singing as they prepared and cooked the food and the tantalizing wafts of their efforts mingled and travelled in the air to where Samuel lay, causing his mouth to water. Quicksilver and Blithe were still gently snoring on the floor beside him. It seemed that Quicksilver was making up for all the sleep he had denied himself on their trek through the forest.

Bruin arrived with a large bowl of water and waited whilst Samuel washed the day's dirt from his hands and face and smartened himself up for the feast.

'How do I look?' Samuel asked his uncle as he stood in his perfectly fitting new clothes.

'Like the true forester you are.' Bruin slapped him on the back.

'Bruin and Samuel,' came Heather's voice from just outside.

'The meal is ready.'

'Thank you, we're just coming.' Bruin replied. 'Ready?' he asked Samuel.

Samuel nodded, a little knot of nervousness tying his tongue. Blithe and Quicksilver needed no encouragement; both sleeping dogs were wide-awake and bolting out of the doorway before either Samuel or Bruin had time to walk across the floor.

'Well!' Bruin laughed and clapped one of his broad hands on Samuel's shoulder, 'I'm a mite hungry myself, what do you say young Samuel, shall we go eat before our companions scoff the lot?' With a great flourish he held back the door-skins for his nephew to pass.

All the people of the village were there, as were their animal companions. To honour the special occasion the women had adorned themselves with their best forest jewellery. Bracelets, anklets and necklaces made from acorns, seeds, teeth and bones, jangled and clattered together as they walked and danced around. The open area in the centre of the rings of tepees had been cleared of all the usual everyday items and occupying the space was a huge blazing fire.

Children ran around squealing with delight, chasing and catching each other. Many danced to the music being played on wonderful instruments beautifully carved from wood and animal bone. The combined sounds came together and lifted into the air with the hazy heat and sparks from the fire.

116

Fire-rosy faces turned to greet Samuel as he approached those responsible for watching and turning the heavily laden wooden skewers of meat that were expertly balanced, close to the leaping flames. Samuel went over to two of the older women in the group who seemed to be in charge and held out the cooking utensils which he had brought along with him from Crossways.

'I wonder if you might find these of use?' he said.

The ladies closely examined what they had been given; they had never seen such things made by outsiders before. It remained to be seen whether these items made from outsiders' metal would do the job any better than those they had been using in the forest village since time began, but the women recognised their intended purpose and smiled at Samuel.

'Well, thank you. We'll see that they're put to good use.'

The woman who had spoken placed them alongside the other forks, skewers and spoons on the serving table behind her and there they lay, looking rather out of place beside the hand-carved forest cutlery.

'Here boy, get this down you. You need to build up those muscles of yours.' A well-built man thrust a thick slab of dark meat on a stick, into Samuel's hand.

Crisp and crunchy on the outside the flame-blackened meat was cooked to perfection in the centre and was the best he had ever tasted.

Finding Bruin in the crowd Samuel sat down by his side and

happily tucked into his food. When it was a little cooler Samuel pulled off a large chunk of the meat and threw it to Quicksilver who caught it expertly in mid-air and chomped it away quickly. The great dog had been sitting patiently eyeing Samuel's prize, saliva threading down from the corners of his silver mouth.

'What a feast! I've never seen so much food.' Samuel said, casting his eyes over the spread of vividly coloured fruits and vegetables that had been laid out on another large table near the fire. Many of the varieties were completely unknown to him, their tastes and textures wonderful new discoveries.

'We don't do this every night, but tonight we have something special to celebrate.' Bruin slapped Samuel on the back and stood, raising his cup to the gathered folk.

'Please friends. Quiet a moment!' A hush fell over the gathering. 'Will you all join with me and raise your drinks to celebrate this wonderful blessing guided to us by the Man In Green; my nephew, son of Lily, grandson of the great Alder, has come home to us!'

A great cheer went up, and for the first time in his life Samuel felt himself to be part of a community that cared about him.

Everyone took another drink and cheered again. Without warning, Quicksilver threw his head back and barked his awful, powerful bark. It was just one single bark but it was enough to cause all those in the village to cover their ears in fright and to send the tiny ones into a chorus of shocked bawling.

118

Bruin stood again, one hand raised to usher calm.

'Forgive me, forgive me. How could I forget? Raise your cups once more, my friends, to honour the great Quicksilver, brother of Blithe, friend of Samuel!'

The people relaxed and the children were comforted. Laughter vibrated around the crowd and all cheered and cried their welcome to the huge silver dog. Quicksilver celebrated in his own way by devouring two huge chunks of deer meat and a massive bear steak all to himself.

Samuel glanced around the crowd. Bruin had mentioned that there were only a handful of people that Samuel hadn't met yet; three young friends and one of their fathers were out in the forest hunting for food. They had left before Samuel and Quicksilver had arrived and were too far away to be connected with to tell them about the feast they were missing. All four were expected back the next day and Samuel was to be introduced to them after they had rested. Then that would be everyone, all the people of the village, his new home, his new friends.

The fire crackled on, sending sparking orange flecks spiralling up into the night sky. Clearly defined against the deepest purple-black, the blanket of stars above were so much brighter than Samuel had ever seen them before. The youngest children began to get sleepy, thumbs in mouths they nestled against their mothers' chests, their eyelids too heavy to keep from falling, the heat of the fire lulling them into their dreams.

The dances, games and singing went on until the sky began to lighten. Samuel only wished that his mother could have been there, she would have loved it so much. It was cruel to think that she had been robbed of this wonderful place and the company of her people.

Everyone ate and drank well that night. Samuel returned to his tepee with Quicksilver, both had bellies that were strained to overfull. Samuel, who had tasted his first forest-brewed liquor, walked a little unsteadily, giggling and whispering nonsense to himself as he went. Quicksilver looked at his young friend suspiciously and gruffed in annoyance each time Samuel bounced off his great silver flank.

Thankfully his uncle had told him that the intoxicating liquid he had been drinking would leave him with nothing more than a deep thirst the next morning. This was just as well as Samuel had agreed, in a mood of high emotion that night as he sat by the fire, that he was ready for his training to begin the very next day.

As Samuel slipped into his bed, and a deep slumber, he was blissfully unaware that Bruin had taken his inebriated nephew at his word and had some stretching work planned out for him.

5

Training

Blithe awoke Samuel very early in the morning with a vigorous and unwelcome face-licking. A wake-up call that she had, there was no doubt in Samuel's groggy mind, been asked to deliver by Bruin. Reluctantly Samuel forced himself upright and slowly made his way to the washing area that he had been shown the day before. Here he met up with Bruin.

Bruin had not long finished his own ablutions; an upturned bucket dripped lazy fat droplets down into one of the cubicles. Already dressed, Samuel's uncle was standing at its door briskly drying his hair, his big broad face ruddy and glowing with health.

'Good morning! Well then, what will it be?' Bruin asked gesturing to a shower stall with one hand and towards the water-pump with the other.

Out of laziness more than anything else Samuel opted for the full shower experience. He was to regret his decision almost immediately.

The water was so cold that Samuel had no chance of feeling sleepy once he had pulled the rope and tipped that first bucket-load down over his head. The effect was to have him wide-awake, alert and intensely grumpy within seconds.

Bruin laughed heartily at Samuel's gasps.

'For goodness sake, lad, you sound like a girl! It's good for you! It'll wake you up and get you ready for a busy day ahead.'

Samuel was rubbing himself down with shaking hands, trying to get the feeling back into his frozen gooseflesh-covered limbs when he heard Bruin's voice again.

'Here comes another one. Don't say I'm not good to you!' he called.

A fresh bucketful appeared above Samuel's head and swung there, ice-cold water slopping over the sides. The rope dangled in front of Samuel's face but he wasn't about to pull on it.

'No! One was qu… qu… quite enough, thanks! Besides, I'm nearly dry now.' He hoped this excuse would save him as he quickly tried to get dry enough to slip back into his clothes. Flicking the droplets off his shivering body with a small piece of animal hide.

'Nonsense! Here, I'll do it for you.' And without further warning one of Bruin's huge hands appeared over the top of Samuel's shower screen and grabbed for the rope.

'No, really!' Samuel tried to bat the rope out of his uncle's reach but he was too late. 'Please!' he pleaded.

'Please?' Bruin mimicked his nephew, pretending to misunderstand his meaning. 'All right, no problem,' he said, and yanked on the rope.

This time Bruin's laughter was diluted by the second bucketful of freezing water cascading down over Samuel's head. The deluge also served to drown out Samuel's rather rude response to his uncle's unwarranted action.

Thankfully a third bucket never appeared and when Samuel emerged from the shower stall, Blithe and his uncle had disappeared. Quicksilver sat grinning at him.

Clean, dressed and ready for his first lesson, Samuel stood with Quicksilver outside his tepee and waited for Bruin to reappear.

'Ready?' Bruin asked as he approached with Blithe by his side. Samuel noticed a quiver of arrows on his uncle's back with a bow slung over it.

'I guess so,' Samuel replied. His mood was a little lighter now that he was feeling warm again and he was looking forward to the challenges ahead.

Bruin's eyes glittered with excitement; he was looking forward to this even more than Samuel. He had a feeling that this boy, his own kin, was going to be a very good pupil indeed. 'You go and fill up your water pouch then meet me at the entrance.'

Samuel did as his uncle instructed then made his way through the cluster of tepees and past the remnants of the previous night's celebrations on his way to where he remembered the entrance tunnel to be.

The village was still quiet, no one else seemed to be up and around yet but as he and Quicksilver neared the entrance a sound behind them made Samuel turn around.

Samuel saw someone leaving their tepee. It was a girl, no, he corrected himself as he watched her, she was a young woman. She didn't look much older than himself but she had left much of what could be called 'girlishness' behind her some time ago. He watched her carefully replace the animal skin that covered the doorway to her tepee and creep past the water barrel that sat just outside. Stretching her arms wide and throwing her head back the young woman yawned extravagantly into the morning air. Suddenly sensing she was not alone she glanced over and caught sight of Samuel and Quicksilver. Samuel saw her face clearly then and knew that he had never seen her before.

'She must be one of the party of hunters that Bruin told us about last night,' he thought to Quicksilver.

There was surprise and a little embarrassment in her look but no trace of fear or alarm; she must already have been told of his presence in her village.

'I didn't know they were back yet,' Samuel thought distractedly as he stared at her.

It looked as if she was headed for the showers as he could just make out a 'soap-root' in one of her slim long-fingered hands and a set of clean clothes lay over her other arm. She smiled and lifted a hand in their direction, put a finger to her lips in a 'hushing' signal, then thumbed over her shoulder towards the tepee she had just left. Samuel understood that there was someone still asleep inside.

Samuel had never been terribly interested in looking at girls. There had been one pretty dark-haired girl back in Crossways that he had occasionally exchanged shy smiles with but he had never spent a great deal of time thinking about her and had never made a move to even speak to her. But, looking at this young woman Samuel felt that he wanted to meet her, to talk and be close to her. Overwhelmed by a strange and new feeling, a tingling in his skin, a tumbling sensation in his stomach, Samuel continued to gape at her thinking that he had never seen anything lovelier in his whole life.

Despite the distance that separated them he could make out the vivid green hue of her eyes, the delicate arch of her eyebrows. Her golden hair was knotted in a haphazard bundle on top of her head, her cheeks were grubby, her clothes smeared with dirt from days spent in the deepest parts of the forest but somehow none of this detracted from her beauty at all.

Quicksilver head-butted his young companion in the shoulder to raise him from the daze he had fallen into. Suddenly realising that he had been staring, Samuel quickly raised his hand and returned her gesture of 'hello'. He watched as she smiled then disappeared between the tepees on her way towards the showers.

'Samuel? What's keeping you?' Bruin's voice slipped inside his mind.

His uncle had connected with him using his gift to communicate. Still standing gawping in the direction in which the young woman had disappeared Samuel suddenly felt embarrassed and hoped that his uncle wasn't able to pick up on what had been going through his mind.

Concentrating hard he sent back his message. 'Sorry, Uncle, I'm on my way.' Samuel hurried along with Quicksilver. 'I wonder what we're in for, old boy,' he mumbled to Quicksilver, under his breath.

Bruin stood waiting at the mouth of the entrance tunnel with Blithe at his side.

'You heard me clearly?' Bruin asked.

'Yes.'

'Good. Soon you'll be more comfortable when connecting with the other villagers too. It must seem strange to you after only being able to communicate with your mother in this way up until now.'

'It is a little strange, but I think that it was just a shock that first time when so many voices were in my head all at the same time.' Samuel explained.

Bruin nodded. 'Come then, let's get going.'

Samuel followed his uncle into the tunnel.

'I see the hunting party has returned already?' Samuel said as casually as he could as they walked.

'Yes. Ahh... I see. Is that what kept you?' Bruin laughed. 'You saw young Willow?'

'I saw someone, a girl,' Samuel replied.

'And you were distracted from your purpose?' said Bruin. 'I can't say I blame you, lad, she's very beautiful and only a little older than yourself you may be interested to know.'

'Interested? Me? No, not at all. Why would I be interested? I mean I...' Samuel stammered.

Bruin laughed again. 'Don't try to deny it, I can feel the heat from your cheeks burning into my back! There's no harm in admiring a pretty face. Willow's a fine girl. She's an exceptional hunter and is blessed with a deep understanding of the gift.'

Willow.

Samuel turned the name over in his mind.

Willow...

When his uncle came to a sudden standstill at the end of the tunnel Samuel walked right into his back.

'Sorry,' he said sheepishly, coming to his senses.

'Right, boy, that's enough of that. I want your full attention for the rest of the day.'

Samuel could just make out his uncle's big friendly face grinning at him through the gloom.

'Yes, Uncle.'

'Good. Now, Ash's mother showed you how this is done, didn't she?' Bruin asked, referring to the procedure for opening and closing the archway.

'Well, I saw her open it but I have no idea what she did. I

supposed it to be some kind of enchantment?'

'Magic? No.' Bruin shook his head. 'Outsiders would see it as that, or worse; "witchcraft" they'd probably call it. Actually it's far more natural than that.'

Samuel listened carefully to his uncle, pushing all other thoughts to the back of his mind, clearing the way for learning.

'Everything has energy inside it,' Bruin explained. 'From the smallest grain of sand to the largest mountain. A thing may not "live" in the same way as we do; it may not breath in and out or need sustenance to exist but still it will have an energy trapped inside it that we can connect with and manipulate with our own energy.'

Bruin waited whilst Samuel considered this.

'Do you mean that we can make anything move or do what we want it to do?' Samuel asked.

'No, not quite.' Bruin shook his head. 'Objects can be moved or manipulated but it depends on the strength of the gift within the person who is doing the moving as to how far this can be taken. There are some amongst our people who struggle to persuade a leaf to turn over and then others who could bring down a small tree if they concentrated on it hard enough. Here, let me show you what I mean and then you can try it.'

Bruin turned to face the tumble of boulders that blocked their exit from the tunnel. As before, when Samuel had watched Ash's mother perform this same task, there was a short pause before the sound of the rocks scraping and grinding against one another began.

A pinpoint of sunlight broke through between the tightly packed rubble as the individual boulders began to separate, shuffle and move out of their way. The spot of light grew to the size of a fist and then larger still, until Samuel could look out, through the archway, and into the green and brown patchwork of the woods beyond. The experience of watching this happen was no less exciting than the first time, but to think that he himself could be taught to do such a thing seemed almost impossible to believe.

The four of them walked through the stone archway into the sweet morning air of the forest beyond. Scents of wild flowers and tree sap greeted them like old friends.

'This is very important, Samuel; every time you open this archway you must be sure that no outsiders are close-by. There's no telling what they might do if they ever found our people. It's your duty as one of us to protect this place and the secret of our home. Do you understand me?' Bruin's eyes were serious and intent as he waited for Samuel's reply.

'Yes, of course. I understand.'

'Good.' The lines around his uncle's eyes softened a little. 'No outsider has ever been known to venture this deeply into the forest, but that day may come and we have to be prepared for the possibility.'

Samuel nodded.

'Now, let us begin. It's your turn. Try to close the opening.'

Bruin took a step back to give Samuel room.

Caught between the desire to succeed and the fear of embarrassing himself if he failed, Samuel stood uncertainly before the opening. Looking to Quicksilver for encouragement, he reached out a hand to pat the dog's coat for luck and received a long steady lick across his open palm.

'Thanks, boy!' Samuel said as he wiped the dog's drool onto his trousers.

Okay, I can do this. Samuel told himself.

He was about to close his eyes to begin when a young girl came skipping along the tunnel towards him. The elfin figure, no more than five years old, Samuel reckoned, came to a stop and stood just on the other side of the archway staring up at him with her big blue eyes, her impish face framed by dazzling yellow hair. She chewed a finger and twisted one foot into the sandy earth as she grinned at Samuel and Bruin through the opening.

'Get along with you Ivy. Run back to your Mama now or I'll come and put you over my knee; you're putting Samuel off.' Bruin called to the youngster.

Ivy turned around and ran off back down the tunnel. She was giggling as she went; not taking Bruin's threat too seriously it seemed.

'Go ahead, Samuel, concentrate. Try to connect with the energy held within the boulders. And take your time, there's no rush.'

130

Samuel calmed his mind and settled into focussing it on the stones that made up the archway. It was nothing like connecting with any animal or human. There was a sense of coldness, of hardness; not the usual gentle heat he felt when he moved into Quicksilver's mind and connected with him. But, as he stood there with his eyes closed, concentrating, searching for the trapped living energy that his uncle assured him was held within each uniquely shaped lump of granite, he found something.

Samuel sensed a hint of warmth, a tiny flickering fragment of heat within each boulder. In his mind's eye he saw them in front of him, not grey and dull, as they were to normal sight but with a sliver of red life just visible through their tough outer layers. Each tiny red flare gently pulsed away deep inside them like a faint heartbeat.

He spoke to these glowing embers, coaxed and almost sang to them with his mind. Stoking them to burn higher and brighter until the archway lit up and glowed like one made entirely of burning coals. Containing his awe and excitement Samuel now worked at asking and coaxing the rocks to move out of their present positions, to let themselves shift out of alignment and fall to the ground once more to seal the entrance. To his amazement Samuel heard the sound of them scraping against each other as they began to move under his will.

Before he had time to check himself, a huge bubble of pride grew inside his chest but this was an interference that the task could not sustain. It diminished his control, taking his mind away from the job of dismantling the archway and blocking his connection with the energy trapped within it. The noise of shifting and falling stones abruptly stopped. To his mind's eye the boulders were cold and grey again. He opened his eyes to confront the truth; the entrance was only half-closed. A tumble of rocks lay over one side of the opening but the other half of the archway still stood strong.

Deflated, Samuel noticed that the little girl had sneaked back again and was peeking out from the tunnel.

'Ivy!' Bruin bellowed in annoyance and she ran off whimpering; she knew from the tone of his voice that this time she was in trouble.

'It wasn't her fault, Uncle.' Samuel said dejectedly, 'I lost it. I'm sorry.'

'Not at all Samuel! That was amazing!'

Surprised, Samuel looked at Bruin to see if he was just teasing.

'Really, that was fantastic!' Bruin confirmed and stepped forward to pat his nephew's shoulder. 'When my father first got me to try this I was older than you and I didn't even get a single rock to wobble.'

'Really?' Samuel grinned, feeling a good deal better.

'Yes, really. But don't you go off telling everyone else that, all right?' Bruin ruffled Samuel's hair.

Samuel nodded.

'Let me finish this off for you.' Bruin said and stood by Samuel's side. 'You save your energy for later, okay?'

Samuel watched as his uncle brought the rest of the boulders swiftly down into their place as easily, and with as little effort, as if he had merely closed an ordinary door.

As they walked on into the trees, Bruin pointed out and explained the properties of the surrounding vegetation. There were plants which were good for eating in their entirety and some of which only the roots or leaves were of use. Some that yielded edible fruit or fruit which could be drained of their liquid for drinking. There were many that, when combined in the right proportions, were used in the treatment of illnesses or to quicken the healing of wounds. Samuel couldn't help but wish he had known these wonders when his mother was still alive. Perhaps there had been some remedy for her pains close-by in the woods, free and abundant and hidden from him only by his lack of knowledge.

There were all manner of animals too. As Bruin strode along he pointed out forest deer, hares, elk and even tiny voles and mice as they scampered about, nosing in their agitated way through the scramble of vines and leaves scattered on the ground. Samuel's uncle talked of how his people hunted for meat and which animals were good to eat and provided not only food but also tough hides, innards and bones that were all put to good use in the hands of the forest folk.

'We only catch what we need, there's never any waste. Waste is wicked. If an animal of the forest is taken by us, then we make sure that its death is swift and that none of it goes unused. That is our way,' he explained.

Samuel thought of all the hanging carcasses in the window of the butcher's shop back in Crossways. He remembered seeing how much of the meat was thrown away when it went bad; Mr Cardell's prices too high for many of the people that lived there to be able to afford it.

'But,' Samuel knitted his brow whilst searching for the right words, 'what about the animals that we hunt? The forest people...' he paused, and then tried out a new phrase; '*Our* people...' it felt good to say that... *our* people... he exchanged a smile with his uncle. 'Our people eat meat but many of our friends are animals. Doesn't that make it difficult when we go out hunting for food?'

'Oh, I see what you mean,' Bruin nodded. 'You're worried that one of our hunters may come back with his catch to discover that he's unknowingly killed one of our animal friends for the pot?'

'Well, yes. I mean, how can you avoid that happening sometimes?'

Bruin scratched the back of his neck where the red dot of a fresh insect bite flared. 'This will become easier for you to understand the more you come to grasp your skills,' he explained. 'Some of our number choose not to eat the flesh of

134

animals, but the majority of us do. We all make our own choices on this matter. But, to answer your question, you come to *know* those animals who have a connection to our people and you don't harm them when they are out in the forest.'

'But, how do you *know* them?' Samuel asked. 'Surely you can't recognise every animal that flits past you when you're out hunting in the woods?'

'No, you're right, we don't know them by sight, Samuel. It's a much deeper instinct that we use. We can *feel* them... with our minds.'

Quicksilver and Blithe were leaping about, play fighting. Bringing their huge padded paws down on one another, pushing, shoving and rolling and lifting themselves up onto their powerful back legs as they wrestled with their forepaws.

Samuel watched them, his mind confused as he tried to grasp what he was being told.

'Perhaps it would be easier to demonstrate this to you.' Bruin said and called Blithe over to him. She came immediately, leaving Quicksilver standing alone and panting great clouds of steamy breath from his exertions.

Samuel watched whilst his uncle held Blithe's head in his hands. Her huge silver eyes staring unblinkingly into Bruin's as the man connected with her. After just a few seconds, Bruin released his hold on the dog and walked over to stand at Samuel's side.

Bruin gave Blithe a nod and she sped off into the

undergrowth. Quicksilver leapt after her.

'Try to feel Quicksilver, Samuel – don't connect with his mind, just *feel* where he is.'

Samuel wasn't sure that he understood but he closed his eyes to try it anyway. Soon he found his mind racing through the ferns and tangled roots, bobbing between leaves and under low boughs, seeking out and pursuing his racing silver friend. Once again he found himself inside Quicksilver, looking out through the dog's eyes. Samuel felt the rushing air tearing passed the dog's face, felt his ears flapping against the side of his head as he watched the muscles working in the backside of Blithe who was up ahead and leading the way.

Samuel could see where Quicksilver was. He could see, through the dog's own eyes, where he *was* – but he could not exactly and definitely locate his precise position in relation to where he himself stood. It became obvious that he needed to pull back a little and try something different.

Reluctantly Samuel forced his mind and thoughts to come back to his own body. He stood trying to do as his uncle had told him for a few moments more but nothing seemed to be happening. Visualising Quicksilver inside his head didn't seem to bring about the new kind of connection he was striving for.

Sadly, Samuel wondered if he was incapable of such a thing.

'Let me help you.' Bruin's voice drifted gently into Samuel's mind as he carefully reached into his nephew. 'It's like listening, but with your mind rather than your ears,' he said.

Samuel relaxed and let his uncle in. It felt very strange, almost like being led by the hand as a child but the strangeness came from the fact that it was his mind that was being led.

'Do you feel this?' came Bruin's voice again, from deep inside Samuel's head, from a place further back than he had been trying to work from, a place he had not known was even there.

'Yes!' Samuel said out loud, then with more control, 'Yes, I do,' this time answering his uncle with his mind.

'Listen from *here*. Try again to sense where Quicksilver is, using this part of your mind.'

Samuel tried again. He listened. Concentrating all his strength and will to the task, he began to feel something. Something was moving fast, weaving between the wrinkled trunks of the ancient trees. It was sweeping through the forest in a great arc around to Samuel's left. Barely containing his joy Samuel realised he had found Quicksilver.

Even with his eyes closed and no telltale sounds giving away Quicksilver's position, Samuel could actually *feel* how far away the dog was and could easily track his position from where he himself stood.

'There!' Bruin's delighted voice resounded inside Samuel's head. 'Now, hold it Samuel, hold onto that sensation. Let's push you a little further. You don't know Blithe nearly so well but see if you can feel her position too. Don't be discouraged if you can't, let's just give it a go.'

Desperate not to allow the excitement of his achievement interfere with this new-found skill, Samuel pushed himself to focus harder.

And suddenly, there she was.

The sense of Blithe's position was far fainter than Quicksilver's but it was there, it was *definitely* there.

'Oh, yes! That's amazing!' Samuel squealed aloud, his face flushed and damp with sweat.

Bruin laughed. 'It's *you* who are amazing, Samuel. Very well done! Let it go now, gently. You can practice this new skill another time. Now that you've found that you can do it, it'll be easier every time you try.'

Samuel allowed the connection to fade and evaporate in the warmth of the forest. He felt tired. Not exhausted, but comfortably tired, like the feeling one might have after a long enjoyable walk in the fresh air.

Samuel opened his eyes to see his uncle grinning widely at him. Without thinking about it Samuel threw himself into the tall man's arms and hugged him hard.

'Wow!' Bruin said, startled. 'And that's just the start, my young nephew. What a pupil you're turning out to be!' Quicksilver and Blithe broke through the trees nearby and came hurtling towards them.

'Well done, Blithe, you're a good girl.' Bruin greeted his companion warmly.

Quicksilver came straight to Samuel and licked his face all

over, his hot steaming breath further dampening the young boy's wet hair. After this new experience, both boy and dog felt a deepening of the bond between them.

'Can you do that with any forest animal, Uncle Bruin, or can you only sense those creatures that are known to you and the forest people?'

'When you have mastered this skill you will be able to sense all living animals nearby. Those known to you will give you a strong feeling of familiarity. They will exude a kind of warmth felt only by your mind. The awareness of their proximity to you will become more powerful as you learn to control this skill. Those animals, which are suitable for hunting, will give off a much fainter sensation, but you'll be able to pinpoint them fairly accurately. That's how it is for me and, of our people, I have the strongest ability in this matter. However, I have a feeling that you'll be rivalling me in this very soon.' Bruin grinned at Samuel.

Samuel felt pride at his uncle's words. No one in his life, except for his mother, had ever made him feel special or gifted in any way.

'It's quite tiring isn't it?' Samuel said, pushing his sweaty fringe out of his eyes and wiping the perspiration from the back of his neck.

'It will become less so with practice. Whenever you have a free moment, try it with Quicksilver. Playing hide-and-go-seek is a fine way to train and improve this talent,' Bruin suggested.

Samuel suddenly remembered seeing a few of the young children back in the forest home playing such games with their animal companions. He had thought it nothing very unusual at the time, had believed it to just be a child's simple game. But Samuel had been unaware that the children were not using their eyes and ears to play this 'game'.

Samuel remembered one time when he had seen his young friend Ash doing this very thing. Ash had been slipping covertly between the tepees, pausing every now and then, seemingly to listen. He would close his eyes for a few heartbeats, and then move on again. After some time of this slow progress, Samuel had watched as the young boy sneaked up on a large wooden water barrel behind which, on the far side and hidden from Ash's view, crouched his animal companion.

Ash had quietly slipped a hand beneath the surface of the cool water held in the barrel. Then, very carefully, he had reached over it, letting fat droplets fall from his fingertips onto the young red fox crouched below. At first, Sly, Ash's companion, had shaken himself, sending the drops scattering from his luxurious thick fur. The water landed on the hot ground and had dried almost instantly in the high heat of the sun. Sly caught on to what was happening as a fresh handful rained down on his pointed ears. He leapt up and scampered around the barrel in a flash, jumping on Ash, yipping in the boy's laughing face and nipping him playfully about the ears. Now Samuel could see the game for what it was; a fun way to learn how to master this skill.

'Let's sit and have something to eat. Watch your step there,' Bruin pointed out a group of odd protrusions near the base of a tree which were nosing their way through some fallen leaves, 'They're breathing roots, lots of the trees near the water and in the boggy areas of the forest have them. Easy to trip over if you're not paying attention.'

Bruin led Samuel and the dogs to the side of the river where he sat down on some huge thick leaves growing on the bank. He gestured for his nephew to sit by his side.

The river seemed even wider and deeper here, the fish swimming by much more plentiful than Samuel had ever witnessed during his often unsuccessful fishing trips.

'You won't have seen the river with so much life in it, I suspect?' Bruin commented, seeing Samuel watching the flowing water.

'No. There are very few fish in the stream near our old clearing and I've never seen any fish at all, not even one, where the stream runs through the village of Crossways.'

'Hmm.' Bruin mused. 'That doesn't surprise me. The fish instinctively know that their chances of surviving in the river outside of the woods are poor. Outsiders from the towns and villages kill far too many of them, trapping more than they need and destroying the balance required to keep their numbers up. Besides, the water is less pure outside of the forest. Outsiders let bad things get into it; they allow their filth to pollute it.

They've no respect for it at all. How they expect the water to stay healthy and provide them with food is a mystery to me.' Bruin shook his head.

The two dogs lapped up water from the stream then came to sit by them, patiently waiting for Bruin to unfold his food parcels, which he had removed from a deerskin bag and laid on the ground.

Bruin unwrapped the first one; a delicious aroma wafted upwards and tantalized all of their taste buds. 'I've brought along some cold cuts of meat left over from the feast last night. Nothing's wasted, you see?'

He threw a strip of meat to each of the dogs who settled down happily to begin working on them. Soon Samuel was following their lead, chewing and chomping till his jaw ached. He was surprised to find himself so hungry, his training had barely begun but it was taking more out of him than he had realised. It seemed that using his mind was going to be even harder work than carting around all those heavy trays of loaves back at the bakery, but he looked forward to every moment of learning that was to come.

Gratefully Samuel accepted another piece of meat and then another. After fruit, some sweet hard nuts and a drink of fresh river water they felt content, their bellies comfortably satisfied.

The sun was past full height in the sky. The morning had been a busy one but Samuel had enjoyed it immensely and wondered what amazing skills Bruin would help him to discover within himself next. He was a little surprised and somewhat disappointed by his uncle's next words.

'I think we should head back now.'

'But we've only just begun, haven't we?'

'Yes, but there's no need to push things too quickly, Samuel. Be patient. There are things to be learnt back home in the village too and besides, I'm sure that you would like to spend some time getting to know those of our number you haven't yet met?' Bruin raised an eyebrow and Samuel reddened a little.

'Well... yes, but...'

'Don't worry, we'll work every day on your skills but you need time to get adjusted to our way of life and your new home.' Bruin stood and offered his nephew a hand. 'Come, let's enjoy our walk back and see how you manage with opening the archway this time, if you feel up to it.'

Samuel took his uncle's hand and let the older man pull him to his feet.

On the way back Bruin took a slight detour to the way they had travelled before.

'I want to show you something,' he explained in hushed tones.

Making their way through the trees to a small clearing, Samuel followed his uncle.

Bruin's voice spoke next in Samuel's mind. 'This is what I wanted to show you. Look over there and tell me what you see. Answer me with your mind, we need to keep quiet.'

Samuel looked. There was grass, blue and yellow flowers, several rocks protruding from the ground – but what was it that his uncle wanted him to notice? He scanned the clearing again.

'I can't see anything unusual Uncle, can you give me a hint at what I'm looking for?' Samuel asked with his mind.

Quicksilver and Blithe both had their ears pricked and were certainly sensing something nearby. Samuel began to feel a tingle of danger in his own senses and looked to his uncle for guidance.

'It's important, boy. Look again, what do you see? Isn't there anything that looks out of place to you in such a wild place as this?'

Samuel looked again. The feeling pushed in on him that whatever the danger was, it was getting ever closer.

What is it? What is it? What am I missing?

Samuel's eyes worked over the ground once again.

Wait a minute... what was that over near the far tree line? It looked like... a *path*. What was a path doing way out here? Samuel followed the route of the furrowed trail that was dug into the mud. It travelled around the edge of the far side of the clearing entering from one side and disappearing between the trees at the other.

'I see it!' Samuel thought to his uncle, 'A pathway, a track. What's a track doing here? Was it made by our people?'

Just as he finished his question the hair prickled on his scalp and Quicksilver moved in front of him in a gesture of protection. Looking across to where the track first entered the clearing to his right, Samuel saw what his uncle had brought him here to see.

A massive fully-grown adult bear, her thick shaggy coat gleaming in the sunlight, broke cover from the trees. She had three young cubs with her; all four bears seemed completely unaware of the two humans and dogs which were watching their slow progress across the clearing. Then the mother bear seemed to sense something. Stopping in the track and lifting her magnificent head she bobbed her nose on the gentle breeze to see if she could catch the scent of whatever it was that her senses were telling her was nearby.

Samuel froze.

They were standing downwind of her and he prayed with all his might that she would not detect them. Her power was obvious, the muscles in her shoulders and legs rippled as she launched herself upright onto her back legs to better survey the area.

'What should we do? Shouldn't we go? Can we go?' Samuel pleaded with his uncle.

'It's all right Samuel, she hasn't seen us. Keep very still, watch and learn.'

Samuel stood rooted to the spot and watched. After a few more moments the beautiful, terrifying bear bounced back down onto all fours, seemingly satisfied that all was well for her and her family to continue on their way. She nipped her youngsters out of their games and barked gently to them to fall in line, which they did, they knew who was boss. Samuel continued to watch as the four bears walked along the well-worn track until they disappeared back into the trees on the other side of the grassy clearing.

'The bears made the track?' Samuel asked incredulously once he found his voice again.

'Yes, it's their way. That type of bear tends to travel the same routes over and over again wearing tracks like that through the forest. We can use them as warning signs to avoid any unwanted meetings with them. It can't always be prevented but knowing what to look for certainly helps to keep you safe in the forest.'

'I'm pretty sure that was the kind of bear that attacked me,' Samuel said quietly, absentmindedly scratching the back of his head.

'Yes, I thought so. If you'd known what to look for, the signs that bears leave on the land, you might have been spared that encounter. That's why I brought you here, I don't want anything like that to happen to you again.'

Samuel looked up into his uncle's eyes. They were slate-grey with flecks of green, not unlike his own, not unlike his mother's.

'Thank you, Uncle.' he said.

6

Fern

They returned to the forest home, Bruin opening the archway and Samuel closing it, this time without assistance.

'Excellent! Next time you can try forming the archway, it's a bit harder but I think you could manage it.' Bruin grinned down at him.

The village was wide awake now and buzzing with activity. Great sides of meat were being cut up and hung to dry in strips; the results of the recent hunt.

'Those will form part of our diet for the winter months.' Bruin explained. 'It seems the hunt went well. Come along and meet Willow and her companions; they should be well rested and ready to see you by now.'

Samuel looked down at himself and brushed away some mud from one of his knees.

Bruin noticed this and laughed gently. 'You look just fine my boy, don't fret. And may I suggest that you bury your thoughts of the young Willow in case she should pick up on them. We wouldn't want you to turn that fetching shade of red again, would we?'

Samuel flashed a look of horror at his uncle.

'Bury my thoughts? But how do I do that?' he asked, feeling his cheeks flush crimson already.

'Just try to keep any... *inappropriate* ideas and images locked away inside your mind. I'm sure she won't go rummaging through your private thoughts but if you go around making it obvious, wearing your heart on your sleeve as it were, then you're bound to have such things noticed.'

'Shhh, please Uncle. I understand but could we *please* talk about something else just now.' Samuel asked, wanting to give himself plenty of time to collect his wits before being face to face with the young woman whose image was still so clearly etched on his memory.

Bruin grinned. 'Certainly Samuel. What would you like to talk about?'

The two dogs had gone off to amuse themselves leaving Samuel and Bruin to walk through the village together. Friendly nods and greetings came from everyone they came across and one large man, whom Samuel remembered as being the one who had constantly refilled his cup the night before, gave him an exaggerated wink and a hearty slap on the back.

'How about telling me about the other members of the hunting party? You told me there were three younger people and one adult, the father of one of them?'

'Yes, that's right.' Bruin stopped walking and gestured to Samuel to stand with him in a quiet space between two tepees.

'There is Flint and his father Rowan, then Willow and her younger brother Fern. Flint and Willow are both in their fifteenth summer, Fern is in his eighth.'

'Only eight? Isn't that very young to be going out hunting?' Samuel asked, wondering why his uncle was keeping his voice low.

'Fern is... different. I only tell you this so that you'll not be too surprised when you meet him. He's a lively lad with a wonderful big heart and loves no one more than his older sister but he behaves... unusually.'

'Unusually?' Samuel prompted.

'Yes. Willow insists on taking him everywhere with her, even on hunting trips and Fern wouldn't have it any other way. They're inseparable. Fern doesn't take any part in the catching of the animals but he helps with other things when they're gone, he'd do anything to stay near to Willow. There was this one time when Willow tried to leave him behind but... well, it was awful... the poor lad was inconsolable and used the gift to connect with his sister and beg her to return. I'll explain more later, in private. He can be quite overpowering but you"ll see that he has a good soul.'

They continued on their way, Samuel once again calming himself down and struggling to slow his heartbeat at the thought of meeting Willow properly.

I hope I don't say anything stupid. I hope I can think of something smart to say. I hope I can manage to speak!

Bruin gave his nephew a pat on the back and a wink of encouragement as they came to stop outside Willow's tepee.

'Here we are,' he said. 'Hello inside? May we come in?'

'Yes, of course,' came the reply from within, 'come on in, we've some fresh berry juice ready for you.' It was Willow.

'Come in! Come in! We've been waiting and waiting to meet you!' came an excited young boy's voice.

Samuel held the door-skin aside to admit his uncle before him. Inside the tepee there were four figures; Rowan, his son Flint, Fern and Willow. They all stood to greet the new arrivals, the space inside the tepee a little cramped for so many. Bruin carried out the introductions, leaving Willow till last.

Flint was a little taller than Samuel, his skin darker from years of fresh air and sunshine, the muscles in his arms and legs more developed than his own. He smiled broadly at Samuel and welcomed him, saying that he was sorry not to have been there when he had first arrived in the village. Although slightly intimidated by the lad's obvious strength and good looks Samuel felt that he could become friends with this boy. He sensed kindness and a gentle spirit behind the strong exterior.

Rowan, Flint's father, was like a larger version of his son. 'I have something for you, a welcoming gift, from our little hunting party,' said the tall bronzed man and produced from the pocket in his tunic a large and beautiful golden feather that he held out to Samuel.

Samuel accepted the gift and turned it over in his hand,

examining it closely. 'It's wonderful, thank you. I've never seen anything like it.'

Bruin peered over his nephew's shoulder at the prize then looked up at Rowan in awe. 'Is that the feather of a Great Forest Eagle?' he asked.

'Yes! Isn't it wonderful? We actually came across a nest out in the forest. Both parents were attending chicks inside; we couldn't get close enough to see how many there were, but I'd guess at three from the racket they made when the adults came in to feed them.' Rowan's eyes were bright as he spoke.

'Wonderful indeed!' Bruin agreed, 'That's a very rare thing, Samuel. I haven't seen any sign of a Great Forest Eagle since I was around your age, treasure that.'

'I will, thank you, Rowan.' Samuel imagined how stunning a bird covered with such brilliant feathers must look with its great wings outstretched beating the air beneath the sun.

'Pretty, pretty, pretty. Me next, tell him about me next!' Fern bounced up and down, tugging on Bruin's sleeve.

Willow placed a hand softly on her brother's head. 'Hush now Fern. Be still. Give them time.'

Fern's reaction was instant. His agitated movements stopped, his arms fell to his sides and he looked up into his sister's eyes. 'Sorry Willow, I'll be quiet,' he whispered, putting a finger to his lips and hushing himself.

'And this fine fellow is Fern. Young brother to Willow.' Bruin ruffled the youngster's hair.

'Yes, I'm Fern. Fern's my name,' he spoke quietly whilst still holding his finger to his lips.

'I'm very pleased to meet you, Fern, my name's Samuel.' Samuel replied in an equally quiet voice.

'Yes, I know. You've come to live with us now. Your mama has gone to be with the Man In Green, the great spirit of the forest, just like our mama, so now you've come here to live with Fern and all his friends.'

Willow took Fern's finger from his lips and looked into her brother's eyes. Samuel made out a faint whisper inside his head and realised that he was somehow overhearing Willow talking to her brother using her mind. He got the feeling that she was telling him that what he had said was impolite.

'It's all right,' Samuel said to Willow, 'Fern speaks the truth,' then turning back to the young boy, 'you're right; my mama has gone.' The words stung a little, 'I didn't know that you had lost your mother too, Fern. I'm very sorry to hear that.'

'Mama's not *lost*. She's not lost, silly, she's with the Man In Green.' Fern said the words slowly as if explaining to a young child. 'She's free, gliding through the trees like a beautiful bird, she can go anywhere now, just like your mama. Not lost, *free*.' Fern spread his arms out as if flying, the smile on his face a wonderful thing to see.

Who am I to say he isn't right? Samuel thought.

Fern tugged on Samuel's hand. 'You and me are going to be friends aren't we, Samuel? Good friends.'

'I certainly hope...'

'But only if Willow likes you,' Fern interrupted him. 'If Willow not like you then Ferny-Fern can't like you. You get it? You got to make Willow like you, all right?' Fern waited for a response this time, his eyebrows raised, his face open and expectant.

Samuel fought the colour threatening to rise in his cheeks, 'Well... I'll certainly do my best Fern as I'd very much like to be your friend.'

Fern seemed satisfied with this, took hold of his sister's hand and grinned up at her.

'Ah, well said.' Bruin patted Samuel's shoulder. 'And now let me introduce you to the young lady in question, our Willow.'

'I'm very pleased to meet you... properly. I'm sorry you saw me in such a state this morning.' Willow smiled at Samuel and bobbed her head in a gesture of greeting.

Samuel braced himself and looked straight into those green, green eyes. When he opened his mouth to speak he was relieved to find that he could. 'You weren't in a state... you were... well... you were very...' Samuel wished he had never begun the sentence.

How was he going to finish it? Certainly not with the truth, unless he could be sure that the floor beneath his feet would swallow him whole without a trace directly after speaking it. Willow had seemed beautiful to him that morning, but now she was breathtaking. Her eyes seemed to burrow right into him and he felt that anything in his mind whether hidden or not could never hope to escape her gaze. She waited patiently for him to continue, a faint smile dimpling the corners of her mouth.

'What Samuel is trying to say, Willow, is that he understands very well that you'd been out in the wilds of the forest for days,' Bruin raised an eyebrow at his nephew, 'and that your appearance... was one of a skilled hunter returning from her work.'

Samuel knew that his uncle had rescued him from an embarrassing situation but still he cringed a little. Bruin's words hadn't been exactly flattering.

'Well... yes.' Samuel gave in rather than get himself into another stammering tangle.

'Well, a 'skilled hunter', I thank you for the compliment.' Willow smiled at Samuel and briefly laid a hand on his sleeve, 'Please, let's all sit.'

The group of six sat around the unlit fire and drank berry juice and ate the fruit which Willow handed around. The hunters spoke about their trip; of the animals they had seen in the forest and how well Fern had behaved during their outing.

'Fern kept ever so quiet, very quiet. Shhhh. And all still like a tree without any wind blowing.' Fern agreed.

Samuel noticed that there were only two rolls of bedding in the tepee both of which had been neatly put aside to give as much floor space as possible for the guests. He wondered if it was only Willow and Fern that lived there, he now knew that their mother was gone but what about their father?

During the time the group spent chatting together Samuel watched Willow and Fern. Whenever Fern became agitated or over-loud all Willow needed to do was to reach out a hand to touch him. She would hold him, stroke his hair, take his head in her lap; Samuel had never seen such a strong bond between siblings before.

Back in Crossways there had been a young boy who had behaved in a similar way to Fern. He was easily excited, always fidgeting and saying strange things or speaking in a way that was difficult to follow. Often Samuel had come across the young lad sitting in floods of tears having been teased or hit by the other children in the village. They would call him awful names and pull at his shabby clothes or knock him down on the dusty road. Whenever Samuel had approached him the boy would cheer up immediately and grin widely. 'Samwell! Samwell!' he would cry and dance all around, so excited to see a friendly face.

No one ever had a gentle word for him or showed him any kindness. No one other than Samuel made the effort to talk to him or try to understand his unusual ways.

Samuel had tried to watch out for the boy but with his own mother ill and with his having to work from sun-up till sundown every day at the bakery it had been an impossible task. It sickened Samuel to think of the young lad all alone and homeless, but what could he do? To his horror, Samuel had learned from overhearing loose talk in the street that the boy's parents had disowned him. They had actually packed up all their belongings one night and moved away from Crossways leaving their son behind, asleep in his bed. Their shame at having brought such a child into the world destroying any compassion or love they had ever felt for him. He had awoken to find himself alone and soon after was turned out of his home by the man from whom his parents had rented it.

Samuel had longed to look after the lad, to take him in and care for him, but his mother had been too ill for him to suggest such a thing. Besides, he feared that if Mr Sanderson found out that he and his mother had another person living in their tiny hut he would either use it as an excuse to lower Samuel's wages or to get rid of him altogether. Sadly he could see nothing more that he could do for the boy. It broke his heart to see the abandoned youngster spending his lonely days wandering around the village, sleeping outside and eating what scraps of food he found lying around in other peoples' rubbish.

One day Samuel had sneaked away from work to go looking for the boy. He had managed to hide a badly risen loaf as it had come out of the ovens and intended to make a gift of it to the boy. The loaf wouldn't have ended up on the shelves in Mr Sanderson's shop anyway, it would only have been wasted or thrown out, but still he took a great risk at stealing it away, hidden under his jersey. Nimbly he had dodged through the streets thinking of how delighted the boy would be with the warm bread. The tantalizing aroma made his own mouth water as he searched all around for his young friend but he was nowhere to be found. Samuel never saw him again after that.

Often he worried what had become of him and wished that he had done more to help. If only the youngster had been able to experience the love and acceptance of the people here or had had an older sister like Willow, how different things could have been for him.

Samuel had drifted off into his thoughts and when he came back to the tepee he found that Willow was looking at him intently. Bruin and Rowan were still talking so it seemed he hadn't missed answering anything but as he smiled politely and looked away he wondered for a moment whether she had been able to read what he had been thinking about.

'Well, it is time for us to be getting along now. Thank you for your hospitality, Willow, and all your hard work.' Bruin stood up.

'And me, and me!' Fern shouted and leapt to his feet.

'Yes, Fern, and you!' Bruin laughed as the young boy jumped around in front of him.

'You've all done very well. Our winter food stock will be blessedly full this year if our future hunts go as successfully as yours. Thank you.' Bruin bowed low to each of them before leaving the tepee, this was a mark of respect and a gesture of thanks to the hunters from their leader, which he would explain to Samuel later.

'Thank you, I enjoyed meeting you all.' Samuel stepped out into the afternoon sunshine after his uncle.

'Samuel.' Willow's voice called out and the young woman came outside to speak to him. She squinted, one eye closed against the glare of the sun as she smiled at him. Without warning she took Samuel's right hand between both of her own and he heard her voice inside his head. 'Thank you for being so understanding with my brother, I'm very grateful.' And with another smile that made his knees weak she was gone again disappearing inside her home.

Samuel stood for a few heartbeats staring at the door-skin before him. Bruin brought him back down to earth with a tap on his back: 'I think it's a fair guess that Willow liked you well enough lad.'

Samuel dipped his head to hide his grin.

Back in the privacy of his new home and reunited with Quicksilver and Blithe, Samuel asked Bruin to tell him more about Fern and his family.

'Fern and Willow's father was a great hunter.' Bruin recalled. 'The best of us. I believe that's where Willow gets her powerful hunting instinct. He was a very close friend of mine and I miss him. He was out hunting alone one day when he stumbled across a trap laid by an outsider. His injuries were horrible.'

'A trap? Do you mean one of the metal-jaws?' Samuel asked.

'Yes, they're cruel devices used by the outsiders. You've seen one?'

'Yes, Quicksilver set one off when we were travelling through the forest. I'd never seen one before that. I would've ended up in it myself if Quicksilver hadn't been there.' Samuel saw again the rusty powerful jaws of the trap waiting for its prey and imagined the pain Willow's father must have gone through.

'They call themselves hunters, the outsiders who set those wicked machines to do their work for them, but they don't deserve the title of "hunter". They show no respect for the life of the forest, give no quick death to the creatures they capture. Half of the animals that are caught in those things are left to suffer in agony for days before the outsiders come to collect them. Some are eaten alive by other animals, as they lie there stuck in the trap. Worst of all they tend to kill off the younger ones who are less wary and carry less meat on their bodies which just causes the outsiders to set more and more traps in order to catch larger numbers to make up for their meagre kills.

'Whenever we come across them we break them up and put any trapped animals out of their pain, but there are always more. It seems that Willow's father stumbled across a particularly well-hidden metal-jaw that day. His leg was badly damaged, the flesh torn right down to the bone but he was a strong and determined man, he managed to get himself out of the trap and drag his way back home to us.' Bruin scratched

Blithe behind one ear. 'Willow's mother was still with child when it happened, still carrying Fern. The shock of seeing her husband all torn up like that had a terrible effect on her. We did all that we could for him but it was no good. Even though we cleaned the wounds and dressed them, used our most powerful medicines to fight the infection that grew in his leg, there was nothing we could do to stop it from racing through his body. He suffered greatly before the end.'

'That's awful. Willow would only have been a child at the time, near eight years old?' Samuel asked.

'Yes, but she did a lot of growing up over those dreadful days as she helped her mother to nurse her father. Willow had always been older than her years, caring and thoughtful, a gentle soul. We all feared that the experience would greatly damage her, that she was too delicate to cope with such sadness, but the opposite became true, her inner-strength surprised us all. She practically reversed roles with her own mother; looked after her and made sure that she ate properly and took enough care of herself and her unborn child.

'Willow made her mother rest each day, turning away offers of help from the rest of us, insisting on doing the cooking, water fetching and watching over her father all by herself. I think she barely slept all that time. She was so determined to do everything that she possibly could and to keep strong for all of them, but her mother handled it very differently, it was simply too much for her to bear. Her husband's passing was an awful thing to witness. We all felt it. His pain was terrible, the infection so rampant by the end that he didn't even recognise his own wife and daughter. On that last day, his cries of agony were heard all around the village, and when they suddenly stopped... the silence was even worse.

'After we buried him in the forest, Willow's mother grew more and more distant. She would sit staring into space, and not respond to her name being called. We all tried so hard to reach her, to bring her back, Willow more than any of us, but it was no good; her loss was too much.

'The baby, Fern, came too early, there were... complications. She only set eyes on her new child for a few moments before she left us to join her husband. I'm quite sure that Fern wouldn't have survived without Willow's care and love. He was so small and weak but she pulled him through and she's taken care of him ever since.'

'Surely they didn't live alone?' Samuel asked incredulously, 'Didn't anyone offer to take them into their home to look after them? Willow was only a child herself.'

'We all wanted to do just that, Samuel, but Willow wouldn't have it. She argued that she knew how to look after herself and the baby. She insisted that she could cope on her own and that we were just a thought away if she needed us. It was something she needed to do; it helped her to deal with her grief to take on all that responsibility. We all did our best to watch over them and help in any way that we could but she and Fern have lived on their own ever since and Willow has always managed. She's an incredibly strong young woman.'

Samuel sat in silence thinking over what he'd been told.

'I must go now nephew, I've to meet with some of the elders. We'll catch up again later.' Bruin left Samuel to his thoughts.

Samuel spent the rest of the afternoon playing with the children in the village and helping to carry firewood and water to the homes of anyone who needed it. It felt so good to be a part of the place, one of the people. Most thanked him and spoke to him using their voice but some of the children, eager to practice their skills of communication, chatted to him using their minds. It didn't feel unpleasant any more, the sensation held no fear for him. Even when they got too excited and all tried to talk at the same time, all demanding this new person's attention, Samuel merely calmed them and explained that they should take turns so that he could understand and answer them all.

Later, when he returned to his tepee, two of the children, twin boys named Moss and Spruce, followed him and asked if they could come inside. They wanted to get a look at the things that Samuel had brought with him from the 'outside'. Explaining that all he had were a few old clothes, his bag and water pouch and his mother's book didn't put them off. They had heard stories of the outsiders during their eight summers in the forest but had never seen anything that had been made by them before and were eager to look at whatever Samuel had.

With their two identical bright blonde heads close together the pair laughed at Samuel's old, worn and poorly made clothes.

'Your new clothes suit you much better, these wouldn't keep you warm come the cold season.' Spruce said. 'You'd end up like an icicle hanging from a branch if you wore these out here!'

'Yes!' Moss agreed. 'And they certainly wouldn't stand up to working hard in the forest either, look, they're nearly worn through in the bottom!' Moss giggled. 'Just as well you came here or soon you would have been showing off your backside to all the girls.' The twins dissolved into explosive snorts.

Samuel grinned.

Next to go under their scrutiny were Samuel's water pouch and bag.

'Not bad,' Moss shook the pouch. 'It doesn't leak?'

Samuel shook his head.

'His bag is well-made too, a forester could have made this.' Spruce said turning over the deerskin bag in his hands, pointing out the tight, neat stitches of sinew that bound it together.

'A forester did.' Samuel smiled as he found himself remembering. 'My mother made it for me from a discarded deerskin we found near the edge of the forest,' he told them.

'Discarded? You mean *left* there, to go to *waste*?' Spruce's tone displaying his disbelief at such a thoughtless act.

'Yes, the hunter who killed the young deer was only interested in its meat. He must have skinned it there in the forest and left what he didn't want.'

The twins looked at each other in horror. 'That's very bad, you should never kill an animal unless you mean to use all of it. Why don't the outsider hunters know that? They should be taught it.'

On hearing this Samuel warmed to the two young boys even more; he felt exactly the same way. How would the outsiders learn if those who knew better and understood the ways of the woods didn't teach them?

When they came to Lily's book the pair fell silent and looked to Samuel for permission to open it. They seemed to sense how precious it was to him.

'It's all right, you can look,' he told them.

Without being asked to, the two young boys stepped outside for a moment to dip their hands in the water barrel that stood there. They wiped their hands dry on their trousers so as not to get the pages grubby and sat quietly again, side by side, tracing their fingers over the writing on the pages. They asked him what it all meant and Samuel gladly read a number of the words and a few simple sentences out to them. When he offered them a pencil so that they could try to write a word for themselves their eyes grew wide with delight.

Samuel tried not to grin as he watched the concentration on Moss's face. His tongue poked out the side of his mouth as he held the pencil firmly and began to copy the sweep of Lily's letters onto an opposite page.

Samuel kept him right. 'Don't push it too hard, be gentle or the point will snap off. That's it, start at the top then straight down...'

Both boys managed to copy the word 'Lily' then Samuel wrote their own names down to show them what they looked like.

'Hey! Your name is longer than mine!' Moss complained.

'That's because I'm older.' Spruce explained irrationally.

'Only by a few heartbeats!' Moss retorted.

Samuel had them copy their own names in the spaces he had left below each on the page and taught them how to sound out the letters which made them up.

The twins were greatly disappointed when they received a mind-message from their mother to hurry them on home for their supper. Moss and Spruce thanked Samuel warmly, their faces aglow and excited. As they made their way through the forest village Samuel listened and could hear them repeating the letters of their names over and over to each other. Even though it had been his first lesson, and a short one at that, Samuel felt a little of the satisfaction and joy that his mother had felt when she had taught him how to write. Carefully he put the book away again in his bag.

'Thank you, Mama,' he said quietly in the stillness of his room.

Samuel dined with his uncle that night in his uncle's tepee. They talked more about his training and of the other foresters and parted for an early night some time after. The sky was deepening from purple to black as he and Quicksilver returned home with full stomachs. He found himself reflecting on what a wonderful day it had been; he had learned a great deal and made new friends. The only disappointment was that he had not seen Willow again since that afternoon in her tepee; she was likely just taking it easy after the past few days, he supposed. But, still he had kept an eye out for her all the time just in case, hoping to catch a glimpse of her once more before nightfall.

Bruin had told him to expect Blithe's wake-up call the next morning and to get himself showered, dressed, ready and at the entrance to the village in better time than the day before. Samuel didn't need to be told that twice, he looked forward to getting back into the forest again.

'Goodnight, boy,' Samuel thought to Quicksilver as he snuggled down under his cover and closed his eyes.

The day had been more draining than he'd realised and it wasn't long before Samuel was deeply asleep and back in the forest in his dreams with Quicksilver by his side. They ran through the undergrowth happy in one another's company, playfully thumping against each other as they dodged and wove nimbly between the tall trees.

A sound like the tinkle of small bells stopped them. Above their heads, sitting on a high branch was a young woman. Her back was to them; long golden hair blazing in the sunlight tumbled over her shoulders like a waterfall. Laughter, sweet light laughter echoed through the still air and at once Samuel knew who it was even before she turned to look over her shoulder at them.

She blew him a kiss before reaching up towards the sky. 'Do you remember your wish my sweet? It has come true, I will always be with you and I *am* better, all better now, my Samuel, I'm free my darling,' she called down to him. He stood and watched as a glowing, transparent image of her leapt upwards from the seated figure and glided off between the branches.

'Mama?' Samuel took several faltering steps forward.

The female figure was still there sitting on the branch but it was a little different now, the frame stronger, no longer that of his mother but someone else, someone he recognised.

'Willow?'

'Catch me if you can!' she called to him and leapt down from the tree to begin running through the forest.

She was so fast, expertly avoiding fallen logs and entwined vines covering the forest floor. They sped after her, the sound of her laughter getting fainter as the distance between them opened up. He didn't want her to get away from him; he wanted her to slow down, to wait.

'Willow, wait for me!' he called, gasping for breath and laughing too as he sped along after her.

Suddenly a vicious metallic sound reverberated through the woods sending the birds leaping into the sky. Rabbits and mice hurtled along the ground, squirrels scattered through the trees above Samuel and Quicksilver, as the creatures all tried to get away from the source of that awful noise. A sickening feeling entered Samuel's stomach as he heard a voice up ahead.

'No! No! Not Willow, not my Willow. Not allowed to happen, not allowed! NO!'

It was Fern's voice.

Samuel could see him now in a little grassy opening between two massive trunks. He was distraught, pulling his hair and rocking back and forward on his heels. In a tangle of thicket in front of the boy, Samuel caught a glimpse of what he was dreading he would see. The gleaming edge of a wickedly sharp metal-jaw, far bigger than the one he had seen before, was just visible above the greenery of the thicket. There was something else to see from where he stood paralysed with horror, there was a clump of something bright hanging limply over a gnarled and snapped branch. A twisted length of something golden... hair...

Willow's hair.

There was no other movement except for a light breeze that stirred a few strands of the golden hair, giving hope where there was none.

'No no nooooooo!' Fern screamed and fell to his knees.

Samuel threw himself upright in bed, frantic to be out of the dream, the nightmare.

Sweat clung to him, his heart pounded painfully in his chest.

It's all right, it's all right. It was just a dream. Just a mixed up jumble of everything I've heard and seen today.

Quicksilver immediately came to him and nuzzled his

tousled hair with his big heavy head. With his friend by his side, Samuel eventually managed to relax enough to lie down again. But he couldn't stop the images from his nightmare loom like ghosts. It had felt like some kind of warning or premonition. How long would it be before another of the forest people were hurt or killed by the 'hunting' contraptions of the outsiders? Wasn't there anything he could do to prevent it? He tried to blot out these thoughts and concentrate on all the good things about the forest but still, in that part of his mind where he stored his problems and fears, Samuel began to gather more and more things that needed to be considered and thought out. Problems that would never go away or get any better until something was done about them... but how... and by whom?

Pushing it all to the back of his mind he turned and stroked Quicksilver's coat.

It was only a dream.

But hadn't his uncle said that dreams had value, that they were important?

He spent the rest of the night fitfully tossing and turning, watching the colour of the sky through the opening in the centre of the tepee's roof lighten with every passing hour.

7

Willow

When Blithe stirred Samuel in the morning it was almost a relief.

He tilted his face upwards to meet the freezing shower-water, anxious for it to cleanse him of his upsetting thoughts. The chill forced his senses into alertness, but the shadow of the dream hung over him throughout the rest of the morning.

'You must focus, Samuel.' Bruin had gently chided him as the archway entrance wobbled and collapsed back into a pile of rubble.

'Sorry, Uncle.'

'Is there something you want to talk about? Something on your mind?' Bruin asked kindly.

Samuel hesitated before replying. 'No, it's all right. Can I try again?'

His uncle nodded.

This time the archway held fast, the boulders perfectly aligned and stable.

Quicksilver and Blithe were off into the undergrowth without so much as a look back over their pounding shoulders, leaving both nephew and uncle in peace to roam together through the trees. They spent time working on Samuel's ability to pinpoint nearby animals. His senses were growing stronger and more reliable every time he tried it. In his mind it became more clearly defined, not only where each nearby animal was, but also its size and species.

'Soon you'll be ready to go on your first hunt,' Bruin congratulated him.

Samuel had only ever caught fish before, all the hunting on his earlier journey through the forest had been taken on by Quicksilver, and he wasn't looking forward to learning how to kill other creatures even if it was for food.

'We all need to play our part in catching and gathering the food for our people, Samuel, it's a necessity out here. If you want to eat meat you must learn to catch it.'

'I understand that, Uncle, it's just...' Samuel tailed off.

'You find it distasteful? The thought of killing the forest animals to satisfy our own hunger seems wrong to you?'

Samuel wasn't sure how to answer.

'We're only one of many meat-eaters that exist here in the forest, and so long as we hunt carefully, with thought and understanding, the forest can sustain our existence. As your senses sharpen you'll find that you can tell the fawn from the ageing stag, the hog that is heavy with unborn piglets from the laboured movements of an injured one who is no longer able to forage for food and will soon die from hunger or be taken by another predator. I will teach you how to determine these things and to take only those animals we need with both speed and respect. Do you trust me to do that?'

'Yes, of course. I only hope I won't fail you.' Samuel said.

Bruin smiled down at him, 'I think there is little chance of that.'

Samuel thought back to the paltry scraps of meat he had occasionally managed to purchase from Mr Cardell's butcher shop. Whenever he had a few pennies left over from his wages Samuel would go to the shop to see if he had enough to buy anything. The fatty, stringy strips of meat were always past their best, old and tough to chew; scraggy ends not good enough to sell to the wealthier folk of the village. How had the animals that had provided that meat met their end, Samuel wondered? He felt quite sure that they had not been given the respect or quick death that the forest people afforded the creatures that they took for food.

'Forgive me, Uncle, things are very different here. I'll learn.'

Bruin gripped his nephew's shoulders, 'There's nothing to forgive. What you have to remember is that we are only one kind of animal that makes our home in the forest, there are a great many others and we all have to learn to keep a balance between us to make it work. Give yourself time, Samuel, this place is in your blood. You'll soon feel more in harmony with our ways.'

Although most of the forest animals moved out of the path of the two humans as they wandered through the trees, Bruin brought their presence to life by pointing out the markers that they left behind.

'See over there?' Bruin gestured towards a thickly trunked tree with deep scratches and gouges dug into its bark. He led Samuel over for a closer look. 'That's where a deer has been scraping its new antlers. At the end of the season they'll shed them again; each year they get larger and stronger as the animal develops through its life. A good sturdy set of antlers can be used to make all sorts of useful things. They're especially well suited for fashioning into digging implements to use when we're planting seeds and saplings in the forest. If you ever come across a set, bring them on home with you and I'll show you how we use them.'

Samuel nodded as he let his fingers follow the scored markings in the tree's bark. Congealed lines of amber tracked down from the gouges where trickles of sticky sap had bled from the tree's open wounds.

Bruin went on with his observations; what had seemed to Samuel to be no more than a simple muddy dip in the forest floor turned out to be a hog's wallow and concealed behind a curtain of glossy green leaves and a mass of twisted vines which hung across its mouth, was a cave. Quietly Samuel followed his uncle, pulling aside the hanging vines and squeezing through the narrow opening, on his belly. Once their eyes were accustomed to the darkness inside the cave Bruin spoke using his mind.

'Look up, Samuel, do you see them?'

At first Samuel could see nothing but a mass of black protrusions decorating the roof above. He thought he was looking at an unusual rock formation and wondered what use or interest they held for his uncle, but then a flutter of movement caught his attention. Another flutter gave away the true identity of what he was looking at.

'Wow, bats!' Back when they had lived in Genesis, Samuel's mother had shown him pictures of these odd creatures in a book on nature, but he had never before laid eyes on the real thing.

They hung there like withered dark fruits, slumbering away the daylight hours, patiently storing their energy for the night of hunting which was to come. Using his gift to *feel* their presence instead of relying on his sight alone, Samuel became suddenly aware how many there were. Hundreds or perhaps even thousands of the tiny life forces sprung into his perception as they hung there, crowding the roof of the cave.

Samuel had always known that the forest was brimming with life but he'd had no idea just how much was all around him all the time, just out of sight. The only thing stopping him seeing or experiencing their wonder was his ignorance, something he was eager to remedy. With Bruin's help he was able to find a badger sett, several anthills, recognise a fox's reddish-pink droppings which had been left clearly visible on a rock in order for the animal to mark its territory and even to spot the sleek tracks made by a snake that had travelled along in the wet mud beside the river. With every new discovery the forest was opening up to him, showing off her secrets.

The lessons were abruptly halted by a single howl that was followed by some miserable whimpering which echoed through the forest air around them.

'Ah,' Bruin stopped and turned to Samuel. 'I'm afraid you'll have to excuse me, I believe Blithe has had another run in with a spineypig. That dog will insist on sticking her nose in where it's not wanted. I'll go pull out the spines and meet you back here soon.' He jogged off in the direction of the wretched sound.

Taking the opportunity to lie in a patch of sunshine that shone through a gap in the foliage high above, Samuel breathed in deeply and closed his eyes. Testing with his senses he discerned that there was no danger close-by. Many small animals and birds, and a few people from the forest village, were nearby but there was nothing to be alarmed about or on his guard for; time for a moment to just lie back and enjoy his surroundings. Lightly he let his senses rise upwards to the sky where he followed the track of a bird circling just above the tall trees. Its movements were smooth and effortless, a joy to witness.

The bird must have seen something that caught its eye because now it was dropping, descending beneath the canopy of leaves to perch high above Samuel's head. Opening his eyes and shielding them against the sunlight with one hand, Samuel tried to get a look at it. Very high up, almost too far away to spot, there was a young hawk peering down at him. He couldn't be sure, still a novice with his new-found skills, but he got the feeling that this bird was a companion to one of his fellow villagers, but to which one he had no idea. The bird let itself fall from the branch and glided effortlessly down to land silently on the forest floor near to where he lay.

'Well, hello there.' Samuel ventured, sitting up to get a better look at it.

A slender yet powerful bird, its long dark-tipped wings neatly folded over his tail, the young hawk looked Samuel over with eyes that were full of quiet intelligence. He held out his hand to it.

I'm mad; it could easily take off one of my fingers at the knuckle if it wanted to! But he held his hand still and spoke to the bird with his mind: 'I'm a friend.'

The hawk took a few steps closer, its beautiful eyes never leaving the boy's face for a moment. Gently it reached forward and touched Samuel's fingers with its beak, then hopped over his outstretched hand to perch instead on his knee.

Delighted that the magnificent creature had found him trustworthy enough to share such close proximity, Samuel kept very still and stared at the hawk.

'I see you've met Swift?'

Bruin walked up to Samuel with a chastened-looking Blithe by his side. The great silver dog stopped, sneezed, snuffled and

176

shook her head then put her nose down to the ground where she could give it a good rub with her front paws. Samuel could see that her muzzle was covered with little dots of drying blood where Bruin had pulled out the spines of the prickly adversary she had tackled.

'Swift? That's his name?' Samuel asked looking back at the hawk.

'Yes, he's Willow's companion. You're very honoured; Swift's a bit fussy about people. There are only a few that he would allow to get as close to him as that.' To offer an example, Bruin reached down to stroke the bird's feathers. Swift turned on him and clacked his beak together a hair's-breadth from his fingertips, warning him off. 'And I'm not one of them,' he laughed. 'Willow and Fern aren't far away, can you sense them?'

Samuel concentrated. 'Yes, I sensed two people but I wasn't sure who they were.'

'They're collecting roots and foraging for fruit. It would be a good opportunity for you to learn about those things, that pair are experts on such matters, another instinct inherited from their father I think. Why don't you go and give them a hand and I'll rejoin you later?'

'Are you sure?' Samuel tried not to let his excitement, at the prospect of spending more time in Willow's company, show in his voice.

Bruin grinned down at his nephew. 'Yes, you've done well today, on you go.'

Quicksilver appeared and came to Samuel's side. He looked a little puzzled at the bird that had now perched himself on the boy's shoulder.

'Don't worry boy, you haven't been replaced, this is Willow's friend, Swift.'

The hawk and the dog looked one another over and seemed to accept the other's presence with little concern as they made their way through the trees towards Willow and her brother.

When Willow saw Swift riding on Samuel's shoulder she froze in surprise. The bird flew to her and nibbled her earlobe gently. 'Why you little traitor,' she giggled, 'imagine sitting on someone else's shoulder!'

'I hope you don't mind, I didn't know he was your friend, I...'

'I'm only teasing, Samuel, Swift can make friends with whomever he wishes, it's not up to me. Besides, you can't be that bad if Fern likes you.' She smiled up at him from where she knelt on the forest floor.

'Samuel! Samuel! And the big silver dog!' Fern ran over to Quicksilver and flung his arms around the dog's broad neck.

'Fern is going to plant trees now, Samuel help?' the young boy asked.

Willow answered him. 'How about you go and get started Fern and we'll catch up with you once I've got some more of these roots here?'

'All righty-right, Fern go and you come soon. Come on, Silky, we go plant baby trees now, make the Man In Green happy.' And off he bounded, his mouse companion bouncing around in the pocket of his tunic.

'So you're here to learn some of the basic stuff are you?' Willow asked as Samuel crouched down by her side to watch what she was doing.

'There's so much to learn, about everything. What are you looking for here?' Samuel asked and watched as Willow carefully pulled aside some tangled ferns that hid the stalks of the yellow-green plants which she had hoped to find.

'Ah, here we are. Do you see this speckling on the leaves? That's the easiest way to recognise this one. If you look closely you can see that the specks are deep green and they're all separate, not overlapping?'

'Yes, I see. Do none of the other plants you collect have that kind of marking?'

'Not exactly the same, no. As you get used to them you'll see the differences between them more easily. Fern is a natural at it. All he has to do is take a leaf in his hands and just with feeling it between his fingers and taking in its scent he can tell you which plant it is. He does it with his eyes closed! We make a game of it sometimes, see who can get the most right, but he always wins.' Willow smiled with pride.

Samuel tried to concentrate on what Willow was saying rather than allow himself to ponder too much on how the sunlight made her hair seem even more golden or how slender her hands were, how nimble and long her fingers seemed as they worked away in the soil. Samuel watched and listened as they gradually stacked up their finds in Willow's basket. He watched as she gently prised up the roots of the plants with a curved wooden implement that had obviously been fashioned especially for this job.

'You made that yourself?' Samuel gestured to it.

'This?' She expertly eased the tool up through the soil, bringing with it a collection of pale fleshy roots. 'No. I *can* make them, but this one belonged to my father.'

'Oh, I see.' Samuel worried that he had raised unhappy memories with his innocent question.

Willow looked at him. 'It pleases me to use it. It was my father who brought me into the forest and taught me all about the plants and trees, all the things you're now learning about with Bruin.'

'And with you,' Samuel said.

Willow smiled and nodded. 'Now for your first lesson.' Twisting off one of the hanging roots Willow wiped the earth from it with her hands then presented it to Samuel. 'Try this and tell me what you think.'

Fern, already having planted all his young trees with great care, had returned to join the other two. But, on seeing this exchange between his new friend and his big sister he ducked behind a nearby tree to watch. Silky perched on his shoulder, her whiskers tickling his ear as she contentedly preened her luxurious fur.

Samuel turned the root over in his palm, brushing more dirt from its pale firm skin. He recognised it. Did she really expect him not to? Without looking at her he could tell she was stifling a grin. In his hiding place Fern controlled his giggles behind both hands, which he had clamped over his mouth.

'What's wrong? Not afraid of a little dirt are you?' Willow asked.

'No, no.' Samuel wiped at the root again.

'I could take it to the river and wash it if you prefer?' she offered.

'No, that's not necessary. I'm merely examining it so that I remember what it looks like. After all, that's the point of this isn't it? You teaching me about the plants so that I can learn to identify them for myself?' Samuel offered her his most innocent expression.

For a moment he felt a flicker of hesitation in her, would she give in and take it from him before he bit into it? Only one way to find out.

He raised the root to his mouth and turned his head away from her slightly as he pretended to bite into it. Willow's hand had flinched in her lap but she hadn't tried to stop him. She would pay for that.

Samuel and Willow were too engrossed with their game of wills to hear Fern gulping back his sniggers as he doubled over behind the tree trunk. Silky chattered her annoyance at the sudden change of angle and dug her tiny claws in to hold on.

'And... how do you find it?' Willow asked. From the corner of his eye Samuel could see that she might explode into hysterics at any moment.

'Hmmm...' he mused as he turned the imaginary mouthful over and over, chewing on it. 'Well,' he said as he mimed swallowing it. 'It's delicious! Would you like some?'

The look of surprise on Willow's face was something to treasure. 'No thanks. I had a large breakfast.' She patted her stomach.

'Oh come on now, this is quite a treat, as you must know having been so kind as to introduce me to it.' Samuel offered the root up to her, holding it in front of her face.

Willow backed off and put a hand up to push it away.

Fern felt his chest might burst if he had to keep quiet much longer. What would his sister do? Would she take a bite? He couldn't bear to look away.

'No, no really. I don't want any, I...' Willow's brow furrowed as she looked at the root in Samuel's outstretched hand. 'Hey! You haven't taken a bite of it at all! What game are you playing?'

'Ha! What game am *I* playing? You're the one who's supposed to be teaching me and yet you try to get me to eat what passes for soap around here!' Samuel bellowed in mock anger and flew at Willow sending her sprawling onto her back. The pair struggled over the root, Samuel fighting to get it to Willow's mouth, both trying to catch their breath between bouts of gut-wrenching laughter. 'No really Willow, I think you should try it.' Samuel managed to catch her thrashing arms by the wrists and held them in one of his hands as he teased her with the soap-root.

'Stop, stop! Please, Samuel,' her face was a patchwork of muddy smears tracked with tears of laughter.

Samuel released his hold on her and the pair lay panting on their backs side-by-side, looking up at the canopy of dappled leaves high above.

Fern was about to run over to them, to jump on his sister and tickle her, to help her pin Samuel down and really make him taste the awful bitter soap-root. It would be so much fun. Fun, fun, fun. But as he broke cover and took his first creeping steps towards the pair lying in the undergrowth he saw his sister do something he had never seen her do before, and it chilled his heart as he stood in the shadow of the great tree and witnessed it.

Willow heaved herself up onto one elbow and peered into Samuel's face. 'So, what have you learned today?'

'Not to trust you.' Samuel laughed.

What happened next surprised them both. Willow hadn't known she was going to do it until she had begun and Samuel wondered for a moment if he was merely having a very vivid daydream. Willow's green eyes stared right into him as she leaned gently against his chest and placed one hand on his cheek. She moved forward, bringing her face closer to his then...

At first the kiss was just a gentle touch of her lips on his, but soon it blossomed into something more, something deeper. The forest spun away taking all its sounds along with it; rabbits thumping in their burrows, the birds in the trees, even the constant rustle of the breeze through the leaves all around them disappeared as they lost themselves in that kiss.

When they moved apart, and the world rushed back in to fill their senses, Samuel and Willow stared wide-eyed at each other.

'Well...' Samuel felt he ought to fill the air between them with words but could think of none.

'Well...' Willow agreed. There was a gentle rosy glow in her complexion just noticeable beneath the streaks of mud.

Samuel reached for her and, with a clean thumb, wiped a patch of dirt from her cheek. 'I guess we should go and wash our faces?'

Fern watched. Confusion and fear erupted into a black anger inside his heaving chest.

What was she doing that *for? Bad Willow. Not love anyone else, only love Fern. Bad, bad Willow.*

Unseen by his sister or Samuel, Fern tore off into the forest away from them, running hard, back to the sheltered space where he had planted the young saplings.

Samuel stood and offered Willow his hand but as she arose, a sudden and vicious pain pulsed through her head causing her to crumple to her knees.

'Willow! What's wrong?' Samuel reached out to steady her.

'I... I don't know. My head hurts. I think it's Fern.' She pushed the heels of her hands into either side of her head, trying in vain to relieve the ache that throbbed there.

'Fern? What do you mean, is he in trouble? Does he need you?' Samuel helped Willow back to her feet and put his arm around her waist to support her.

'No... he's... shouting... he's angry, very angry. I'm trying to connect with him but he's blocking me. I didn't know he knew how to do that; he's never done it before. What does it mean Samuel?' Tears were pearling at the corners of her eyes, either from pain or worry, perhaps both.

'Come and sit down over here, I'll go and find him.'

'No! *I* must go, he'll need me. It has to be *me*.' But as a fresh spasm seized her mind Willow gave in and allowed Samuel to lead her over to sit beneath a nearby tree.

'Trust me. I'll find him. He'll be all right.' Samuel squeezed her hands.

Willow opened her mouth to argue but closed it again and nodded miserably.

'Quicksilver, I need you.' Samuel sent out his thought and within seconds his friend was by his side. 'We need to find Fern, something's wrong.'

The great dog gruffed once and together they left Willow behind and began to run through the trees to where they felt Fern was.

'Fern? Can you hear me? I'm coming to help, hang on.'

Dimly, Samuel sensed Fern's presence up ahead as he used his mind to try to communicate with him. The boy was trying to block out Samuel's connection. 'Talk to me, Fern. Are you all right? Don't block me out, I want to help.'

'Go away!' came the angry reply booming inside Samuel's head. 'Bad Samuel, go away. Leave Fern and Willow alone, we not need you, we only need each other.'

Samuel felt the force of the boy's anger, but also sensed in it an edge of sadness and, more than that; fear. The strength of the contact was enough for both him and Quicksilver to pinpoint Fern's whereabouts. The pair bounded into the small sheltered area that Fern had lovingly prepared for the planting of his saplings. Samuel saw that each young tree had been damaged. Some had been stamped on, others ripped out of the carefully prepared soil and thrown around. A number had been snapped, their fresh green insides lying mashed and exposed.

'Go away, not need you, not like you any more. Go away.' Fern was sitting, his back to a tree stump, his face wet with tears. As Samuel looked at him, Fern wiped them away roughly with his sleeve.

Samuel approached cautiously and hunkered down to Fern's level but kept out of range just in case the youngster should choose to lash out at him with a hand or foot.

'Are you hurt, Fern?' Samuel asked.

Fern looked into Samuel's eyes for a long moment before shaking his head.

'Can you tell me what's wrong?'

The boy cast his eyes downward and a fresh flood of tears spilled down his nose. 'Fern did bad thing, Fern bad. No one like Fern now, Willow not love Fern now.' His face distorted in anguish.

'That's not true, Fern,' Samuel said gently. 'You know that Willow loves you very much and she always will, no matter what.'

'No! Willow love Samuel now, not want Fern no more, Fern did bad thing.'

Now Samuel realised what Fern was upset about, he had either seen Willow and himself together or had sensed it. Fern must have seen his sister's show of affection for another person as a kind of betrayal of her love for him.

'Look at me Fern.' Sad, confused eyes met Samuel's own. 'Listen to me. Willow will *always* love you, no matter what. Nothing and no one can change that, Fern. She and I, well, we like each other, but that doesn't change how she feels about you. People can care for more than one person at a time. You know that, don't you?'

A look of hope came into the boy's eyes as he listened. His tears stopped and he wiped his face again. Samuel moved a little closer and sat cross-legged before him.

'You love Willow but you also care about all the other people in the forest village, don't you?'

Fern nodded thoughtfully.

'And you love Silky, too?' Samuel added, feeling that he was onto something here, Fern was beginning to understand. But then the boy's face crumpled in renewed distress and he hid it beneath his crossed arms as a new bout of weeping seized him.

'Told you, Fern did bad thing, very bad thing.' came his muffled voice, 'Silky hurt, Silky dead!'

Quicksilver gruffed and flicked Samuel lightly on the back with his tail. Turning, he saw his massive silver companion gently nosing at something that lay on the ground between his paws.

'What have you got there, boy?' Samuel asked, moving over towards the dog. As he got closer to the object that Quicksilver was examining, Samuel felt his heartbeat quicken.

Oh Fern, what have you done? he thought.

It was Silky. She was lying still and silent, her silky-soft fur ruffled and damp with perspiration, or perhaps it was tears. Samuel looked at Quicksilver, the dog's big silver eyes full of concern mirrored his own.

Lifting the small creature carefully into his palm Samuel cupped his other hand over the top and went to sit at Fern's side. The boy lifted his head but fell into a long groan as he realised that Samuel had found the source of his shame.

'Not mean it, Silky friend, so sorry, sorry, sorry!' The boy wailed.

Samuel's heart felt heavy in his chest. Studying the tiny creature in his hand he thought he saw a twitch of whiskers.

With eyes closed, he quickly slipped into that place within himself that allowed him to connect with other beings.

Silky was not dead.

Fern's sobs subsided as he became aware of the silence that Samuel had slid into at his side. The boy wiped his face, gave a stout and noisy sniff, then watched.

Visualising the small rodent within his mind Samuel found that wonderful red glow of energy and life that still throbbed away inside the creature. She was quite badly hurt, that was true, Fern must have squeezed her then thrown her down to the ground in his fury. A tiny rib was cracked, some organs bruised and there was blood there inside where it should not be. Should he put her out of her pain? A quick twist of her tiny neck would extinguish that glow and send Silky off to scamper freely again with all those that had joined the spirit of the forest, the Man In Green.

I will do that if I have to, but not yet. Samuel vowed this to himself as he began to try to help her.

Moving closer towards that red light in his mind Samuel pushed deeper, his senses finding a way *inside* the warmth of that glow. With all his will he pleaded with the life-energy still held within the creature's injured body to grow. He tried to tease it out, to stretch the energy further to cover the tiny injured organs, to bind the fragile bone of its rib. The shape of the warm red light moved this way and that, and it did grow a little, its colour brightened slightly like the way the energy in the boulders of the archway did when he concentrated and made them move, but try as he might Samuel could not force it to fill the whole body of the mouse in his hands; it seemed she was too far gone for that.

I'm not giving up on you yet, Silky, hold on.

Pulling back in his mind, so that he could see not only the mouse but also his own hand and arm, Samuel began to try something else, something he had never thought of before. He had no idea whether it was possible or not. Unlike the now weak and flickering light in the animal's body, when he concentrated on his own limbs Samuel saw that they were radiating a brilliant red aura. It seemed unfair that he should have so much life when the defenceless animal in his hand had hardly any. Moving into the flame-bright energy of his own body Samuel pushed and forced a thread of it out of himself and watched amazed as it obeyed his will and moved snake-like into the body of the mouse. This twisting line of energy connected with the centre of Silky's own feeble glow stoking it like a poker prodding a dying fire causing it to bloom and grow once more. The glow grew in size and deepened in colour until it filled the mouse's every extremity from the tip of her twitching nose to the end of her trembling tail.

'How you do it? Samuel good, Samuel very good. My Silky, oh my Silky!'

Fern's voice brought Samuel back to the here-and-now, back to the forest, spiralling out of the depths of his own mind. His breathing was hard and laboured, he felt as though he had been running through the forest racing Quicksilver. Then Samuel looked down at the mouse in his open palm.

Silky was sitting on her haunches busily licking her paws and grooming away at her dishevelled fur coat, putting it back into good order.

'How Samuel do it?' the boy asked again, his voice quiet and full of awe and respect.

'I... I'm not sure, Fern.'

Samuel brought Silky over to Fern's outstretched palms. The rodent looked up into the face of his companion, into the expectant face of the one who had so nearly taken away her life and she hesitated, remaining in Samuel's care.

Fern's face fell. 'Silky not love me now, Fern bad.'

'You did a terrible thing, Fern. Silky is afraid you might do it again.'

'No! No! Never again, never hurt Silky again, never hurt anyone or anything, not ever.'

Samuel looked seriously at Fern. 'No matter how angry or sad you feel you must never take it out on any other living creature. It's wrong. Do you understand that?'

Fern nodded miserably. 'Never done before, never do again, bad Fern.'

'It's all right,' Samuel placed a hand on the younger boy's shoulder, '*you're* not bad, Fern, what you *did* was bad but you're never going to do it again, are you?'

'Never, never ever.' Fern turned his attention back to Silky and offered his hand to her again. The mouse sniffed at it and touched one of his fingers tentatively with her forepaw. 'So sorry Silky, Fern did bad thing but not ever again, forgive Fern, Fern love you.'

Silky considered for a moment, twitched her nose-whiskers thoughtfully then leapt onto Fern's hand and scampered up his arm to sit in her favourite spot on his right shoulder.

Fern's broad grin and wide eyes dimmed a little as he asked, 'Samuel tell Willow? Samuel tell Bruin?'

'You mean, tell them about what you did?' Samuel asked.

Fern nodded.

'I don't think so. If you've learned your lesson then there's no need to tell anyone about it.'

'How you do it Samuel, how you fix Silky?'

Samuel thought about what he had done and wondered if he could do it again. Could such a thing help other creatures or maybe even people? But he felt incredibly weary and it had only been a tiny mouse that he had healed this time. He felt as if he had been a full cup of water but had poured himself out, almost draining himself completely after giving away part of his own energy to Silky.

'I'm really not sure, Fern, but perhaps we should keep it as our secret too? For now at least.' Samuel replied.

'Ok Samuel, me good at secrets, shhh!' Fern threw himself against Samuel's chest and hugged him fiercely, Silky chattered and squeaked away as she clung to his shoulder. 'So sorry, sorry, sorry. Thank you Samuel for fixing Silky and for being Fern's good friend.'

Samuel wasn't sure which touched him more; the boy's words or the hug. He gestured to the strewn debris around them. 'What do you say we sort out this mess then go and find your big sister? She'll be worried about you.'

A few of the saplings were salvageable and Samuel watched as Fern apologised to each of them in turn and replanted them carefully with his skilled hands. Those that couldn't be saved, the pair broke up and buried. Samuel agreed that he would help Fern to bring more out from the nursery and plant them later that afternoon.

As they neared the place where he had left Willow, Samuel fixed her with his mind and connected with her, doing his best to shield this conversation from the boy at his side. 'We're on our way Willow, Fern is fine.'

'Oh thank goodness! What was it? What happened?' She asked, the sound of her voice inside his mind full of concern.

'Perhaps it would be best for us to talk about that later, in private.'

'But...'

'Please Willow, trust me on this.' Samuel thought to her.

She hesitated for a moment before replying, 'All right, Samuel.'

'Willow! Willow! Fern love you!' Fern ran to his sister and

she took him in her arms, flashing a smile of gratitude at Samuel over the youngster's shoulder.

'You're all right Fern?' Willow asked him.

Fern nodded and looked to Samuel for guidance on what to say.

'Fern had a problem with some of the saplings didn't you?'

Fern nodded uncertainly.

'We need to head back and get some more for planting. I'll help Fern if you're all right to carry on here on your own Willow? We could meet back up with you a little later, after we're done?' Samuel gave Willow a look to encourage her to agree.

'Oh... all right then. I can manage here just fine. But wait a minute...' Willow rummaged in her deerskin bag and handed a parcel of food and a water pouch to Fern. 'There's plenty in there for the two of you if you don't mind sharing.'

Fern kissed his sister on the cheek. 'See you sis. Me and Samuel going to plant beautiful trees, trees that'll grow up high and touch the sky!' he leapt into the air pretending to grab a handful of blue sky above. Silky dug in her tiny claws to the fabric of his tunic to stop herself from falling off.

Samuel and Fern shared the lunch that Willow had prepared and made quick work of fetching and planting the replacement saplings in the small clearing. The stumps of the trees that had been cut down for use by the forest people would provide the new young trees with added protection from the wind as they grew and got stronger. Soon their heads would rise above the stumps of their felled neighbours and they would grow, year-by-year, ring-by-ring, taller and broader, enriching and replenishing the forest. It amazed Samuel to think that these tender shoots would one day be as strong and wide as the ancient trees of the forest, with luck they would outlive both himself and Fern and provide for a future generation.

'Good luck, little ones,' Fern whispered to the saplings before they left to meet up with Willow again. 'I hope the Man In Green watches over you.'

They helped Willow to carry all her findings back to the forest village and to wash and prepare them for storing in the food hut. Although still tired, Samuel was much recovered from his earlier experience with Silky. When Bruin came to say that he wouldn't be able to spend that evening with him, Samuel had been delighted when Willow overheard and invited him to share the evening meal with her and Fern instead.

Fern fell asleep very soon after the meal was over and Willow quietly suggested that they leave him to dream whilst she and Samuel had that talk that he had promised her earlier.

8

T a l e s

Willow and Samuel slipped out into the forest and walked to the river where they sat on the bank dangling their bare feet in the chilly shallows. The setting sun threw a spangled trail of liquid gold across the water, dragonflies and flitting bugs danced on the surface. Hungry fish lurked in the shadows below, rising up to gulp in some of the less wary insects from above.

'Samuel, tell me what happened with Fern.' Willow placed a hand on his arm.

Looking into her deep green eyes Samuel wished he could tell her everything, not just about what had happened that day, but everything that was in his thoughts.

'Fern... saw us.'

'Oh.' A shadow of worry crossed her face. 'I see.'

'He was very upset, confused. He thought that it meant you didn't love him anymore. I think he got it into his head that you would leave him, not want him anymore, something like that.'

Willow nodded, 'I understand. Poor darling. He must have thought that we would go away, like the others, and leave him behind.'

'The others?' Samuel asked.

Willow looked at him. 'You don't know about them? Bruin hasn't told you?'

'Who do you mean? Do you mean the outsiders?'

'No... perhaps I should leave it for Bruin to tell you, I expect there's a reason he hasn't.' Willow looked uncertain.

'Please Willow, you tell me. Who are the others?'

Samuel saw the struggle in her eyes. Should she tell him or wait until Bruin, the leader of her people, told him? Finally she decided.

'I can't see what harm there is in telling you, it's no secret in our village. It happened a long time ago, when I was very small. Nearly all of what I know is what I've been told, or picked up from talk around the village, but the only thing that I actually remember from when it happened is that they took my friend Brook away with them when they left. I don't remember what she looked like, I was too young, but we had a strong bond and I remember missing that for a long time. I've no recollection of how many others left with her or who they were.'

'But why did they leave at all? Do you know?'

'I've been told that it was getting too overcrowded for us all to live comfortably within the secret forest village. There were many more families and homes back then, so Bruin and the elders met and decided which families and couples should leave us to make a new settlement elsewhere.'

'I suppose that makes sense, but where did they go? Didn't

the two settlements keep in touch? Didn't you ever see Brook again, or the others?'

'No. Bruin thought it safer if they moved far away, in case the outsiders ever found our homes. That way at least one of our groups would still be able to carry on our ways and look after the forest. I believe it was mostly young couples and the younger families that left. I expect Fern worried that if you and I... well... if you and I became a "couple" that maybe we would leave and go to join them. It's a story the children tell each other and add to, the way children do. If you don't behave you'll be sent away to the "other place" or your parents will go there and leave you behind. Fern takes things like that a little too seriously, you understand?'

Samuel nodded, 'It's easy to see why he would worry about it, Willow - you're everything to him.'

'Yes, I often worry about that myself. If anything should ever happen to me...'

'Nothing will, I won't allow it.' Samuel's face darkened, the dream about Willow and the metal-jaw rising fresh in his mind.

'Samuel the great warrior will protect me?' Willow joked.

A little stung by her tease Samuel looked directly into her eyes in the fading light. 'If I can, yes.'

'I'm sorry,' Willow reached a hand out and stroked his cheek lightly, 'I believe you would. But will you promise me something? It's a lot to ask, but I feel that I can ask it of you.'

'What is it?' Looking into Willow's eyes Samuel found it

unbelievable that he had known her for only two days.

'If anything does ever happen to me, would you look after Fern for me?'

'But, Willow...'

'I know we barely know each other but... please, will you say that you will. It would put my mind at rest.'

'I'll do anything I can for him, of course I will, but for tonight can we not think of such things? Fern is safely tucked up in his bed, the night is beautiful, and the forest is peaceful...'

'And we are all alone?' she smiled at him.

'Well... I didn't mean...'

'Samuel the great warrior is blushing. There's no one to spy on us now.' She leaned towards him.

That second kiss was just as sweet as the first had been.

The sun had dipped a little further in the darkening sky before they started to make their way back to the forest village, hand in hand.

'There's another story that the children used to tell each other. I'm not sure where it came from or who started it but when Bruin heard it he called a gathering and forbade it to be told any more.' Willow spoke as they walked along.

'He *forbade* it?'

'Yes. I thought it strange at the time but Bruin's our leader and I supposed that he had a good reason, though I couldn't see any harm in the tale.'

'Will you tell it to me?' Samuel asked.

'So long as you don't let on to Bruin, I don't want to get into trouble.'

'Of course not.' He gave her a nudge with his shoulder. 'Go on.'

'Well, it was about a young forest man who committed a terrible act and betrayed both himself and his kin, forcing them to turn their backs on him. They threw him out of their village, shunning him forever. But as he walked away through the woods, he turned and swore that one day he would have his revenge on them all. His anger was so fierce that with every step he took flames were said to have leapt from his feet scorching the ground and leaving his footprints burned there forever into the forest floor as a warning and a reminder of his curse.' Willow tickled the back of Samuel's neck. 'Spooky, huh?' she giggled.

A chill ran down Samuel's back as he recalled the markings he had seen in the woods just before Quicksilver had run off and found Ash. Everything that had gone on after that time had wiped them from his mind.

'What did the story say that he'd done? What was so terrible that his people turned him out, do you know?'

'Well,' Willow tilted her head as she thought, 'that varied depending on who was telling the tale. It ranged widely from him having eaten all the winter food supplies, leaving the village with nothing to face the cold season with – I think that version was thought-up to warn the children against greed — to his refusal to take part in any of the work in the village — again I think that was more of a warning, this time to frighten the young ones into not being lazy. But, the most popular reason for his being sent away was that he fell in love with the wrong girl.'

'The wrong girl?'

'An outsider.'

'That's a "terrible act"?' Samuel asked in surprise.

'It's forbidden to us, we aren't even allowed to go near their towns and villages. Anyway, the story goes that he wouldn't give her up and so he was put out of the village, never to be seen again.'

'That seems very harsh.'

'It's only a story, Samuel.' Willow squeezed his hand.

'I wonder...' Samuel thought again of the markings he'd seen. He put his arm around Willow's shoulder and they moved on together through the trees.

Before returning to the village Samuel took Willow to where he had been shown the cave full of bats earlier in the day. They sat quietly, bathed in moonlight, the sky above clear and studded with a thousand specks of brilliant white and they waited for the small creatures to begin their nightly outing.

The rumbling, flapping noise began deep inside the cave then rose in volume to a wonderful ear-splitting din as the bats burst out into the open in a black cloud of wings and squeaking.

'Where have you two been?' Bruin's voice startled them both as they left the tunnel behind and entered the forest village.

'We took a walk, Uncle.' Samuel answered. Bruin's face was furrowed with what could have been either concern or anger.

'It isn't wise to go out into the forest alone at night, Samuel, without telling others where you are. Willow, you should know better.'

'I'm... sorry, Bruin, it was such a lovely night and...' Willow tried to explain.

Bruin interrupted her. 'That may be, but we can't afford to take any chances. What if there was a group of outsiders nearby hunting in the woods and they came across you two?'

'We were alert to our surroundings Uncle. I sensed no danger.' Samuel answered.

'Samuel! You're only just learning to use your skills, what if you made a mistake? What if you were distracted and didn't sense the danger because your mind was on other things? You could have put Willow and yourself in danger.'

Samuel looked at Willow but she had hung her head and was looking at the ground. She was just taking this from Bruin without standing up for herself. Even if Bruin was right about his skills Willow was more than capable of looking after herself. Why was his uncle being like this? Careful not to let his feelings show on his face, Samuel felt it best not to push further on the matter.

'I'm sorry, Uncle, it was foolish of me.'

'It's late,' Bruin sighed, his features softening a little. 'Off you go, both of you,' he added before walking away.

Lost in their own thoughts about Bruin's words the two companions walked to Willow's tepee.

'Why didn't you say something to him?' Samuel asked Willow quietly.

'Like what? Bruin must be respected and listened to. Perhaps we shouldn't have gone out without letting anyone know.'

'But Willow, we're not prisoners here, are we? Why can't we be free to go into the forest when we want to?'

'Please, Samuel. I don't want to argue, it's been such a lovely night. Bruin is my leader and what he says I must follow. You'd do well to remember that, after all he's your leader now too.' Willow leaned toward him and kissed him lightly on the mouth. 'Goodnight Samuel, we'll see you tomorrow.'

That night, as he tried to recall every moment he had spent with Willow, the image of Bruin kept looming in his mind. Had Bruin been right in what he'd said? Had Samuel really put himself and Willow in danger by being alone outside the village at night? He didn't think so. Of course he had been a little distracted by Willow's presence, but he felt sure of his skills, of his gift. If any danger had been close by that threatened them he would have known it. But his mind flitted back to his encounter with the bear.

But I'm different now. My gift is stronger... isn't it?

Why would Bruin lead him to doubt himself and his abilities? Was he just trying to protect him?

It niggled at him that Bruin's fears about the threat of the outsiders were unjustified. Why was his uncle always so sure that they meant the forest people harm? Samuel had lived as an outsider all his life before coming to this place but he had never heard any talk of the 'forest people', only folklore and tales that were designed to spook those who heard them and keep them from going too far into the woods. It made less sense the more he pondered it.

Eventually falling asleep with his mind churning, Samuel began to dream of the young man that Willow had told him about. He dreamt the story as he had been told it; the angry outcast cursing the village that had shunned him, his flaming footsteps full of anger and hatred burning their promise of revenge between the trees.

Then Samuel dreamt of the outcast again... Samuel was looking into a beautiful clearing ringed with bluebells and daisies. A young man sat on a boulder playing a wooden flute, stopping every now and then to listen for something. A slight, pale girl with hair the sheen and rich blackness of a raven's wing entered the clearing and the two embraced. They kissed, their arms wound tightly around each other, her long sleek hair draped over his shoulder. The contrast against his stark golden curls both vivid and startling. Samuel watched as they sat together talking, their smiles and tender touches showing their deep affection for each other. He felt he should leave, give them their privacy, but suddenly he sensed something, someone, who was also watching and in that figure a dark anger was growing. He longed to call out to the young couple, to warn them that someone was coming, but he couldn't make himself heard. He could only look on as a shadow fell across the pair of lovers.

The girl's face crumpled in fear, her eyes filling with tears as she pleaded with the unseen figure to release the hold he had taken on her young man's arm but she was roughly pushed away and fell to the ground. Samuel wanted to reach out his hand to help her up but there was nothing he could do, he was only an observer here. He watched as the dark-haired girl scrambled upright and ran off into the trees weeping, fleeing back to her own people. When Samuel turned to look once more at the young man, he was nowhere to be seen. The hidden figure had taken him away, dragged him off through the woods, leaving the ground churned and muddy from the struggle.

Around him, the clearing in the forest quickly faded away into blackness. The darkness persisted for a few minutes before Samuel fell gratefully into less disturbing dreams and then came one which he wished would continue forever: he and Willow were alone together, side-by-side on the riverbank as the sparkling water tumbled by.

9

A P a i n f u l L e s s o n

The next morning Bruin came to Samuel's tepee and woke him.

'Tell me Samuel, do you know how to climb a tree?' Bruin grinned widely at his nephew's quizzical look, all signs of his discontent from the night before were gone.

'I've never had much cause to try.' Samuel said, wiping the sleep from his eyes with the back of his hand and struggling to sit up. 'Once I did, when my mother and I were out for one of our days together in our clearing, but I stood on a weak branch quite high up and nearly fell, so I didn't try it again.'

'Why, were you afraid?'

'No.' Samuel replied, now upright and gathering his clothes together. 'It's just that if I got hurt and couldn't work...' he trailed off.

'Of course, forgive me.' Bruin paused a moment. 'Well, climbing a tree out here could save your life. Not only that, but it can also give you a good view of the surrounding forest. It may sound simple enough, but there are mind skills and a great deal of physical strength involved. You wouldn't want to find that you'd trusted your weight to a weak branch if you were standing on the uppermost limbs of one of the great ancients.'

Samuel knew what Bruin was referring to; he had shown him the 'great ancients' out in the forest. Massive trees that disappeared into the sky like giant's arrows that had been fired from the heavens to burrow deep into the fertile ground below. They were the oldest trees in the woods.

'Do you feel up to trying?' Bruin asked.

If he had been honest, Samuel would rather have stayed in his bed until the sun had risen much higher into the sky, but he nodded and Bruin left him to get ready.

Soon they were out in the woods once again with the dogs. Samuel was thankful that Bruin didn't choose to begin his climbing lessons on any of the great ancients. Their trunks were so straight and their branches started so high up from the ground that they looked to be the hardest of all the trees in the forest to climb, certainly not for beginners.

Samuel thought about what he had learnt from Willow the evening before. Questions about the other settlement were burning away inside him but now didn't seem the right time to bring the subject up.

They walked on for a little way, Bruin naming the trees that they passed, explaining the uses and the nature of the bark and timber of any types they had not discussed before and testing Samuel's memory about the ones they had. Samuel was studying the trees now in great detail, paying close attention to everything he was being taught and seeing them in their full glory for what seemed to be the first time. Suddenly he was seeing them all as the individuals they were; so many different shapes, sizes and heights. Small variances in the colour of their bark, leaves and buds; picking up on minute differences that he had not fully appreciated before. He had always thought them beautiful and magical, years of time trapped and numbered within their powerful trunks, but now he could distinguish the different varieties and see how they all lived together, side-by-side, as diverse as people.

Bruin stopped and patted the bark of a twisted old tree.

'This will do for a start,' he said, as he looked upwards.

Samuel studied it. The old tree bristled with branches. Some even wound their twisted limbs along the ground, snaking through the vegetation before reaching up again towards the light. It was a fairly high tree, Samuel estimated it to be about the height of ten grown men standing on one another's shoulders, but it looked so easy to climb that Samuel felt a little disappointed. Did Bruin think so little of his abilities?

'It's not as easy as you think, nephew.' Bruin said, having read Samuel's face, or perhaps, his mind. 'You need to learn never to underestimate anything in the woods, to give it your full attention, let nothing distract you.'

If Samuel had heeded this last instruction, taken it for the warning it was, then perhaps things would have gone differently that morning. But, as Samuel stepped between the knotted limbs of the tree, he thought the task ahead of him was an easy one and instead of giving it his full concentration he allowed his mind to wander off.

A child could climb this old thing, he thought as he placed his two hands on its gnarled trunk and looked up.

Apart from a few larger gaps, most of the branches were no more than a step apart, like the rungs of a massive twisted ladder reaching up to the patchy blue sky above. How this could be an important part of his training was beyond him, but Samuel began to climb, his mind on other things.

Bruin stood watching, his face set like stone, one of his hands absentmindedly rubbed at the back of Blithe's neck. He made no comment as he waited for Samuel to make his first mistake. It was important for Samuel to learn some things for himself, hopefully that way he would never forget the lesson that might one day save his life. But still, it wasn't an easy thing to watch.

Samuel made his way up, stepping easily from one branch to the next. He moved quickly on, up and round he went, anxious to get the climb over and done with so that he could move on to more interesting things. In his rush to complete the task he ignored every hint of danger on his way up.

Seeing the tree just as an obstacle to be overcome rather than as a living part of the forest, Samuel didn't treat it with the respect it was due. This lack of watchfulness caused him to miss several important signs. The first of these was that there were obvious areas of decay within some of the branches that he passed by on his ascent, branches that he should have taken the time to remember as it would be sensible to avoid them again on his way down, rather than trust them once more with his weight. Secondly, above the constant buzz and whir of the insects that flitted around beneath the canopy of greenery above, there was another closer sound, a sound not picked up by Samuel's inattentive ears or senses as he ploughed on. And lastly, the one oversight which could prove the most costly of Samuel's errors that day; he did not notice the huge, delicately woven webs that adorned the higher limbs of the old tree.

There were only three more branches between Samuel and the first of the Fierce Spiders. Bruin had told Samuel about this species of spider on their first venture into the forest together. The bite of the Fierce Spider, Bruin had explained to his nephew, was not fatally poisonous but was surprisingly painful. Bruin himself had been unfortunate enough to have experienced it when he was much younger and had told Samuel that the sensation was akin to having a fingernail shoved into an open wound and then twisted.

Unluckily for Samuel, the pattern on the body of a Fierce Spider makes them almost indistinguishable from the bark of the trees that they choose to inhabit, the type of tree that Samuel was now climbing. Although the male spider, that was as big as one of Bruin's large strong hands, was keeping completely still and as such was all but invisible to the eye, Samuel would have been able to sense its presence and the threatening aura it was emitting if only he had been concentrating more on his surroundings and putting his gift to good use.

The spider had been watching the boy's ascent as it had held its position in the tree, faithfully guarding the nest of eggs that nestled in the hollow just above it. Some moments before it had sent out a message to its fellow guards and workers, who were stationed further up the trunk, informing them that a large predator was approaching. The others had immediately ceased their collection of the insects that had been caught and wound in silky thread and had begun the short journey back to protect their young from the impending danger.

Samuel had hardly broken a sweat on the climb. He was around halfway now, perhaps a little more and was looking forward to the view he should get once he reached the top. It never entered his thoughts that he might not actually make it that far. Looking down on the faces of Quicksilver, Blithe and his uncle, Samuel gave them a wave before carrying on. Bruin's face looked tense and worried.

He thinks I can't do this.

Samuel would prove him wrong.

He began a chant inside his head: *lift up foot to next branch, slide hand up the trunk, step on up to next branch, slide hand up trunk...* there's nothing to this... *place foot, slide hand, place foot, slide hand...*

'Yowww! Aaaahhh!' Samuel screamed. The pain that shot

through his hand was so terrible and unexpected that before he realised what had happened, he found himself falling. The instinct to pull his hand away from the source of the agony and then to clamp his other hand over it had surpassed anything and everything else, including maintaining a hold on the tree.

The massive Fierce Spider was still attached, its jaws deeply embedded in Samuel's hand, in the fleshy part between his thumb and forefinger. Samuel's body thumped and bashed past splintering bone-breaking branches, his torso and limbs twisting and bruising as he fell.

At last the spider was thrown clear. Spatters of blood from Samuel's wound flew past his face as he scrabbled to catch a hold of the branches that were fleeting by at a terrific pace as he tumbled ever-downwards. But next he was cracking through the decayed limbs of the old tree; these weakened rotten branches were unable to stop his fall, his weight at such a speed was far too much for them to stand.

Samuel had just got to wondering if he was going to travel the full height of his climb and land in a bloodied and broken mass at his uncle's feet, when his fall was suddenly and gut-wrenchingly halted. He lay there, beaten and oozing blood from many cuts, on the thick healthy branch that had finally arrested his downward journey. In a blur of excruciating pain he wondered if his back was broken.

Looking up at the devastated limbs of the tree above him he saw just how far he had fallen. The sound of the forest around

212

him buzzed with the disturbance he had created. Startled birds screeched and warbled, afraid for their young, thinking themselves under some threat. Leaves and snapped twigs spiralled down in the shafts of morning sunlight; airborne debris from the destruction he had inflicted on the old tree. Ear-splitting screams came from other nearby trees, the animals that voiced them unseen and unknown to him. Rabbits drummed their warnings through the forest floor.

Below him Samuel heard Quicksilver's frantic barking. The great dog was leaping and scratching long strips off the tree's trunk in a desperate attempt to climb up to his friend. His heavy, muscular frame was no match for the task; he kept getting up onto the first spindly branch, then his paws would slip, and down to the forest floor he would tumble. Samuel tried to connect with him to calm him and say that he was okay, but his head was so clouded with pain that he couldn't manage it.

There was something wrong with his hearing too, it seemed. There was a buzzing, rumbling noise, which was getting louder. Samuel tried shaking his head to see if the noise would clear. A jolt of pain ran down his neck but the noise was still there, louder now.

Then he saw it. The real source of the noise.

How could he have missed *that* on the way up? He was lucky not to have landed right on top of the thing or else he would likely be dead already. Lying there, so close to the throbbing hive that dangled precariously from the damaged remains of the branch above him, he realised he was still in terrible danger.

The hive was swinging slightly, like a great pale fruit, but a fruit writhing with hidden dangers. Its movement was not due to the gentle breeze, nor was it an aftershock of Samuel's descent; the massive hive was seething from the activity of its angry inhabitants.

Samuel wondered how long it would take to die from a hundred stings. Perhaps, this deep in the forest, the bees or wasps would be more vicious, their stings more potent and would bring the end quickly for him rather than drag it out.

Lifting his damaged hand before his face, Samuel examined the spider's bite. It was red and angry, the two puncture wounds deep and ragged. The skin around the wound was the purple-brown of congealed blood and early bruising. Shame overcame him. What a fool he had been. Bruin had quite plainly told him to respect the forest and be prepared for anything. What had his uncle said to him just before he had begun to climb?

'You need to learn never to underestimate anything in the woods.'

Well, he had certainly learned that lesson, a lesson he would not forget for the rest of his life... but how long would that be? Samuel pondered on this horrible question as he lay there waiting for the first 'stinger' to emerge from the hive. The idea to try to climb further down, away from the source of danger, occurred to him, but only for a moment. He was quite sure that there were broken bones in a few areas of his body, where exactly he wasn't sure, the pain seemed to come from everywhere at once, but in any case his legs refused to move. Whether this was out of fear, or from the damage they had sustained, he did not know.

Samuel became aware of his uncle's voice. Somehow he must have managed to silence Quicksilver, as the dog's barking and noisy attempts at reaching him had ceased. Bruin's voice was firm yet quiet, more than a whisper but only just loud enough for Samuel to make out that it was indeed his uncle. Samuel tried to move his head over to one side so that he could hear him better. He would try to warn him about the hive, Bruin and the dogs should get far away before the insects attacked or else they might get stung too. Sudden panic filled him at the thought of harm coming to them because of his own foolish actions.

'No Samuel, do *not* move. They'll see you as a threat and attack for sure.' Bruin's voice, very close now.

What was Bruin talking about? The insects? Surely whatever lay within the hive wouldn't wait to see if the idiot boy lying outside their home was a threat or not, they would just attack him on sight. Samuel cast his eyes back up at the hive and then to the trunk of the tree above.

That was when he saw what his uncle was *really* referring to.

He saw only one at first and only because it twitched and

215

rubbed together two of its hairy front legs giving Samuel something to focus on. A shiver ran down his aching spine. As his eyes began to adjust to the tiny differences in the pattern of the bark compared to the colouring of that one spider, many others sprang into full, horrifying view.

I'm done for, there must be about fifteen of them! Samuel thought.

The pain in his hand pulsed harder, the memory of how it had felt to be bitten by just one of those things made his stomach contract.

'Keep completely still, Samuel. I'm coming for you.' Bruin's calm voice, inside Samuel's mind now.

Samuel didn't want to keep still, everything inside him screamed at him to move. Even rolling over and slipping off the branch to take his chances with the remainder of the fall seemed a better option than lying there waiting to discover whether it would be the stinging mass from the hive or the vicious biting jaws of the spiders that would descend on him first.

Bruin moved into Samuel's field of vision like a rising mist.

'Stay still,' he mind-whispered to his nephew.

Samuel lay completely still and watched transfixed as his uncle secured himself against the trunk of the tree. Bruin kept one foot on a lower branch then lifted and locked his other leg at the knee over the next branch up, using the strength in his powerful thigh to hold him there. Now he was free to use both of his hands for what he had to do.

Reaching slowly and carefully for the hive, Bruin placed his open palms on its heaving papery sides. The buzzing inside changed pitch almost immediately and a line of angry wasps flew out.

This is it, thought Samuel; *I've now caused not just my own death but my uncle's too. What a fool I am.*

He closed his eyes, not wanting to see the black and orange cloud that suddenly swarmed around Bruin.

The forest grew quiet. The dreadfulness of what was happening was like a thick awful taste in Samuel's mouth. Taking a deep breath he forced himself to look once more on the face of his uncle.

He could not see it.

He couldn't see any part of Bruin at all.

His uncle's form was still there before him, he was still holding onto the hive, but every inch of him was covered by a thick living cloak of buzzing, moving insects.

They hummed as they crawled all over Bruin's body and head. Samuel felt sick, how could Bruin keep so still? Were they attacking him? Was he being stung to death right now? But how was he managing not to scream or even to move?

As Samuel watched, wide-eyed in horror but unable to look away, the cloak of brightly coloured bodies began to lift into the air on a thousand wings. The wasps formed a humming cloud just above Samuel's head and hovered there for a moment before streaming off to file back through the opening in the great hanging hive that was still held firmly, yet very gently, in his uncle's large hands.

Samuel forced himself to look again at his uncle's face.

Bruin was unhurt.

There didn't seem to be one single sting on him.

Slowly, Bruin released his hold on the hive; it hung there, the sounds from within no longer menacing but just those of forest wasps going about their usual duties.

One danger passed, now for the other.

Keeping a watchful eye on the soldier spiders positioned above, Bruin offered a strong arm to Samuel.

'You're going to have to hold on to my neck, boy, and support your own weight while I climb down. Come on,' he said.

Samuel grabbed for his uncle's hand. His sudden movement disturbed the lead spider who sprang forward, closing the distance between itself and Samuel's face alarmingly. Samuel waited for it to pounce on him but it stayed put, legs twitching, watching.

'Careful, slowly does it. You don't want to frighten it.' Bruin whispered.

Frighten IT? Samuel felt like saying, but held his tongue.

This time Samuel moved more fluidly and slowly, taking his uncle's strong hand and biting back a yelp of pain as he was pulled onto the big man's back. He locked his hands, knitting his fingers together below Bruin's chin, praying that he could bear the agony long enough to get down to the ground without letting go. Squeezing his eyes tightly closed he buried his face between his uncle's shoulder blades, tears of pain and shame forcing their way out between his creased eyelids.

The army of spiders held their position and watched as the humans got out of their tree and back on the ground where they belonged.

Bruin laid his nephew down gently on the cool ground and wiped the grime and blood from his face with a damp leaf.

'I think that's enough training for today, Samuel,' he said quietly.

Samuel smiled weakly up at his uncle. 'Yes... I'm so sorry...' he managed.

'Don't be sorry boy, just learn from this. I'll take you home and we'll get you all fixed up. Time will help your bones to knit together again, and Willow will wash your wounds and see to them. But Samuel, if a bear had been after you today or if the wasps had attacked...' Bruin left the rest of his sentence unfinished.

Samuel was only too aware what his uncle meant. He would never forget that morning's lesson for the rest of his life.

'I understand,' was all that Samuel was able to say before the tender loving licks being applied to his face by Quicksilver's massive pink tongue eased him gratefully into a healing sleep.

Settling In

It had been nearly a whole year since Samuel's experience in the tree. A year filled with learning, training and of coming to understand what it really meant to live surrounded by nature in such a wild place.

He had learned many of the ways of his fellow foresters during that time; some had been unpleasant, some plain hard work and others great fun. The most enjoyable and revealing of these ways had been the great tradition of 'The Tests'. This consisted of a string of events that took place annually during the cold season.

Every year when the signs came around that winter would soon be with them, the forest people would get together and begin construction of a huge tent that stood proudly in the open space at the centre of their village. This area was to provide a place to come together, out of the biting wind and snow. It was a space in which to gather, talk and to give the children room to play, but best of all it was to be the arena for 'The Tests'.

Everyone looked forward to these events and practiced long and hard during the lead up to them, especially the children.

There were three different trials or 'Tests'; Communication, Movement and Concentration. Bruin had tried hard to persuade Samuel to take part in them, as had Willow who had been hoping to pit her skills against his, but Samuel had decided against it. With his promise that he would enter the next time around they had eventually stopped pestering him about it. At that time, Samuel had thought it best to avoid any situation that might prove difficult by putting his new skills on show. There was a great deal more he wanted to know and understand about them before he would be ready to even consider doing that. Bruin, Willow and his other close friends had been disappointed by Samuel's decision but the excitement of the games had proved too intoxicating to keep them downhearted for long.

When asked, Bruin had eagerly explained the elements of The Tests to his nephew. 'Communication' consisted of the entrant having to communicate a set of instructions to their animal companion using only the mind. The instructions could be to have the animal retrieve hidden items or behave in a certain way. These instructions were decided upon by those in charge of the judging and were relayed to each entrant well out of earshot of their animal companion.

This particular Test was entirely entered by the children of the village as the adults were all considered to be far too adept at communicating with their companions for there to be any real competition for them in this section. To make it fairer on the children they were grouped by age and Samuel had watched as they all awaited their turn with barely contained excitement. There were minks, foxes, wild-cats, rabbits, hedgehogs, squirrels and many more animals.

The connection between each pair was almost palpable as the child communicated the instructions to his or her companion animal. Creatures darted here and there digging up nuts or acorns – buried earlier in the sandy floor of the tent by the judges – or finding hidden items secreted in the pockets of members of the watching crowd. Samuel and Willow had whooped with delight as they watched Fern come in first place, having scored top-marks in his age section after a perfect round with his little mouse, Silky.

'Movement' was a good deal harder, but both adults and children alike took part in this section. On each of five tables there was an item; a leaf, an acorn, a small pebble, a rock and then on the last and largest table there was a huge bowl of water. Each contender would take their turn to approach the tables and try to 'move' the item on it, using only their mind-skills.

Without exception, a hush would fall like a thick blanket over those within the tent as all eyes studied the item in question, watching for the slightest flicker of movement. If movement was seen, and agreed upon by the judges, the entrant was free to continue on to the next table and try his or her skills there.

Most of the children and younger folk struggled with the leaf on the first table. Of these, only Ash, Heather's son, managed to get on to the next table but even though he made the acorn wobble slightly and was permitted to move on to the pebble on the third table, he was exhausted and chose not to try it. A cheer went up for him nonetheless, as his was a great achievement for one so young.

Those of the forest people most blessed with the gift progressed past the acorn and the pebble, until their number was diminished greatly when many fell away having failed to move the rock; the second most difficult of the items available. Bruin, Rowan, Finch, Flint, Willow, Heather, and just a handful of the others, were the only ones left out of all the foresters to attempt the final hurdle. All of these contenders, still in this section of the competition, were the same ones who had gained the ability to open and close the archway at the entrance to the forest village and so were known to be strong in the ability of 'movement'. But, water was the last trial in this Test and not only was it the hardest of all the five tables but it was second only to fire in its awkwardness to handle using the gift.

Bruin had explained to Samuel before, that due to its fluid state, water was an extremely difficult substance to move and manipulate into any given shape and hold it there using just the power of one's mind. And what was required at this last table of the 'Movement' Tests was far more complicated than the others had been. The contender was not just to make the water move, but also to have it shift over to occupy only one half of the large bowl. Half of the bowl was to be full, the other half empty. With the power of their mind and their will alone, the contestant was to connect with the energy trapped inside the liquid and persuade it to move over and hold this unnatural position for a count of ten.

Children watched wide-eyed as the finalists began their attempts. The very young ones were lifted up onto shoulders to get a better view of the proceedings. There were a number of differing results. Some managed to make the surface of the water ripple or jiggle about as if an unseen hand had shaken the bowl. One older man called Robin, his face red and damp with perspiration, had actually caused tiny droplets of the water to lift upwards into the air, hover there for a few moments, and then rain back down into the bowl, much to the amusement of the watchers. It hadn't been the desired effect but he got a cheer anyway.

Flint's attempt was rather overenthusiastic. Anxious to impress his friends he connected far too quickly with the liquid's energy and, without properly directing his gift, caused the whole bowl of water to tip up onto its side and empty its contents all over the sandy floor. Grinning red-faced through his embarrassment, Flint had meekly accepted Samuel's help to right the bowl again and refill it for the next competitor. When Flint rejoined his father in the crowd he was welcomed warmly and congratulated on his efforts.

Willow and Bruin were the last ones left to try.

'All the best, gorgeous.' Samuel thought to Willow as she stepped up to the table and took her place before it. She flashed him a small shy smile before beginning.

Samuel held his breath as he watched the water begin to move, willing with every part of his heart that Willow would succeed. The surface of the water in the bowl tilted on a diagonal plane and held that position for a moment. Everyone in the tent held their breath along with Samuel as they looked on like a crowd of statues. Tiny beads of perspiration broke out on Willow's brow as the water began to shift again, this time sideways in the bowl, rippling over to gather in one half only.

She's going to do it! Samuel had thought.

But suddenly the spell was broken. Willow's connection with the tricksome substance was lost and the water slopped back in the bowl and levelled out again.

It had been by far the most impressive attempt up until then. Samuel and Fern hugged and lifted Willow off her feet in celebration when she stumbled, a little light-headed, away from the table.

Calmed and quiet again, the crowd returned its collective attention to the last competitor; their leader, Bruin. Samuel felt the intensity of his uncle's gift like a pulse of heat emanating from Bruin's body as he slipped his mind into the task of connecting with the energy held inside the water. The bowl shifted very slightly on the tabletop, then the water began to slide away from one side of the bowl and gather at the other in a purposeful and fluid action. After only a few heartbeats the liquid was completely stored in one half of the container, the other half left bone dry, reflecting back the flickering light of the candles set all around them. Eyes flicked from the bowl to the judges who had begun their count up to ten.

Slowly, slowly, one ancient-faced old judge lifted a hand out to his side. The crowd watched as his arm went up and hovered above his head. The excitement continued to mount until the moment when he brought it down in a sudden rush; the count was complete.

'All done!' the old man cried.

'And agreed!' shouted another judge.

A raucous cheer went up as Bruin was declared the winner of the second Test and was hoisted high on the shoulders of his friends, his victory marking the end of the events for that first day. Everyone needed time to relax and recover from his or her exertions; the excitement of being a spectator at such events was in itself hugely tiring. Food and drink were shared around and time was spent simply enjoying each other's company. Strengthening bonds between friends and neighbours whilst chatting and listening to the musicians of the village play the traditional tunes which had been handed down through the elders of the past. The haunting sounds of their instruments echoing the true life and spirit of the great forest.

The next two days were taken up with the hardest and most

impressive of all the Tests; 'Concentration'. Everyone in the village wanted to try their hand at this. The first day would see the children entering the arena, but on the second day the most skilled of the foresters would compete. Those able to have any real chance of succeeding in this Test were those particularly strongly blessed with the gift. Mostly this consisted of the same final contenders of the first two Tests, but there were some exceptions to this as there was a whole different approach to this last event. The object was to use your mind skills to concentrate all your will into a burning flame and force it to travel along the ground from one point to another.

'Fire is the hardest element of all for us to control,' Bruin had told Samuel before the event had begun. 'It is our most important ally here in the forest, providing us with life-giving heat and the ability to cook our food, but it can be the most dangerous too. Fire is the thing that the forest, and all its many inhabitants, fears above all else. It holds a fierce power which can not be completely tamed but, with enough training and skill, it can be manipulated.'

The adults coached and willed the children along, as they sat cross-legged before the small dancing flame desperately trying to make it move. Determined young faces turned bright red as they put everything they had into the attempt. All the villagers were well aware of how much the youngsters wanted to be the first to have that flame move on their command. They had all been in the very same position themselves, nothing

227

made a forester more proud than seeing that very first flicker of the flame as you finally learned how to use the gift given you by the Man In Green to affect this most powerful of elements.

As he watched them, Samuel longed to try it but forced himself to hold back and stick to what he had decided; he would attempt to do this in a quiet moment when he was unobserved by anyone else. It wasn't the sort of thing he felt confident enough to try for the first time in front of an audience.

The day went well. None of the children managed to have an effect on the flame but they were consoled with games and treats and all went off to bed that night with a smile on his or her face knowing, just *knowing*, that next year would be their year.

The final day came around. Everyone seemed to be up and in the arena early, a sense of anticipation hung in the air. Samuel watched carefully as each forester sat on the sandy floor and began his or her communion with the waiting flame. Most of the more experienced of them could affect the flame enough to make it flicker or bend slightly as if pushed by a gentle breath, which was impressive enough to watch, but the effort it took showed on their faces and in the veins which stood out at their temples as they focused their energy. Some of them gave up, covered in sweat from their labours, their friends or family members pulling them out of the way to revive them with a strong drink or a whiff of Stinkroot.

When the first successful forester managed to get the flame

not only to flicker or bend but also to *travel* a short distance, it was a breathtaking thing to see; that orange lick of flaming energy slowly begin to move along the sandy floor.

After each attempt at this Test was over, the flame was extinguished at the point where it stopped moving and a new one was lit at the start point. First, the distance travelled was but a few fingers-breadth, then further and further still, until the delighted gathering was witnessing each freshly lit flame travel at least the length of a man's arm. Samuel felt he might burst with pride when Willow, Rowan and Finch all managed to get the flame to travel even further; more than three strides distance, and their attempts were greeted with loud applause and cheers. Then there was only one more person left to try.

The sun had gone down outside, the air had chilled and fingers of ice were working their way across the surface of every water barrel outside each home. The wind moaned through the tepees and set an unclosed door on one of the washing-stalls to creak out a lonely tune, but inside the tented arena the air was warm with the body-heat of those watching, the only sounds the gentle murmurs of the crowd discussing and debating the outcome of the very last attempt at the last event of that year's 'Tests'.

It didn't surprise Samuel at all to see that the last contestant to step up was his uncle. Bruin smiled at Samuel as he sat down before the new flame. The gathering fell quiet one last time. The murmuring stopped and was replaced by the sound of the wind tugging at the corners of the tent and that of Bruin's deep breaths as he calmed himself into the trance-like state necessary for the task ahead.

Barely any time passed before the flame began to move. It travelled steadily along the ground and made it all the way to the finishing point, which no other contender had gotten close to. It moved as if carried there by a ghostly hand and although this was the ultimate goal for the contender in this event, it seemed that it wasn't enough for Bruin. Just as everyone was poised to cheer and clap their hands to congratulate their leader on his amazing feat, the flame circled the finishing point and began to travel all the way back towards where Bruin sat. As it came closer to him, it lifted up from the ground, slowly and purposefully rising up into the air. A series of gasps went around the crowd as they watched but hardly believed what they were seeing. The flame rose higher, to the level of Bruin's face, and hung there in the air in front of him.

Opening his eyes, which he had closed in concentration, Bruin put his thumb and forefinger into his mouth to wet them. Samuel watched in awe as his uncle reached out his damp fingers and snuffed out the flame that hovered before him. It hissed out of existence. After a pause of utter disbelief and silence, the tent suddenly exploded with whoops, cheers and screams from the forest people.

'I've never seen anything like that, Samuel. I didn't even know it was possible.' Willow sent this thought to Samuel over the commotion all around.

Surprised, Samuel looked into her eyes.

'He's never shown you that before or tried to teach you how to do it?' he thought back.

'No, never,' Willow replied, still staring at Bruin who was receiving hugs and backslaps aplenty. 'I don't think I *could* do it and I'm not sure I'd want to anyway.'

'Why not?' Samuel asked puzzled, almost shouting to her with his mind as the crowd raged on.

'I'm not sure, it just doesn't seem... I don't know... safe. Perhaps he's the only one who can do it, what with being the leader and everything he's bound to be more skilled than the rest of us. He is in most things, as you've seen.'

Something new niggled in Samuel's head, but the excitement all around was infectious and overpowering, causing him to push it to the back of his mind for now.

'He's quite the showman isn't he?' he gestured to his uncle, the broad man's arms were outstretched, palms upward, basking in the adoration of his people.

'Isn't he just!' Willow agreed, but her expression, Samuel noticed, was tinged with uneasiness.

The close of that day marked the end of The Tests for another year. It was easy to understand why everyone in the village felt a little sad after the excitement had passed and the cold season stretched out before them. The events had certainly helped the villagers to take their minds off the bad weather that was to come, for a short while at least, as they had enjoyed one another's company and shared stories within the great tent. But even having immersed themselves in the wonderful distraction of The Tests, many of them had known, only too well, that there were likely to be troubles ahead during the freeze-up.

There was often a price to be paid for living in their beloved forest, so deep within the heart of the Man In Green's territory.

Even though the forest village was somewhat protected from the worst of the weather, its cliff-walls offering shelter from the full ferocity of the howling winds and falling trees, which were often a casualty of the worst storms, the people still suffered some difficult times.

The hard rains that year had hit suddenly and been harsh. Many of the forest people were washed out of their tepees in a surge of mud and sand. Samuel, his uncle and all those able and strong enough, had worked through raging storms to help those affected by the fierce weather to salvage what they could from their ruined homes and to erect new dwellings whenever a break in the weather allowed it. Everyone had pulled together, making room for their neighbours within their own homes when necessary, and sharing their supplies of food and water equally and fairly with them without complaint.

The winter had also been uncommonly harsh. The snow had come suddenly out of the frosty air one morning, steadily burdening the branches of the forest trees, forcing them into submission, sending them bowing before its accumulative might.

During that first snowfall Samuel had received an urgent mind-message from Willow, calling to him for help. He had rushed to where she said she was and found that she wanted him to assist her in the delivery of a baby. The baby was arriving sooner than expected and the woman who usually attended to the births in the village had been called away to attend to a sick child, leaving Willow in charge of the situation. Willow had helped with several births before and knew what to do but had wanted Samuel nearby to help should things take a turn for the worse.

'But why me? What use will I be?' Samuel had thought to Willow, as he had looked on the scene before him in mild horror.

'The father is too distraught to help, he'll only get in the way. You can do this, Samuel.'

The young woman lying on her bed on the floor of the tepee looked to be in terrible agony. Her face creased and red, her eyes scrunched shut, sweat standing in defined beads on her forehead.

Willow had ignored Samuel's protests that he had no experience in the matter of childbirth or any desire to take part in such an event. Instead she had thrust a damp piece of hide-cloth into his hands and told him to cool Poppy's brow with it. Samuel had watched in awe as Willow talked the first-time mother through each contraction, her voice calm and steady as she gently willed Poppy along the way with kindness and patience. At last it was over and a screaming, blood-smeared tiny human lay in Willow's hands. Both mother and child had made it through the experience healthy and well.

Willow handed the bundle over to Samuel telling him to look after the wailing little girl whilst she helped Poppy to get cleaned up. Samuel had awkwardly washed the baby and swaddled it in fresh fleece and hide blankets as best he could, terrified that he might hurt the tiny fingers or the delicate stick-thin arms.

Moments later, the door-skin of the tepee was pulled aside to admit one anxious father who was followed by the other members of the village quietly filing in to be introduced to the new addition to their number. Poppy and her husband embraced, the new father wiping tears of joy from his eyes as his tiny daughter took his rough finger in a vice-like grip. Poppy had looked up then and caught a glimpse, past Samuel and the other well-wishers, of the sky outside. There she saw the winter's first flurry of silent powdery snowflakes as they twirled their way down through the cold air to lie on the ground.

'Flake,' Poppy said and smiled contentedly up at Willow.

Willow grinned down at her, 'Flake...' she repeated, 'Yes, that's beautiful, Poppy.'

'Flake?' Samuel asked.

'Yes,' Willow confirmed. 'Say hello to Flake, first-born

daughter to Poppy and Finch.'

'And helped into the world by Willow and Samuel,' added Finch, Flake's father, first taking Willow and then Samuel into a bear-hug of thanks.

'No, really, I didn't do anything. It was all Willow.' Samuel protested.

But Willow laid a hand on his arm. 'You did plenty, Samuel, more than you know.' And she had kissed his cheek tenderly, right there, in front of them all.

On some days, during the height of the cold time, it was foolish to venture outside at all. Staying inside their tepees, the people huddled around their crackling fires to stave off the freezing temperatures outside. The snow lay deep out in the forest, smothering the undergrowth, silencing the footfalls of any animals hardy enough to be moving about. Young trees were hidden from view, large bushes reduced to mere humps beneath the thick white blanket. The air was cold enough to freeze the breath in a person's lungs and turn fingers and toes to useless blue digits inside gloves and boots, even on the shortest of treks. The great trees groaned and sent resounding 'cracks' like gunshots, echoing out across the woods as their timber strained and contracted in the freezing conditions. Many limbs eventually gave way to the silent white power, snapping clean away from their trunks and crashing down to the forest floor.

During these winter months, when the conditions were less

hazardous, a few of the forest people would venture out to hunt. Their attempts provided little more than a few shaggy-coated goats and snow hares. The snow hares, white on white in their thick winter jackets, blended invisibly into the deep carpet of snow that blanketed the more open areas of the forest floor. Samuel's new hunting skills were put to the most extreme of tests as he lay on the frozen ground waiting, listening and concentrating his mind to find them out. Striking straight and true was imperative if he was to kill them quickly without causing pain or suffering. The forest people had their dried meats, fruit and roots to see them over the freezing months but it was good to have a meal of fresh hot meat in their bellies once in a while to stave off the icy fingers of winter and guard against illness.

Many forest animals died of hunger or from the extreme conditions during those months. Packs of wild dogs and wolves padded through the great trees with hunger burning their bellies. Fresh meat was what they craved but more often than not they had to make do with the half-frozen corpses of those animals that had succumbed to the intense cold. Most of the time the members of these hunting packs looked after one another within their group, but when things were particularly harsh and starvation seemed imminent they were known to turn on each other. Sometimes, though rarely, the smallest or weakest of the group might be set upon by the others and devoured by its ravenous companions.

Occasionally, the packs would get lucky and come across a small group of elk, or the more common smaller deer, who's habit it was to stand with their flanks against each other between the trees. They would stand there for long periods of time, sharing their body heat and sheltering as best they could from the worst of the wind and snow, waiting for the weather to subside enough for them to continue their mostly unsuccessful foraging for food.

After a day of hunting in the forest, a couple of snow-hares slung over one shoulder, Samuel himself came close to falling foul of a pack of roaming hunters, looking for such a clutch of deer. That day, he had been eternally grateful for his many lessons on how to climb trees swiftly in any conditions. Trudging through the knee-high powdery snow, the effort of it raising sweat beneath his thick winter clothes and cloak, Samuel sensed a circle of creatures closing in on him from a distance. They were moving slowly, stealthily, seven of them in total. Samuel knew instantly that he was being stalked.

Sending out a mind-message to these creatures was not going to help him; he picked up on their hunger, their mouths dripping saliva onto the virgin snow at the thought of the feast of warm human flesh so close at hand.

Then they came into view: wolves. Grey and white coats with a tinge of beige across their bellies, they were both beautiful and terrifying. Even hampered by the depth of the snow, Samuel knew they could be by his side in a few moments, sinking their teeth into his calves, bringing him down onto the ground to tear him apart with their viciously sharp white fangs. They stopped and surveyed each other, hunters and their prey. Fourteen wolf-eyes burned into Samuel as they all waited to see who would make the first move.

He picked out the leader of the pack; he faced Samuel across the clearing, amber eyes gleaming like two setting suns burning gently in his magnificent face. His coat was thick and looked incredibly soft. Under other circumstances Samuel would have loved to touch it, to have run his hands through the luxuriant depth and warmth of it.

If I'm not careful that wolf's fur might well be the last thing I ever feel in this lifetime, he said to himself.

Quicksilver was a considerable distance away chasing his own meal; Samuel sent him a mind-message to warn of the danger and to tell him to keep well away. He hoped that the great silver dog would do as he was told, his turning up to save him would probably mean that Samuel would make it home in one piece but even with Quicksilver's great strength and size, the pack of starving wolves would soon bring him down and settle for his meat instead. For a moment Samuel considered trying to connect with the pack-leader, to convince him that he was not a fitting meal, but the strength of feeling from the other six wolves was enough to confirm that even if he managed to get the leader to change his choice of prey, the remaining wolves would still act without him.

Time to move.

Tensing the muscles in his legs he began to feel out the manoeuvre he needed to make to get up into the boughs of the most suitable nearby tree. As if sensing his very thoughts, the pack reacted instantly, from their observant positions; front legs splayed, heads slightly down, ears pricked, they sprang forward as one, closing the space between Samuel and themselves at a terrifying pace.

Throwing the two dead snow-hares behind him as he ran, Samuel raced as quickly as he could to the frozen trunk of the tree that he had chosen to climb.

The wolves snarled and howled behind him as they arrived at, then fought over, the hares, buying him a few precious moments to struggle up the slippery bark. But a rush of air at Samuel's back had his hair standing on end as the wolf-leader lunged for him as he began climbing the tree.

The wolf thumped into Samuel's back, nearly loosening his fragile hold on the branch he had managed to get up to. The great beast tumbled towards the ground again but grappled with Samuel's cloak and managed to secure a grip on the very tail of it with his sharp teeth. The wolf's body hung there, teeth embedded in the tightly woven fabric of the cloak, his back legs just touching the ground at the base of the trunk as he wrestled and tugged, desperately trying to get his escaping meal down from the tree.

Spittle flew from Samuel's mouth as he roared and forced

himself to pull harder on the branch. He had to get up higher and to do that he would have to shake loose the extra weight. But he didn't have a free hand to untie his cloak that was now threatening to throttle him with the weight of the wolf pulling it hard against his windpipe. For the first time, Samuel cursed at how well made it was.

One foot slipped, came within reach of the other pack members who had now joined in the attack, having made quick work of the snow-hares, then found purchase again on the trunk. Even though the wolf-leader was probably half his usual summer weight, the ferocity with which it was yanking on Samuel's cloak made it feel far heavier. Now another wolf got its teeth in and began to help the first; jerking wildly, pulling, heaving. Samuel managed to get one of his arms around the broadest part of the branch he had been trying to haul himself up onto and realised his only hope of escape was to cut away the tie that held his cloak.

The knot at his neck had been pulled so tight that there was no point in trying to untie it; it would have to be cut. It was a risky decision; if he was tugged in the wrong direction he might lose his grip with his one arm and fall down to the pack below or cut his own neck with the blade, but he had to try this or else wait until he weakened or blacked-out from lack of air.

Locking one arm around the branch, he let go with his other hand and swung there precariously with the two wolves still tugging at him, their weight seeming to increase with every racing heartbeat. Reaching to his side, he managed to release his knife from its sheath and bring it up to his face. Turning the blade sharp-edge outward he awkwardly slid it between the back of his neck and the cord that held the cloak. Bracing himself for the inevitable kickback, he sliced quickly through the cord and silently thanked whatever had caused him to sharpen his knife the night before.

The two wolves tumbled to the ground along with his cloak. They snarled and flew at each other in a mixture of temper and frustration. The other members of the pack attacked Samuel's cloak, ripping and tearing it to shreds as he looked down on them from the relative safety of the tree.

They crowded around the trunk and looked up at him, tongues lolling and saliva still dripping. Some tried flying leaps and snapped their jaws at him but there was no way they could climb up to get him. He was safe, for now, but wondered how long he could stand the cold air without the protection of his cloak. Eventually his body would give in to the bitter climate and his chilled body would slip from the branch, down to the waiting pack.

The jowls of the wolves below were tinged with the blood of the two snow-hares which they had torn up between them. Samuel forced himself to look away. He needed to think of something, and quickly. He felt confident that he could summon enough energy to send a mind-message back to someone in the village but he knew of no one strong enough in the gift to pick up on it. Quicksilver could go back for help, but what if only Willow or Fern came back with him? *They* might be killed.

He rubbed at the tender red marks left on his neck from the rubbing cord. There were still his arrows, he could kill the wolves one by one, but that went against everything that he believed. These animals were only doing what they knew, they needed to eat, they too were hunters. It was his own fault that he was in this situation, he should have been paying more attention to his surroundings. Killing them was not the only answer to his predicament, he would try to think of another way out. Just then Samuel sensed Quicksilver and heard his awful, mournful bark. The wolves below him pricked up their ears and turned towards the sound. On the far side of the clearing Quicksilver had appeared between the trees.

'No! Go back. Run boy, they'll kill you!' Samuel had shouted with his mind, frantic at the thought of losing his best friend.

Quicksilver moved out of sight and for a moment Samuel thought he was going to leave but then he returned, and his great mouth was clamped around the neck of a large limp creature. The dog dragged the dead stag further into the clearing, keeping an eye on the pack the whole time, and dropped the carcass onto the snow. Panting from the exertion of pulling such an immense weight, Quicksilver sent billowing clouds of breath into the icy air, then barked once again.

The wolves moved forward, eyeing Quicksilver with a mixture of confusion and menace, but soon the smell of fresh blood on the air overcame any thought of trying to bring down this strange beast, besides, there was far more meat on the stag.

The pack loped then sped up into a run as they made for the offered meal. Quicksilver watched them for a few moments before skirting the clearing and guarding Samuel as he got down from the tree. None of the wolves left their ample meal to try to stop the human and his strange dog from leaving the woods.

'I ca... ca... can't believe you did that. Thanks, boy.' Samuel chittered as the two companions moved quickly back towards the forest village.

Quicksilver nuzzled Samuel's neck and licked at the blood that was congealing on a small wound he had made when cutting away his cloak.

Bluebell scrunched up her face in disgust on hearing that Samuel was in need of a new cloak. She huffed and puffed as if it were the last thing on earth she had either the time or the inclination to do. Yet, only the next day, a brand new cloak appeared outside Samuel's tepee. He found it neatly folded and perched on the top of his water barrel. It was, if anything, even more beautiful than his first one and without thinking he had run through the village, knocked on the old woman's door and embraced her warmly when she answered it. Bluebell had not received a kiss on the cheek from any man, young or old, not since she had been in her very early years. In shock, she whacked Samuel on the shoulder after he planted his kiss on her rough old cheek but as he ran off again, his cloak burling out behind him in the breeze, she had allowed herself a secret smile that made a hundred wrinkles dance on her ancient face.

Spring brought along lessons of her own. She had arrived quietly, tiptoeing through the snow and had breathed new life into the forest. Waking the flowers from their snug beds beneath the soil, rousing the badgers in their setts. Bear cubs born during the hibernation time, their mothers waking long enough to give birth and suckle their young, now wandered into the fresh forest air, eyes blinking against the force of the bright ball of light above the treetops. They snuffled and gambolled their way around, happy to be out in the open and to have room to play their games.

One crisp clear morning, Samuel saw a pair of courting birds from his lookout high up in a tree. These birds were larger than any he had seen before, their wingspan as wide as a fully-grown man was tall. The orange-red tint of their feathers burnished by the rising sun, set the two ablaze in the sky above. Samuel thought of the feather that Rowan had given him the first time they had met and realised that he was looking at two Great Forest Eagles.

Samuel had become quite an expert with a bow and arrow by then. Combining his senses, concentration and the use of his gift to see the life force that beat in the very centre of all creatures, he had become an adept hunter. His skill was such that he could have taken both eagles with a single arrow, ending their lives so quickly that they wouldn't have felt the sting of the arrow piercing their flesh or had time to realise what had happened. But these magnificent beauties were not destined for any cooking pot. They held the key to the future of their kind. With luck they would mate, lay their eggs and, with the help of the Man In Green, hopefully new life would come to swell their diminished numbers.

Delighted at the spectacle, Samuel watched the two great birds as they carried out their mating ritual. It was a magnificent and breathtaking thing to see. The two massive birds climbed gracefully into the pine-scented air. Turning towards one another, their huge wings beating as each approached its mate in the air. Just as it seemed they were to collide, they thrust their feet at each other, locked talons, and fell like heavy stones, their grip on one another displaying a trust so deep and passionate.

Samuel didn't think about what he did next, he simply allowed it to happen. He was inside the male eagle, hearing the screaming air tearing through his feathers, feeling the force of it, as if against his own body. Samuel and the great eagle were as one, plummeting towards the treetops at a horrifying pace. Talons gripping, each bird holding fast to the other, the feeling of togetherness oddly comforting. The sensation both exciting and terrifying at the same time.

Samuel forced himself not to take control of the bird, he told himself that he should trust it to know when to break out of the freefall, but it was so hard. He knew he should return to his own body in case something should go wrong, he wasn't sure what would happen to him if the bird crashed into the ground while he was so deeply connected to it.

I must leave him. I must leave him... now!

But Samuel stayed right there, inside the bird.

Feeling the sudden release of talons on the eagle's legs, on his own legs it seemed, Samuel saw through the bird's eyes how close it had come to crashing into the forest below. The tops of the trees leapt up to meet him, their tips and outstretched boughs waiting to catch or impale him. Samuel felt the immense strength course through the eagle's shoulders, the effort of lifting out of the downward spiral and into upward movement, sucking energy from every strand of his being. And then they were climbing again, up and away from danger.

Samuel watched the eagles go through the same ritual again and again, before they flew off to their eyrie.

Bruin had been amazed by his nephew's speedy recovery from his injuries after his unpleasant first encounter with the Fierce Spiders. The boy had suffered several broken ribs, one broken wrist and a collection of cuts and bruises not to mention a huge dent in his self-respect.

For a long time Bruin had wondered if he had pushed the

boy too hard, too soon, and perhaps Samuel had not yet been ready for such a painful lesson, but his nephew never once complained or blamed him for the fall. Samuel fully understood how the event had caused his awareness, and sense of respect for the forest and all the creatures who live there, to grow and blossom. Since that day, when Samuel had come down so unceremoniously from the tree, he had studied well, worked hard and was now a very different person to the one who had climbed up it.

As soon as he was fit enough, in fact a little earlier than was sensible, so eager was he to return to the task; Samuel was begging Bruin to take him out into the woods again. With his new and hard-earned respect for his forest home deeply rooted in his heart, Samuel had excelled in all his training. In most skills he now surpassed even his uncle and none of the other forest people could cast the merest shadow over the oneness Samuel had begun to achieve with the energy and life of the woods.

Along with his hunting abilities, Samuel had also come to know other skills, skills that his Uncle Bruin had not spoken of or hinted at, but skills that Samuel had discovered within himself. As he spent time nurturing and testing these new powers, Samuel had come to suspect that they were his alone; not shared by any of the other forest people, so he had kept them to himself, not wanting to seem to be boasting or risk making Bruin feel that he no longer needed him as a teacher.

'The Man In Green has certainly blessed you, nephew.' Bruin would often say to him, and Samuel frequently wondered just how much truth there was in this.

Samuel and Quicksilver were as inseparable as ever. They slept, ate and hunted together. Their bond now so strong that Samuel had only to think of his faithful friend and he would immediately know Quicksilver's exact position. The skill that had caused him to break out in a sweat the first time he had attempted it was now no harder for him than finding the sun in the sky by lifting his face to its warmth.

Although Quicksilver was still the closest friend he had, other friendships had blossomed over time too. Often Samuel would go out into the forest with Flint to hunt, just the two of them. They had become firm friends, as Samuel had hoped they would. But over time, Samuel had sensed an awkwardness beginning to grow between them. Fearing that their friendship would be tainted by not discussing it he had eventually asked Flint if everything was all right and, after some persuasion, Flint had finally come out with it. Ashamed as he was, Flint admitted that he was jealous about how close Samuel and Willow had become.

Samuel hadn't known what to say but Flint had slapped him on the back and laughed. 'She never had eyes for me anyway, my friend. She never had eyes for anyone before you stumbled into our midst. Just be sure you take good care of her or you'll have me to deal with, all right?'

After that, he and Flint never spoke of it again and the air between them cleared, leaving a close and special bond that they both greatly valued. Their friendship had been further sealed when Flint had presented Samuel with a gift; a small pouch containing several pieces of tinder and a beautifully shaped flint.

'I know you're good at setting a fire, but these make the job easier and faster.' Flint had said as he had handed the present to Samuel. 'Besides, you'll think of me every time you get a fire going when you use this. "Flint" that's me, a real bright spark!'

Spring gave way to Summer. Sitting high in the branches of the very tree he had fallen from all those months ago, Samuel surveyed the treetops around him. The wind ruffled and stroked the lush green leaves with its fresh cool breath, sending branches gently swaying and bobbing in its wake, the movement fluid and tranquil.

Quicksilver and Blithe's morning hunt had gone well. Samuel had felt a twinge at the passing of the old grey hare that the two silver dogs had caught and shared. It had been despatched quickly and without unnecessary suffering. The sibling dogs were now lying by the edge of the river, their meal finished. Content, and with full bellies, the two were passing the time gently taking turns at grooming each other's face, neck and shoulders with rhythmic strokes of their great pink tongues. Nearby, a number of lacewings flitted around the burbling water, their vivid green and blue bodies suspended so delicately beneath their intricately patterned wings.

Samuel began to make his way nimbly back down the tree, moving through the branches so swiftly and gently that barely a leaf shifted behind him. The family of Fierce Spiders were undisturbed by his passing. They had come to accept his unthreatening presence as if he were one of their own. A few wasps, lazy in the warm sap-scented air made their way to the hive, which was bigger and heavier than it had been the year before.

Using his mind, Samuel called to the squirrel who was nibbling on the remnants of an acorn a few branches away from him. 'I've got something for you, Scamp.'

The squirrel's ears pricked and swivelled. Spotting Samuel grinning at him, Scamp began scampering fluidly along the spindly branches towards him. Reaching into the pouch at his side Samuel brought out a handful of deep crimson rowanberries, which he had saved especially for his small friend. Scamp munched his way happily through them, his feather-light touch resting on Samuel's fingers as he skimmed through the berries with his free paw, picking out the best fruits.

'You're such a perfectionist, Scamp, they're all good ones, and tasty.' Samuel stroked the creature behind his ear then ran his fingers gently down his sleek back and up the twisting, twitching tail. 'Good?'

The red squirrel observed him carefully with wise eyes as he chewed a mouthful. Pink juice dribbled down his tiny chin. When the berries were all gone Scamp gave a 'pip' of thanks, leapt to Samuel's shoulder to nibble his ear affectionately, then disappeared off up the trunk in that wonderful flowing motion.

Samuel could think of nowhere he would rather be. For the first time in his life he felt he was in the right place. He was home. But although he had tried to push it to the back of his mind, something dark was looming over his more contented thoughts. Bruin.

Bruin had struck out of camp at dawn. He had asked Samuel to take care of Blithe whilst he went on a journey into the forest, saying that he was going on a hunting trip with two of the other men from the forest village. Samuel had pretended to accept his uncle's explanation, but he knew better than to believe it, having used one of his newly discovered skills to do a bit of digging.

Samuel had stumbled across his latest talent quite by accident one day as he sat in the sunshine watching Willow. She had been playing a game with Fern and as she turned his way and flashed him a dazzling smile, Samuel had slipped effortlessly into her mind. He and Willow had become very close and were able to talk to each other using their minds over greater distances than most of the forest people, so he was used to connecting with her, but this was something very different.

Samuel instantly sensed that he was in a part of her mind that he hadn't reached before, and he felt that she didn't know he was there. Inside Willow's mind he heard her *thoughts*, not just what she wanted to say to him but what she actually thought *about* him. Suddenly he was privy to all her deepest, most personal musings. Blushing deeply, he had looked away and ceased his unintended intrusion immediately. Right then he had made a promise to himself; he would learn how to master this new ability so that he would never stray accidentally into someone's private thoughts again.

On the next few occasions when Samuel tried to use this skill, the people whose thoughts he was attempting to dip into had complained of a strange stirring and tingling sensation in their heads. They would look about them perplexed; complain of odd vibrations or of feeling suddenly 'a bit giddy'. Not wanting to let his secret out, or to frighten folk into thinking they had some kind of strange illness, Samuel had thought it best to stop trying it for a while.

He had learned to go more slowly, stealthily. Spacing out his attempts over time and trying it on different foresters, Samuel found that it came more easily to him and now he was so accomplished at it that he could look into someone's thoughts as easily as looking through a doorway into a room; the effort no more testing to his mind than moving aside an animal skin hung over a tepee entrance was to the muscles of his arm and hand. Samuel had stuck to his self-promise not to misuse this ability, only trying it out now and then to keep it trained and limber in his mind and on call should he ever need it. It worked with animals too, but their thought patterns were irregular and flitting and were, more often than not, about getting food or finding shelter.

Quicksilver had been surprised at first when, without having begged for it, his human friend tossed him the odd extra scrap of food when his belly wasn't quite full enough or when Samuel had scratched him in the exact right spot without having been pointed to where the inaccessible itchy bug bite was.

So, that quiet morning, when the sky was still more night than day and many of the forest birds were still asleep in the trees, when Bruin had told Samuel that he couldn't go along on the hunting trip with him and the two other men, Samuel had seen the deception in his uncle's eyes and had gone back on the promise to himself not to use this new skill to pry. He had skimmed his uncle's thoughts briefly, just enough to see that hunting was not the only thing that Bruin was planning to do whilst away from the forest home.

Samuel had been on many hunting trips with Bruin, and from the time he had loosed his first arrow he had grown rapidly to become a skilled tracker and one of the most successful hunters of his people. So how was it that Bruin did not want him to go along this time? His uncle had said that he needed time alone with the other two men in order to train them, their skills needed improving and he wanted to give them his full attention.

'Your skill is formidable, Samuel, it will likely make them feel inferior. It would be better if I teach them on their own. Don't take it so hard boy; we'll go together next time. Just you and me.' Bruin had said.

But it made no sense to Samuel. If he was one of the best with a bow and arrow, why couldn't he help to teach those men? Bruin himself admitted that Samuel had a special flair for hunting; he had said on many occasions that Samuel was born to it. And apart from all that, there was Blithe. Why was he leaving her behind?

No, something was definitely going on. For some reason, Bruin was trying to shield him, to keep him in the dark about... what? Justifying his actions with the belief that he might be able to help his uncle in some way, Samuel had slipped silently further into Bruin's private thoughts. What he found there confused and chilled him.

Bruin was going to Crossways.

Revelations

Bruin, and the two men that were to travel with him, were planning to venture right into the village of the outsiders.

What for? And why is he keeping it from me?

Samuel managed to keep the questions inside but he was greedy for more information. Carelessly, he ploughed further into Bruin's thoughts, his eagerness making him clumsy. Samuel watched in horror as his uncle frowned down at him and shook his big head, patting one bronzed temple with an open palm. Samuel cursed himself for being so foolish and pulled back, abandoning his search before his uncle became too suspicious.

But still the questions whirled around in his mind.

What possible reason could Bruin have for going to Crossways? Why can't I go along? Is he worried that I'd be recognised by the villagers there? But if so, why not just tell me? There's something more going on here.

There was no way of asking his questions without giving his new skill away, so Samuel reluctantly watched the three men leave, having promised to take good care of Blithe during

Bruin's absence. A mixture of anger and confusion filled him as he stood there with the twin silver dogs by his side. The anger he felt arose from the belief that his uncle didn't trust him enough to tell him the truth about his plans. His confusion stemmed from the deep love and trust that had grown within him for this same man who was now, it seemed to him, shutting him out.

At that moment, Samuel decided that on his uncle's return, he would confront him about the true nature of his trip and, he felt quite adamant now, that it was well-past time for Bruin to tell him all he could about another subject that he'd been patiently waiting to hear about; the story of what had happened to the rest of their family.

Bruin had only mentioned his father, Samuel's grandfather, on a few occasions since that first time when Samuel had entered the forest village and begun his new life with the foresters. Patiently, Samuel had waited for the tale to be told to him but although he had tried, on several occasions, to bring his uncle around to the subject, Bruin had always sidestepped it or said that the time was still not right.

His patience was now at an end. Recently, in his thirst for knowledge, Samuel had considered attempting to rummage through his uncle's memories to find the answers for himself but his respect for the leader of the forest people had stopped him. For the last few months he had bitten back his questions and managed not to ask any of the older folks in the village about it, though he was sure they could answer him. But enough was enough. Either Bruin would tell him when next they met or Samuel would find out the answers for himself, one way or another. He had waited long enough.

Leaving Blithe and Quicksilver to amuse themselves, Samuel headed back to the forest village to find ways in which to distract himself. For the rest of that day he did as much as he could; he cut up logs for firewood, told stories to the young ones to keep them amused whilst their mothers were cooking or washing clothes, and fetched water to fill the barrels of the older folks who were less able to do such things for themselves.

Playing hide-and-go-seek with Quicksilver had lost its appeal for both the dog and himself since their connection had become so strong that they instinctively knew where the other was. But it was still great fun helping the younger children to learn how to play it with their own animal friends, and Samuel loved to watch their obvious delight as their skills improved.

Out of respect for his uncle's wishes Samuel had stopped teaching the younger ones how to write. Ever since that first time when the twins had asked to see his mother's book, the word had spread amongst the children and Samuel had found great enjoyment instructing them and seeing their pleasure at learning the alphabet. Whenever he had a free moment he had been more than happy to gather them together for a lesson. Samuel hadn't thought that there was any harm in it and the children certainly enjoyed learning how to spell their names, scratching out the letters with fingers and sticks on the dusty ground. But Bruin had asked him to stop.

One day, whilst walking past the group of children who were crowded all around his nephew, Bruin had paused to see what game was keeping them so attentive. On seeing the writing lesson in progress, the children busily forming the letters to spell out the names of different forest animals, Bruin's face had darkened and he had taken Samuel aside.

'I understand that writing was something your mother shared with you, but you're in the forest now, Samuel. The children here mustn't think that learning the ways of the outsiders is something they should do. I'd be grateful if you kept this skill to yourself and don't show them any more,' he had said.

Samuel had tried to explain that the children enjoyed it, that it was only for fun, but his uncle had stood firm on the point and Samuel had given way. From that day on he had kept his writing book and pencils to himself.

Samuel greatly missed the lessons and the children often pleaded with him, whenever Bruin was away, to continue with his tuition. But Samuel never went back on his promise to his uncle, although he couldn't help but smile whenever he overheard the forest children secretly whispering away about words and letters or keep himself from laughing whenever he stumbled across their names scratched in the dirt on the forest floor.

Returning to those lessons would have been a welcome distraction during the days of his uncle's absence. But Samuel managed to fill those days to the brim with other things, leaving himself exhausted each night so that he could fall straight to sleep, leaving no room or time for brooding.

On the day of Bruin's return, Samuel couldn't settle to do anything constructive; he was too on edge. Every time anyone entered the village his heart skipped a beat in anticipation. In the end, he sensed his uncle's presence well before he saw him. Bruin's towering and usually imposing figure, looked very weary and somehow older than his years as he walked back into camp with the two other men.

'Welcome back, Uncle.' Samuel greeted him. 'I need to speak with you.'

'Not just now Samuel, perhaps tomorrow. I'm very tired.' Bruin had answered and offered an exhausted smile.

Samuel felt sorry for him, it looked as if whatever had happened on their journey had taken its toll. For a moment he considered letting it go for just one more day, but something inside him stood up to this thought and pushed it aside. He must be strong or else he would just be put off once more.

Samuel steadied his voice and found the courage to speak again. 'I'm sorry, Uncle, but my mind is set on it.' Bruin raised his eyebrows in surprise but listened as Samuel finished, 'I'll wait until you've eaten and are more rested, but I must speak to you today.'

Bruin opened his mouth to protest, but seeing the look in his nephew's eyes he paused. There was a maturity there that had grown over the past year.

'Very well,' Bruin placed his large hands on Samuel's shoulders. 'After the meal. You're right, our talk is overdue.'

Samuel nodded his thanks then let Bruin go on his way to wash and ready himself for the evening meal.

As if to confirm Samuel's knowledge that hunting was not all that the three men had been doing whilst away from home, he watched as only one wild pig and two rabbits were handed over to the women whose turn it was for gutting and preparing the evening meal. The blood on the animals' wounds was still fresh; Samuel sensed that they had been caught recently, probably only that morning.

What have you been doing during all that time you've been away, Uncle?

Samuel sat in the flickering firelight of Bruin's tepee and watched his uncle closely. He had not needed to voice the sentence that he had been practising over and over in his head during the previous days. The tall man seemed to know what Samuel needed to hear, at least part of it anyway. And so Bruin began to put into words the events that had taken place many years before, the events that had claimed the lives of the other members of Samuel's family and a large number of the other forest people.

'It is time to tell you of Alder, my father, your grandfather. Alder was the leader of our people before me.' Bruin's face was serious in the dancing amber light, his eyes downcast. 'He was a good man, the powers of the forest worked strongly through him. Many said that the Man In Green himself had specially blessed him. Most of the skills that we now use were taught to us by him. My father was the first to push the connection between us humans and our animal friends further than ever before. Not only could he enter the senses of his animal companion but he found that he could actually *manipulate* what an animal did, how it behaved. He found a way to move into the very life-spirit of the creature and use its body as if it were his own.'

Samuel looked down at his clasped hands. For a long time he had experienced this very gift but now he worried that he had been wrong to keep it from his uncle.

Quicksilver had never complained when Samuel joined him inside his mind and body, in fact he seemed to welcome the closeness, but he was disconcerted when Samuel had learned to take over him completely. Samuel could only imagine how strange it must be for Quicksilver to suddenly lose control over his own four legs. The dog had shown his annoyance when Samuel had practiced on him; preventing him from hunting, cutting into his play-time with Blithe to have him walk around in circles or forcing his body into a run when all he had really wanted to do was lie on the cool damp earth beside the river and doze in the sun. But, although Quicksilver did not like it when Samuel used this intrusive ability, he loved the strange boy more than anything or anyone else and so he had put up with it, every now and then.

Samuel understood that his companion found this particular type of connection unpleasant so he had kept his training sessions short and explained to Quicksilver that this skill might come in useful in the future but that he would never use it to cause him harm. Eventually Samuel had tried it on other forest creatures and after much trial and error had discovered that he could control any lone animal he chose. He had not thought that this was a talent anyone else had, now he was learning that he had inherited it from his grandfather.

Samuel realised that Bruin had stopped speaking and was staring over at him. He looked up and met his gaze.

'You have this gift?' Bruin asked. His voice had an edge to it.

Samuel chewed his lip and nodded.

Bruin smiled sadly, 'I see. I myself do not. It's a dangerous thing, Samuel, that 'skill'. It caused the death of your grandfather, your aunt and many of our people.'

Samuel was shocked at his uncle's words but needed to hear it all, however difficult it might be.

'What happened?' he asked gently.

Bruin pulled a ragged piece of loose hide from one of his boots and wound it round and through his fingers as he spoke.

'Back then, the forest was much bigger than it is now, but every day it was being eaten into by the saws and axes of the outsiders. They cut indiscriminately, paying no heed to the age or condition of the timber. Their ignorance serving only to clear great areas of forestland, leaving it barren and bereft of any shelter for the forest animals. My father, and those of our people who shared this particular gift, left our home to walk through our forest to meet with the outsiders in the surrounding villages.

'They decided to begin with the closest: Crossways. They went to tell the people there, to try to make them understand, that the way they were destroying the trees and the forest creatures was causing great harm to the energy and life of the woods. He tried to explain their responsibilities to the forest, that they should plant trees to replace the ones they cut down; how important it was that they learned to be selective when choosing which animals to hunt for food, leaving the young to grow and produce the next generation. As things were, the outsiders were hunting some animals almost to extinction; killing off the new-borns and those heavy with new life because they were easy targets.

'My father also told them that the river needed to be cleared of the waste that choked it and would have to be kept clean and free from disease if they ever wanted fish to thrive there again.

Through their ignorance, laziness and stupidity the outsiders were destroying the very things they relied upon.' Bruin's face darkened with anger as he pulled on the piece of hide snapping it into two pieces, which he threw into the fire.

'Did they listen to him? Did they understand that what they were doing was wrong?' Samuel asked.

Bruin gave an exasperated grunt, 'No. They laughed at him. They said that the forest had always provided them with food and shelter; they saw no reason to change anything they did. They said his stories of the Man In Green were nothing but fairy tales, not even fit for their children. Your Grandfather and the rest of our people who had travelled with him were beaten out of Crossways, chased away, back into the forest. The outsiders said that they were mad, that living in the forest had addled their minds.'

'What did my Grandfather do?'

'Part of him had expected such a reaction, but he'd wanted to try to talk sense into them first. Father was always like that; patient, ready to give even the most stubborn a chance. That was his downfall, his compassion for those people who deserved none.' Bruin stared into the fire, his face slack and tired.

'You said "first", he wanted to try talking sense to them "first"? Before what? What did he plan to do if they didn't listen to him?' Samuel asked.

Bruin looked into his nephew's eyes. 'Before he left to return to the woods he faced the crowd and warned them that if

264

they didn't heed his warnings and take more care of the forest, that its animals would be sent by the Man In Green to have his revenge on them. They would rise up against their village and tear it down around them.'

Samuel nodded thoughtfully, willing Bruin to continue whilst imagining his Grandfather's face as he stood so bravely before a whole village of outsiders.

'Everything my father had told them made perfect sense, wisdom that would have meant the outsiders could have found a new kind of harmony with the forest, a new way of life that would have benefited them all... But they were too blinded by greed and laziness to see it. Alder returned to the forest with the rest of his group, the jeers and laughs of the outsiders at their backs.

'They camped there for a few days, one of them slipping silently into Crossways each night to see if their visit had had the desired effect. Any sign of change might have stayed my father's hand. Even to find the people there discussing the possibility of altering their habits would have meant that there was some flicker of hope, but it was no good. Their traps continued to be set, the trees chopped down, the river polluted. My father had no choice but to carry out his threat.'

Bruin's brow creased, the sense of his loss almost palpable. 'My father and his people sat together in a circle, linked their arms and, using their newly discovered skill, sent their animal companions forward to destroy the village.'

Samuel closed his eyes and pictured the scene as his uncle spoke. There had been twenty of the forest people in that linked circle. Two of them Samuel's own blood-relatives; a grandfather and an aunt, both of whom he'd never known, or ever would, after what happened that day. His aunt had been the oldest child of her family; Bruin and Lily's older sister. Samuel wondered if she had looked anything like his mother.

His aunt had only been fourteen summers old when she lost her life that day, Bruin told him, younger than Willow was now. She had begged the leader of her people, her own father, for the chance to go along with him on that journey and to stand beside him in the name of her people and the forest that she loved so dearly.

Their intention had only been to frighten the outsiders, to make them believe that the forest would no longer put up with their mistreatment. Perhaps if they saw the power of the forest creatures they could be made to see that the great spirit of the forest deserved their respect. No real harm would come to the outsiders; they were to be taught a lesson, that was all. But as their animal companions broke through the tree line and entered the village of Crossways, outsiders, with guns, met them.

Every animal, from the great bear who was Alder's animal companion to the beautiful black-backed jackal linked to Bruin's older sister had been felled mercilessly by an onslaught of flesh-ripping bullets.

'That was when we came to understand the full strength of the link my father had discovered, and how dangerous it was to connect so deeply with an animal. I'm sure he had no idea that joining so completely with another being meant that you would suffer the same fate if they were harmed or killed. The instant it happened, we knew. Even over that great distance, the pain of the passing of so many of our people and their animal companions cut through the senses of every one of us who had been left behind in the forest village. We felt so helpless; there was nothing we could do to help them. We formed a group, I insisted that I go along, and we travelled swiftly through the woods to where they were.

'When we found our people their arms were still linked. They looked unharmed, as if they had just fallen asleep; one body slumped against the next, quiet and peaceful within the ring of tall trees that skirted the clearing. My father's closest friend, Wolf, was the only one still alive. He used his last few moments to tell us what had happened… and then he too was gone. We did our best to find the bodies of their animal companions, hoping to give them their rightful burial in the forest, but the outsiders had taken most of them away.'

'I'm so sorry, Uncle.' Samuel sat in shock unable to find the right words of comfort. He could only imagine how the young Bruin must have felt when he helped to bring the bodies of his friends and family back to the forest village that day.

'That is the evil that we face in those people. They can't be reasoned with, you can't explain to them the value of Nature.' Bruin rubbed a hand over his eyes and coughed, clearing his throat.

'What happened was awful, terrible,' Samuel said cautiously. 'But the outsiders couldn't have known what they had done.'

Bruin looked up sharply at him as he thrust the poker into the fire and threw on a fresh log to bring the flames leaping up again.

'What I mean is,' Samuel continued, 'they killed animals, they only *saw* the animals. Perhaps they were afraid for their families. Surely they had no way of knowing that their actions would cause the deaths of our people.'

Bruin straightened his back. 'You're *defending* their actions?' he asked angrily.

'No. Not defending, but perhaps if they'd known... if my Grandfather had gone about things differently...' The look on his uncle's face stopped Samuel mid-sentence.

'You dare to suggest that you know better than my father? He was a great leader of our people! You think you could have done better? You foolish child!' Bruin stood up and stared down at his nephew.

Samuel felt his anger like a fierce burning aura all around him. 'Forgive me, Uncle, I didn't mean to offend you. I was just trying to think how things could have been different; maybe there's still hope? Perhaps we could still get through to the outsiders, try something else?'

'Stop! I've heard enough! I was wrong to think you were ready for this. You obviously still have doubts about where your loyalties lie!' Bruin bellowed.

Samuel could hardly believe how badly this was suddenly going. He had meant to help, not to send his uncle into a rage.

'My loyalties lie with the forest, with our people, you know that, Uncle Bruin.' Samuel also got to his feet now in an attempt to feel less like a child being told off and more like what he believed he was: a young forester with a valuable opinion which should be heard by the leader of his people, however hard he found it to hear.

'I only want what is best for us all and if that means approaching the village of Crossways again and all the other villages and towns of the outsiders to make them listen to sense then I think we should try. Doing nothing will never stop the destruction. I thought that was why you travelled to Crossways today? To try again? I want to be part of it, Uncle, that's all I'm saying.'

Bruin's jaw slackened for a moment, the shock of what Samuel had said about his trip to Crossways obviously hitting him hard.

'No, we didn't go there to 'try again,' Bruin said, once he'd recovered his composure. 'It didn't work before and I don't believe it would make any difference this time. We went to observe, to watch how they're living. To see what harm they're wreaking on our forest now. What we saw was far worse than we were expecting. They have learned nothing and made things even worse. The time for teaching has long since passed.'

The look on Bruin's face was full of hatred.

'What do you mean to do?' Samuel asked.

'The time has come for action. I only hope I haven't left it too long, but I had no choice, it took us a long time to recover from the loss of so many. When I took over after my father died I had to lead our people, bring them together as a community again and to train our skills to a level at which we can fight back.'

'*Fight* back?'

'What choice do we have, Samuel? Violence is all these outsiders understand. Surely you don't have fond feelings for the place? Why, you told me that you were glad to get away from that village. You caused some destruction there yourself before you left, didn't you?'

'Yes, but that was... different. And I'm not proud of it. I wasn't trying to hurt anyone. What do you mean to do?' Samuel was annoyed that his uncle was throwing his story back at him and manipulating it in such a way.

Bruin brushed his words aside. 'Our message this time has to be quick and brutal. We will destroy their village completely and without further warning. There will be signs left to show that it was done in revenge for their misuse of the forest. Maybe, just maybe, if the story travels to other villages that border the great forest then perhaps it will cause the outsiders to think again.'

'And if it doesn't, what then? What if the outsiders rise up against us and use violence in return?'

'So be it. If we must fight to preserve our forest then that is what we shall do.'

'But, Bruin, surely you wouldn't harm anyone? You won't... kill?'

'So you think I should just sit here and allow those damned people to continue to damage the forest. When they have decimated the great ancients, killed the animals and finally arrive at the entrance to our forest home, what then boy? What would you suggest then?' Bruin's voice was crackling with rage.

The fire fizzed and spat in the silence between them.

Samuel could see the weight of responsibility on Bruin's shoulders. Ever since he was barely more than a child this great man had been the one that his people had turned to. He had had to bear the loss of his family and find the strength to lead his people at the same time. 'But there must be another way, you can't just...'

Bruin's face darkened again. 'We will do whatever we have to, Samuel. Either you are with us or not. Your skills are very powerful, we could use them in the fight. I have thought on this for many years, this is the only way, and the right time to strike. Are you brave enough to stand with us? Will you join us in what must be done?'

'I would follow you in almost anything, Uncle, but I won't knowingly bring harm to anyone. I can't believe you would ask me to do such a thing.' Samuel's head spun, was this man before him the same one he had come to love and respect? It seemed his reason had been devoured and distorted by his loss.

Bruin's face twisted into an expression that Samuel had not seen before and one he couldn't read. 'Perhaps the "outsider" half of you is stronger than your love for the forest?'

His uncle's words cut Samuel deeply. Unable to find a response inside him he just stood there staring into his uncle's eyes, watching the flames that were reflected in them dance and leap.

'You should think very hard on this matter, Samuel. I am weary of this talk and of this day. We will speak about this tomorrow.' And with that, Bruin left Samuel's tepee, nearly tearing the door-skin away from its stitching as he did so.

Blithe, her ears tucked flat against her head, glanced at Quicksilver, then trotted after Bruin. Quicksilver came over to stand by Samuel and tenderly licked his friend's cheek.

'What are we going to do, boy?' Samuel hugged the great dog around the neck.

There was no way Samuel was going to sleep after that. No way he was going to stay there in the forest village. He had seen another side to Bruin he would never have believed existed. And he sensed that there was little point in staying around to try and talk to his uncle the following morning. If

272

Bruin had been training his people to sharpen their gift just to use it to rise up violently against the outsiders, then Samuel felt sure there was nothing he could do to sway him from his decision.

He knew he had to leave. His heart felt heavy and full of sadness but he heard the forest calling to him. To get out and away from that place and into the fresh air of the forest to be alone with Quicksilver, to have time to think and to be his own council again; that seemed the most important thing to do right then. But he couldn't leave without first seeing Willow.

Sitting on the floor of his tepee, until all sounds of the village around turned to that of slumber, Samuel quietly gathered his belongings together, doused his fire and crept silently through the rings of tepees towards Willow's. Fearing that Bruin might still be awake he forced a veil over his thoughts, blocking out any attempt that could be made to track his whereabouts or his feelings. This was another skill he had discovered within himself and one that he was very glad he had not told his uncle about, especially now.

From a place deeper down, he connected gently with Willow's mind, raising her slowly from sleep until she flipped the door-skin of her tepee aside to admit him. She lit a small candle so that they could see one another as they spoke. For privacy, and so as not to disturb the sleeping Fern, they conversed using their minds.

'Whatever is wrong, Samuel? You look so...' She lifted a hand to brush his hair from his eyes.

'I have to leave, Willow.'

'*Leave*? Why? What's happened?' her voice, full of concern, filled his head.

'There's so much to tell you, so much I've learned but I need to get away and think things out for myself.' Samuel answered.

'But, where will you go? Do you mean to go alone? Does Bruin know?' Willow pulled on Samuel's hands to bring him down to sit by her side on the sandy floor.

'No, he doesn't. He's mostly the reason I need to leave, Willow. Things have changed here lately... at least I've noticed things aren't quite what I thought they were, perhaps they never were...'

'Samuel, I don't understand you. You're frightening me.' The flickering candle sent shadows dancing across her beautiful face.

'I'm sorry, I don't mean to. It's just that since I've been here, everything I've known and learned has been taught to me by Uncle Bruin, I haven't had any time to think for myself. I've accepted everything I've been told without question, now I fear that Bruin's judgement isn't all that it should be.'

'But Samuel, Bruin's our leader, whatever he teaches you is only done to help you. He's simply guiding you to be the very best that you can be. When you take over his position and become our new leader...'

'*What?*' Samuel interrupted.

'Surely you knew that was his plan?'

'No. I had no idea... his *plan*? What about *my* plan, what about what *I* want? I'm no leader, I'm not really even one of you, I'm half and half; half forester, half outsider.' Samuel scowled and looked away from Willow, remembering Bruin's cruel words.

'Samuel!' Willow took his face in her hands and turned his head so that she could look into his eyes again. 'Why do you say such a thing?' she waited for a reply but Samuel just stared at her miserably.

'Please,' she continued, 'you're upset, go back and sleep on this tonight. In the morning we can go someplace quiet and talk it out together. You'll feel differently in the morning.'

Taking her slim hands in his own he smiled at her sadly. If only she was right. Perhaps she was; he might feel differently in the morning. Bruin might come and apologise for what he had said, blame it on his weariness, beg Samuel's forgiveness. But would that change how Samuel felt about his decision to attack the village of Crossways? No. Even though his uncle had hurt him deeply Samuel still loved him but he couldn't afford to stay around and be pressurised into taking part in his cruel plans. Talking to the other foresters might win him a little support, perhaps amongst the younger men, but Bruin's people were loyal to him and he was too well respected for everyone to disobey his orders. There had to be another way.

'I can't Willow. I know in my gut that it's the right thing for me to leave. Something's calling to me from the forest, I feel the answers to all my doubts are out there somewhere but I need to find them for myself.'

Willow could see there was no point in reasoning any further with him, 'All right, if you're adamant about leaving then I'm coming with you.' She made a move to get up and ready her things.

Samuel held fast to her hands. 'No,' he said gently. 'I would love you to come with me, you know I would, but it wouldn't be fair on Fern.' There were tears in her eyes now; she had known he would say this. 'You couldn't leave him behind, Willow, and I've no idea what awaits me out there; we couldn't take him along. Please, trust me. This is something I have to do, alone.'

Biting her lip, 'You're planning to leave right now? In the dark?'

'Yes. I have my reasons for not wanting to see Bruin again before I leave. Don't worry about me, Quicksilver will be with me all the way.'

Willow threw her arms around Samuel's neck and pressed herself close to his chest. 'But I *will* worry about you Samuel, I won't be able not to,' she buried her face in the hollow between his neck and shoulder, breathing in the comforting scent of his skin. 'I love you.'

Samuel knew that she did, he had felt the warmth of her love grow daily since that sunlit afternoon in the forest when they had shared their first muddy-faced kiss, but she had never actually put it into words before, neither of them had.

'And I love you, Willow. I'll come back for you, you know that.'

'I know. And you should know that Fern and I will come with you wherever you lead us.'

'I do, but let's hope it doesn't come to that. I'll be careful. Explain to Fern that I'll be back. Tell him not to worry.' Samuel reached into his pack and pulled out three items. 'Give him these to look after for me.'

Samuel handed Willow the feather from the Great Forest Eagle, a pencil and his mother's writing book.

'Are you sure? I know how precious these are to you.'

'So does Fern. It'll give him something to hold on to and help him to believe that I really do mean to come home to you both.'

'I'll see he takes good care of them.'

'Tell him he can write in the book; will you show him how to?'

Willow's eyes filled again with tears and this time she didn't try to hold them back. There was nothing else to say, so they said nothing. Rising to their feet they held tightly to each other.

Willow kissed every inch of Samuel's face and, as he forced himself to leave her tepee and walk quietly through the village towards the forest, her tears mingled with his own on his hot cheeks.

Daniel

Samuel closed the archway behind himself and Quicksilver and the pair moved into the dark forest beyond. Without any warning Samuel was stunned to receive a forceful whack across the backside. It took a moment before he understood the source of the blow; Quicksilver had thwacked him with his great strong tail.

'Ow! That hurt boy, what was that for?' Samuel thought to him angrily, only glad that he'd had the presence of mind not to have shouted out loud and roused the foresters from their beds.

Peering through the gloom Samuel looked into his friend's silver eyes and guessed the answer. Quicksilver had always shown confidence in Samuel, he would follow him anywhere but this time he had sensed Samuel's self-doubt and it troubled him.

Knowing that he had made the right decision to go didn't help Samuel when he thought of everything he was leaving behind. Willow, Fern, Ash, Heather, even baby Flake; he would miss all of them and many more besides. He would miss Bruin too, greatly, and wondered what his uncle would think when he awoke the next morning to discover that he had left during the night. Would he care?

Where am I going to go and what do I hope to find?

He didn't know where this new journey might lead him, but he did know where he was going to begin it; he was going to travel back into the forest to the place where he saw those scorch-marks on the ground. Perhaps it would be a waste of time, perhaps it was just some silly old tale that the children told each other, having made it up on seeing those same marks out in the forest; but something deep inside Samuel pulled him that way. The story that Willow had told him about the markings and the vivid dream he had had afterwards had never left him. They had burned themselves into his thoughts just as deeply as the 'footprints' had scorched the ground.

They moved carefully through the darkness, the light of the moon just enough to illuminate their way through the more dense areas of the forest. Just as the sun dawned the next day Samuel heard Willow's voice very faintly in his mind.

'Go well, my love. Take care.'

It made him stop in mid-step and once more reconsider his decision to leave. Before moving onwards he replied to her, marvelling all the while at how far she had managed to send her mind-message, once again it proved that their skills were well matched.

They hadn't found the time to pack any food to take along with them so Samuel caught a rabbit for their breakfast and cooked it over a small fire. It made him feel good to provide for Quicksilver for a change after all the times when he had done the hunting for the pair of them. Samuel ate a handful of wild raspberries and they both took a long drink from the river, Samuel taking the chance to refill his water pouch before they continued on to find some shelter to rest in. Both were tired from the sleepless night of travelling and Samuel felt confident that they were far enough away from the forest village for it to be safe for them to have a nap to restore their strength and senses. Curling up together on a bed of soft, springy moss the pair slept deeply, the rabbit meat refuelling their limbs with energy for the next part of the journey.

The nap turned into something far longer and when Samuel felt the finger that tapped him on the shoulder to rouse him from his slumber it took a moment for him to recall where he was. A voice whispered in his ear. 'Up now lad, time to be moving on or be discovered.' A deep gentle laugh followed the words, but by the time Samuel's eyes were adjusted to the brightness of the sun all he could see was a shimmer of leaves disappearing between two old pine trees.

He sat up and immediately his senses flicked into action, warning him that there were people nearby.

'Quicksilver, wake up, boy. You need to run up ahead and wait for me, we're not alone.' Samuel thought to the sleeping dog.

The dog raised his big silver head and looked intently into

Samuel's eyes, his silver ears swivelled, his nose twitched, as he processed the information from his senses about the men who were closing in on them. He gave a single gentle *gruff*, then sped off between the trees in the opposite direction. Samuel quickly composed himself and blotted out his thoughts, he pulled down the defences that he had learned to use, which made his presence invisible to the searching mind-skills of the other foresters.

Then he listened with both his ears and his mind.

'I lost him, Bruin.' Samuel recognised the voice of Rowan, Flint's father.

'Yes, so did I. It seems that my nephew has even more skills that he's kept from me.' Bruin this time.

'Samuel?' Bruin called out loud, 'Come out, boy, whatever's the problem, we can talk about it.'

Bruin waited for Samuel to respond but Samuel held his position and closed his mind completely to any possible intrusion by his uncle, or the two men that were with him.

'Samuel? This is Finch, come on home with us.'

That was Poppy's husband; he knew all three of them so well, had come to love them over the time he'd spent in their company. Bruin was his *uncle*, he had helped to deliver Finch's first-born child and Rowan had helped Willow to nurse him back from his injuries after his fall the previous year from the old tree... was he mad to be hiding from them?

No, I'm not.

'Blithe, can you go and find Quicksilver?' Bruin's voice came again and Samuel froze. He couldn't bear the thought that they might catch Quicksilver and force him to help them track him down. Or perhaps they would use Blithe to lure her brother out of the woods and take him back to the forest village with them; leaving him alone, without his companion. Sending Blithe to find Quicksilver was cruel; what would the dog do if made to choose between his human friend and his own sister?

'Quicksilver,' Samuel pushed his thought past the veil he had drawn over his mind and out through the forest, all the way to where his companion darted sinuously away through the undergrowth. 'Blithe is coming to find you, it's your choice whether you go back with her or not. I'll understand whatever you choose to do but I must go on, don't let them find me boy.'

With her mind fixed on Bruin's request, Blithe thundered past where Samuel was hiding and hurtled after her brother. Samuel tried not to think of how it would feel to be all alone if Quicksilver decided to return with her.

'We'll wait around here for her. If Quicksilver's anywhere nearby Blithe will track him down.' Bruin's voice was confident and Samuel feared that he was right.

He could see the three men now, could just make them out through the twisted branches and undergrowth. They had come so close to discovering him. They were sitting down, sharing a drink of water from Bruin's water pouch.

'Do you know why he left, Bruin?' Finch asked.

282

'I don't understand it, he's been so happy living with us. What happened to make him feel differently?' came Rowan's question.

'I'm not sure, he's young and still has much to learn. Perhaps he's had a lovers' tiff with Willow. Who knows?' Bruin smiled and took a gulp of water.

The hairs on the nape of Samuel's neck bristled with anger.

Why is he lying to them?

Forcing himself to control his temper for fear it would interfere with his ability to hide himself from their alert minds, Samuel thought instead of Quicksilver.

Although the dog was safely out of range of Bruin and the others, the bond between the twin animals was very strong and it wasn't long before Blithe found her brother, who had actually stopped to wait for her. With their heads together the two silver dogs greeted and licked one another's faces tenderly. When Blithe ran back to Bruin, Samuel saw that she was alone and his heart leapt up to soar like an eagle in the sky.

Bless you, Quicksilver, for not leaving me!

But Samuel's concentration lapsed for a moment as he thought this and that moment was long enough for Bruin to leap to his feet and to be staring in Samuel's direction.

'I sensed him – follow me.'

Cloaking his mind once again, Samuel began to run towards where Quicksilver was waiting for him.

Fool! If I'm caught now...

He left the rest of his self-reprimand for a more appropriate time as he sped between the trees.

The three men followed the right course for a while and Samuel feared discovery. He began to wonder what he would say to them when he was caught. Could he betray his uncle and tell the other two the awful things he had said to him the night before? Did they already know of Bruin's plans? Would they believe Samuel's version of the truth over their leader whom they had followed and respected all this time? Thankfully he didn't have to find out. Veering off to the left, homing in on where Quicksilver waited patiently for him, Samuel sensed that the three men and Blithe were continuing on their same course and so were now headed in a different direction to him. He thanked his luck, if it was that, that neither Finch nor Rowan had a bird for a companion or else he may yet have been discovered.

Samuel threw his arms around Quicksilver. 'Thank you, boy. You'll see her again, I promise. I'm so glad you chose to stay with me.'

A massive and hot pink tongue licked Samuel's face and neck. Quicksilver's tail swept back and forth, cutting through the air like a furry sword as he greeted his friend.

Keeping a safe distance, to avoid Quicksilver being detected, they began to follow the men through the forest. Samuel wanted to hear more of what his uncle had to say about his departure. As they went along, Bruin and his two friends would stop every now and then to 'read' the forest around them; send out their skilled senses to search for the boy and his dog.

'Wait!' Rowan's thought was directed at Bruin and Finch but Samuel easily overheard it and stopped. 'Up ahead, over there. I'm sure there's a human, it doesn't feel like Samuel, seems smaller but we should check to be sure.'

Following their lead Samuel couldn't see anything of what they saw but he listened to their thoughts as they moved closer and discovered what Rowan had picked up on.

'It's a trap, a pit.' Finch arrived at the scene first.

'Hey look, down there. It's a child.' There was deep concern in Rowan's voice, the concern of a good father.

'That's who I was sensing. Are you all right down there?' Finch's voice, this time not using his mind so Samuel could barely make out what he said as he was so far away. Forcing his skills to work harder Samuel pushed his mind deeper, to bring him closer to the feelings of the men up ahead.

'He doesn't look badly hurt, there's some blood on his leg but I think he's been down there a long time, his energy is low. Help me get him out, Finch.' Samuel intercepted Rowan's thoughts.

'No.'

That was Bruin. But what did he mean "No"? Samuel listened with heightened interest.

'But, the lad needs help, Bruin.' Finch reasoned. 'He could die down there.'

'Any of us could have fallen down there but do you really believe that an outsider would help one of *us* to get out of one of their damned traps if we had?' Bruin's words were cold and detached.

'But... he's only a child Bruin, it's not his fault...' Rowan this time.

'Is it ours, then?' Bruin's tone was confrontational now and he didn't pause to let either of his friends answer, 'No! The outsiders are blind to the dangers that their traps cause. Perhaps if they come across one of their own young caught in one, then they may reconsider using them.'

Then there was silence. Samuel felt a chill run down his back. The atmosphere between the three men up ahead in the forest permeated and tainted the air all around.

'We can't leave him here, Bruin,' Finch, cautious, spoke gently as if trying to placate a wild animal. 'You know that the outsiders rarely check their traps, it could be days before the boy is discovered, if at all.'

'Are you questioning my decision, Finch?' Bruin, steely determination gilding his voice.

'Bruin, calm down. Listen to him.' Rowan tried to defuse the situation.

'All I'm saying is...' Finch tried once more.

'Enough! Am I your leader or not?'

'Of course, but...' Rowan tried to answer but was quickly cut off.

'We are here to find Samuel, not to save foolish outsiders from their own handiwork. Move on with me and do as I tell you, or don't bother to return to the forest village today, or ever again!'

Samuel couldn't believe what he was hearing. Had this terrible hatred and loathing for the outsiders always been so strongly rooted within his uncle? Could he really mean to leave a helpless child in such a situation?

Samuel could sense the boy's presence in the pit up ahead, could feel the fear in his small body as he shook with cold and hunger.

There were no more words exchanged between the three forest men. Samuel felt them move away, continuing in their previous line of pursuit, further away from him into the woods. They had left the child alone to his fate.

Quicksilver and Samuel stayed where they were for some considerable time until it was obvious that Bruin had no plans to come back the same way; Samuel's sense of their whereabouts was now so faint that he knew they were a great way off. Someplace inside him, another piece of his love for his uncle faded as he realised that Bruin had been serious; he really had no intention of returning to help the boy trapped in the darkness of the animal pit.

Moving through the great trees, the leaves whispering to each other above them as they went, Quicksilver and Samuel arrived at the mouth of the trap. It was very large, big enough to catch a full-grown bear. The pit had been dug to a depth of nearly three times the height of a man, and in the gloom below Samuel could see that wooden stakes had been driven into the earth to point skywards, ready to impale any unwary creature unlucky enough to stumble into it. The branches and ferns, which had lain across the opening to hide it from view, were scattered below, sent crashing down as the young child had broken through them and fallen into the pit.

'Hello?' Samuel called down to the boy.

No answer.

'Are you hurt?' Samuel tried once again.

He knew the boy was there, even though he had dragged himself right up against the earthy side of the pit and was out of sight, Samuel could sense his presence and the life force that pulsed within him.

It seemed that the youngster had fallen through right at the very edge of the pit. This was extremely lucky. If the camouflaging had supported his weight, just a little longer, he would surely have suffered the painful and slow death of having his body pierced by the wooden stakes. He had escaped any serious injuries but still, Samuel could feel, he was hurt in some way.

'Don't be scared, I want to help you. I'll be back in a moment, then I'll come down there to get you out. Hold on.'

Quicksilver fetched a long and strong vine which Samuel pointed out to him. Using his hunting knife, Samuel cut and secured one end of it around the trunk of a nearby tree.

'Wish me luck, boy,' he thought to Quicksilver before beginning to lower himself backwards into the pit.

'Here I come, don't be scared.' Samuel heard a slight movement in the dimness below but still the child kept quiet.

Keeping close to the wall of the pit he dug his feet into the crumbly earth to slow his descent and make sure he didn't swing out backwards and land on the stakes. Landing safely, he looked up at Quicksilver's concerned face that peered over the edge above.

'I'm all right, boy.'

The young lad was sitting with his back against the pit wall. He was hugging his knees, which were pulled up tightly against his chest, his head bowed over them. Samuel could see congealed blood on the boy's right leg where his trousers were torn and ragged and smeared with dirt.

'Your leg is hurt. Will you let me have a look at it?' he spoke quietly so as not to frighten the boy any more than he already had.

A miserable face lifted to look at him. 'My father is going to be so angry,' he sobbed. 'I promised not to go off without him.'

The boy could be no older than seven or eight years old, his small tired face smeared with mud and tears.

'I'm sure your father will just be glad to see you again.' Samuel moved slowly towards him. 'Let's get you home to him, shall we?'

'Please, don't come any closer.' The boy looked distraught and jerked himself back to push harder against the earth wall.

'I'm not going to hurt you, honestly, I just want to help.' Samuel hunkered down to bring himself to the boy's level and looked into his puffy eyes.

'I know, it's just that...' the boy bit his bottom lip and looked down at the ground. 'I had... an accident.' he explained timidly.

Samuel had been aware of a faint odour of urine since entering the pit but hadn't thought much about it. The poor boy had wet himself and was too embarrassed to have Samuel come closer because of it.

'Hey, that's okay.' Samuel tried to reassure him, 'I'm sure I would've done the exact same thing if I'd been through what you have. Don't worry about it.'

The boy looked up sheepishly.

'Let's get you out of this horrible place and then we can fix that leg for you, all right?'

The boy thought about this, then nodded and let Samuel examine his injured leg.

'I'm Samuel, what's your name?' he asked to take his attention away from the pain.

'Daniel. Father calls me Danny. Ow!'

'Sorry,' Samuel apologised. 'Do you think you could hold on to me while I climb us out of here? You'll need to hold on tight; I'll need both my hands and I wouldn't want you to fall again.'

'Yes, I can do it.' The boy seemed brighter now; the prospect of getting back into the fresh air and out of the pit had lightened his spirits.

Samuel sent a thought-message to his friend. 'We're coming up Quicksilver, perhaps you should hide yourself until we're safely there, just in case the lad gets a shock at the sight of you.'

He sensed the dog move off to conceal himself behind a tree.

'Here we go,' Samuel said.

Daniel held on tightly around Samuel's neck and after a few minutes of straining the pair were safely up in the warm sun where Samuel could get a better look at the boy's wound.

'There's nothing broken, but I think you should take some of this to stop any infection getting into that gash.' Samuel took off his medicine necklace and held it in front of Daniel's mouth. The boy sniffed it and wrinkled his nose.

'Smells funny.'

'Yes, but it's good for you. Chew one of them off the leather and swallow it down, then we'll get some food into you.'

The boy did as he was told but Samuel couldn't help but laugh at the expression of disgust on his face at the taste of the tree-fungus.

After a quick forage, Samuel returned to the boy with a handful of fruit and berries. Daniel gobbled them down gratefully and slurped deeply from Samuel's water pouch.

'I've a friend with me I'd like you to meet.' Samuel said. 'He looks quite fierce but he's very gentle so don't be alarmed, all right?'

The youngster nodded and followed Samuel's gaze as he called to Quicksilver.

'You can come on out now, boy.'

Daniel's eyes nearly popped from their sockets as Quicksilver ambled over towards them.

'He's your *friend*?' Daniel asked in wide-eyed awe.

Samuel nodded and stroked Quicksilver's gleaming coat. 'The best I ever had.'

Quicksilver dipped his head down towards the boy and sniffed at his hair. Daniel, at first wary, began to giggle as the great dog's long pink tongue found the back of his neck and licked it copiously.

'I think Quicksilver's saying that you need a bath.' Samuel sniffed at his own clothes. 'In fact, I think we could all do with one. Let's go to the river.'

Samuel helped Daniel onto Quicksilver's back and the three made their way towards the water.

Samuel had considered trying to heal Daniel's wound using the same skill he had found to work on Fern's little mouse, but decided against it. It might not be sensible to weaken himself just now with such an act, and he didn't want to scare the boy. Besides, once his wound had been well washed, it looked a great deal better.

Daniel lay contentedly in the sun; a spray of fern leaves affording him some privacy whilst his newly washed clothes dried on a nearby rock.

'Where are you from?' Samuel asked, he was standing in the river and helping Quicksilver to wash behind his big silky ears.

'We live in Crossways now, me and Dad, moved there a while back. Dad works in the forest, cutting down trees. I'm supposed to be learning how to do it so I can help him out when I'm a bit older but I keep getting into trouble.'

'Trouble?' Samuel asked, leaving the river to lie out his own wet clothes in the sunshine.

'I keep wandering off. I don't mean to, it's just that I'd never seen the forest before and when I did... well, I just wanted to explore it. It's just so beautiful and there's so much to see.'

Samuel smiled to himself.

'Father says I'm a daydreamer and a lazybones but I'm not, least I don't mean to be. I'd just rather learn how to do something else, that's all. They don't even make use of all the timber they cut down, it seems such a waste.'

Samuel wished that his uncle could hear this young boy's words. The child of an outsider, an outsider who is paid to help destroy the forest, yet still this boy seemed to care about the forest; was he so unlike a forester child?

Are we so very different, outsiders and forest folk?

That thought kept coming back to him over and over again.

Covering Daniel's gash with leaves that speeded the skin's ability to heal, Samuel secured them in place with reeds tied neatly together. The colour had returned to the boy's face and looking into him, using his gift, Samuel felt confident that there was no infection in the wound or any lasting damage from his experience.

'You'll take more care in future when you're off exploring in the woods?' Samuel asked him.

'I certainly will. That's if my father ever let's me again.'

'Have you ever told him what you've told me? How you feel about the forest?' asked Samuel.

'No,' Daniel grinned and shook his head, 'I don't think he'd understand. He'd just say I was being silly.'

'You might be mistaken, you should try him. Why not take him with you on his day off work and show him all the things you've come to enjoy? Maybe you'll surprise him? Perhaps he'll find that he likes them too?'

Daniel looked dubious. 'Maybe.'

'He's a good father?' Samuel asked.

'Oh yes.' Daniel answered without hesitation. 'He's strict and gets angry with me sometimes, but he's good to me.'

'He loves you?'

'Well,' Daniel reddened a little, 'he doesn't say it much now that I'm bigger.'

'But you know he does?'

Daniel nodded.

'Well then, give him the chance. What's there to lose?' said Samuel.

Daniel fell quiet as he thought it over and the two of them shared a few minutes of companionable silence. Then

Quicksilver galloped over towards them, bounding from the water to stand right between them where they lay comfortably soaking up the sun's rays.

'No, Quicksilver!' Samuel shouted realising what the dog was about to do. But he was too late. The massive dog shook himself vigorously, scattering river water over both boys and their drying clothes.

'Thanks a lot, boy.' Samuel grimaced up at him.

'Gruff,' Quicksilver responded. *No problem.*

Once they had dried off... again, the great silver dog carried Daniel on his back without complaint for the rest of that day as they headed in the direction of Crossways.

'I'm sure I could walk.' Daniel said as they moved along.

'No, you save your energy. We can't take you all the way there so you'll have to walk later on.'

Late that afternoon, Samuel helped the boy down from Quicksilver's strong back.

'Are you sure you'll manage by yourself from here?' Samuel asked, handing Daniel the crutch that he'd been whittling for him along their way.

Daniel trusted his weight to it and grinned up at Samuel. 'Thank you, this is great! I'll manage fine from here. I know this part of the woods very well.' Daniel gave Quicksilver a hug and received a face-lick in return. 'Thanks for carrying me boy,' he said to him. 'You're not at all how they describe you, you know.' Daniel said to Samuel.

Samuel looked at him quizzically.

'Back in Crossways, there's a story that they tell about you.' Daniel explained.

Samuel's jaw dropped, 'About *me*? Are you sure?'

'I wasn't sure at first but once I'd met this chap... ' Daniel rubbed Quicksilver's side, 'I knew it was definitely you two that I'd heard about.'

'But, what do they say?'

'The story goes that a witch and her boy had lived in the village a few years ago. The people had taken them in and treated them just like two of their own for years, but one day they turned against them and tried to burn the village down.'

'Treated us as two of their own?' Samuel muttered incredulously.

'They say that, using his magic, the boy started a fire in the village bakery. It was his intention that it would spread throughout the other shops and houses, bringing death to all the sleeping inhabitants. When the witch and her son left Crossways behind, they stole away the butcher's prize animal, who was a massive and fierce silver dog, luring him away into the forest to help them with their wicked spells.'

Samuel's eyes were wide in surprise. It seemed that the forest village was not the only place where stories and events were wildly twisted out of shape to suit the teller.

Daniel nodded, grinning widely, obviously enjoying the

absurdity of the tale. 'Mr Sanderson, the owner of the village bakery, single-handedly put out the flames and saved the whole village. Or so they say.'

'Is that so?' Samuel didn't have to think too hard whom it might have been that had come up with that particular detail of the fictitious story. 'Quite a yarn.'

'Isn't it? But I don't believe everything I hear.'

Samuel ruffled the boy's hair. 'Then you're a wise lad.'

'Perhaps you can tell me what really happened... when we meet again?'

Samuel laughed gently, 'I'd like to do just that Daniel, if we *do* meet again.'

'Oh, we will. I'm pretty sure of it. Sometimes I can sort of foresee things like that, Father's not too keen on it, but it happens, sometimes.' Daniel hugged Samuel around the chest with his free arm. 'Thanks for helping me, I won't forget it.'

As Samuel stood with Quicksilver watching Daniel move off between the trees, in the direction of Crossways, he sent a thought-message to him, 'Good luck Daniel, go well.'

The boy stopped, and looked over his shoulder at them. He lifted a hand to wave before moving off again and Samuel wondered, for a moment, if it had just been a coincidence or... could Daniel, an outsider, possibly have heard him...?

An Old Friend

Samuel turned to his companion. 'Well! Quicksilver, my friend, what do you think about that? We're the stars of our very own fairy tale! Imagine thinking that anyone could lure *you* away anywhere against your will. And as for saying you were *fierce...*' Samuel pounced on the dog and tickled him until they were a mass of limbs tumbling over one another in the bracken and undergrowth.

'Mr Sanderson must have loved making himself out to be the hero that saved Crossways from my 'evil magic'. From their story, I guess they don't know that Mama is...' Samuel stopped short of saying it. He mused aloud as he chewed absent-mindedly on a long blade of grass, lying with his head against Quicksilver's side in the fading light, feeling the rise and fall of his friend's every breath. 'As if the fire could have spread to the houses, the bakery was too far away for it to have done that.'

Samuel could feel himself starting to get angry as he thought about it. He would never have harmed any of the people of Crossways; not even the cruel and stupid Mr Sanderson. The people had never shown kindness to him or his mother, neither had they made them feel welcomed, but still it was unpleasant to think that they believed he had intended to cause them harm, or even worse.

As far as being known as the 'Witch's Boy'... that just made him smile. His mother had been magical and mysterious and beautiful, let them call her by any name they wished, pointing out how different she had been to them, and their blinkered ways, only served to confirm what a special person she had been.

Quicksilver gave his companion a light flick with the tip of his tail.

'I know, I know. Time to set up for the night.' Samuel got to his feet and followed his friend through the dappled forest to find a suitable place to set up camp.

It was a pleasant night, no sign of rain, it wasn't cold and there were hardly any biting bugs flying around.

No need for a shelter tonight, Samuel decided.

With the fire set and a dugout for two prepared below a gentle old oak tree, the pair were ready to go to the river and catch themselves a fat fish for their supper. Samuel marvelled at how different things were now compared to that first time when he had met Quicksilver in the river on the night the bear had attacked.

Using his skills, Samuel could now not only feel assured that no danger was nearby; no bear or other kind of hunter ready to steal his catch away from him, but he could also *feel* the fish that were travelling down the fast-flowing current of the river towards them. Quickly assessing their choice, Samuel made his decision and homed in on the fish he was going to catch, as it sped towards him. It was an older fish, one that had given life to many young and would yield enough food for both himself and Quicksilver. It was a good choice, quickly made.

Eyes closed to enhance the connection Samuel leaned forward towards the water, hands steady, waiting, waiting. Up to his thighs in the cold river he timed the moment perfectly; grabbing the fish as it was about to scoot away down the river between his open legs. Powerfully he heaved his catch out of the water and over to where Quicksilver waited to perform his part of the ritual. There was a flash of water-bejewelled scales, burnished by the orange glow of the evening sky then the great dog caught the fish in his jaws and delivered a quick bite that ended the fish's life before it knew what was happening.

Quicksilver's chops glistened with drool as he patiently waited for his dinner to cook in the embers of the fire. After a delicious meal of juicy salmon stuffed with red berries and wrapped in tasty sweet leaves, the two companions lay down against each other, warm and contented by their fire.

Samuel stared into the dancing flames and thought back over his time in the forest village. Forcing his thoughts away from Willow as much as he could, because it hurt so much to be away from her, he found himself remembering the last of the three 'Tests' when his Uncle Bruin had manipulated the flame.

Samuel had wondered at the time if he would ever be able to do such a thing but had never got around to trying it out for himself. Sitting up again, he leaned forward and pulled a burning log from the fire. Quicksilver groaned his complaints as his human companion moved away and left a cold spot where he had been lying against his side.

'Sorry boy, just want to try something.' Samuel explained, before placing the still-burning log on a level and cleared piece of ground before him.

He sat cross-legged in front of it and stared into its energy. Talking quietly to himself he calmed his thoughts, cleared his mind of anything other than the flames, and gently let himself fall into a trance-like state. Looking into the flames with his mind, he visualised the energy vibrant within them. They were glowing red-hot, full of fierce power, hungry for fuel to make them bloom and grow. Samuel concentrated on them, poured his will into those flames and pushed them to move along the log away from him. Quicksilver lifted his head to watch as the flames danced and flickered away from Samuel as if blown by an unfelt breeze. Deeper, harder, Samuel felt his way inside the energy that was held in the fire.

Move. Move!

The flames began to shiver. Then, very slowly, they started their way along the log. They travelled over the bark like a living, breathing creature. Samuel had intended to have the flames stop at the far end of the log then make their way back towards him but it felt too good, this power, this control. He pushed further.

Go on. Keep going.

He pushed and coaxed the fire with his mind, pressing it to continue past the end of the log and to move along the forest floor. Quicksilver groaned gently and pulled himself up to a seated position, watching the events unfold before him with trepidation. The flames moved on, a little faster now, skimming over leaves and moss, stones and bracken, under Samuel's instruction they caused no devastation on their way; they ate nothing of the fuel that lay so tantalizingly close at hand.

Samuel's eyes were full and round; he was doing it! He could have beaten even his uncle at this if he had put himself in for The Tests.

This is easy!

Quicksilver tried to send his feelings to Samuel; he wasn't happy about this. The great silver dog shifted uneasily on his muscular backside, his ears flat against the sides of his head. But try as he might he had never been able to figure out how the lad spoke to him inside his head, he always heard and understood what Samuel said but had never been able to begin the connection himself.

'*Gruff!*' he decided to try a gentle sound to try and rouse the boy a little; to bring him back down to earth so he could clearly see that what he was doing was both foolish and dangerous. It hadn't rained for some time and they were in the middle of the forest surrounded by dry kindling; if Samuel lost control of the fire it would be off like a wild animal ripping through the trees before they could do anything to stop its fearful appetite.

The flames moved on, Samuel was transfixed by them. The great dog got to his feet and padded quietly closer to the moving flames, his eyes flicking from Samuel, to the moving fire, and back again.

This is amazing! Samuel pushed on.

The excitement of discovering yet another ability, filling his mind and forcing out any common sense or caution. Recklessly he wondered if he could make the flames lick and hover their way along the limbs of a fallen tree that lay nearby and pushed them to move towards it. A pile of twigs and leaves lay against the rotting trunk, blown there by the wind they had gathered to a depth that equalled the height of Quicksilver's knees. The dog moved over, shadowing the moving flames on their journey towards the debris.

Samuel was beginning to tire. The effort of controlling such a wilful element was taking a great deal out of him. He had not noticed this during his growing excitement, but now he began to feel the fingers of weariness prodding at his mind. Lifting his hand to wipe the sweat from his brow was the only break in concentration that was necessary as the flames reached the dry pile of kindling and at last slipped from Samuel's control.

'Oh, no!' Samuel struggled to regain his command over the energy within the now leaping flames but it was too late, they greedily gobbled at the twigs, leaves and other dead matter that had gathered by the side of the fallen tree. Samuel's brain screamed at him to get up and fetch water from the river to douse the flames but another part of him knew that he could never gather enough water fast enough to stop what he had set in motion. He watched, transfixed in horror at his own stupidity, as the flames grew.

What have I done?

A steady gush of yellowish water streamed down from above the growing blaze. The liquid cascaded in a perfectly controlled arc that quickly subdued the worst of the flames. The dying fire hissed like a cornered and threatened snake as its will was first thwarted, then extinguished altogether, as it fizzled and died out to nothing more than steam and smoke.

The stream of liquid diminished to a few drops then stopped. Samuel looked up to find the source and saw Quicksilver through the clearing clouds of smoke. He was standing three-legged on the broad trunk of the fallen tree. Quicksilver had saved the day once again.

Cursing himself for his stupid pride Samuel looked with renewed admiration at his silver companion. The moonlight shone down on them, its gentle white light illuminating Samuel's great friend as he stood looking down on him with silver reproachful eyes. Quicksilver was now back on four legs again, his saving stream of urine now fully expended.

Samuel hung his head in shame, 'I got carried away. I'll be

more careful in future, I promise. Thanks, boy.'

Quicksilver surveyed his friend for a moment longer then bounded down off the fallen trunk and padded over to where Samuel still sat cross-legged on the ground.

'*Gruff*,' he said gently and licked the back of Samuel's neck. Samuel accepted his friend's affection gratefully. With a look of mild satisfaction on his big sleek face, Quicksilver snuggled back down and made room for Samuel to join him in their sleeping hollow. They lay there in companionable silence, listening to the sounds of the woods.

It felt good to be out in the forest again. There was something far more peaceful about sleeping out here, surrounded by the wonderful smells and familiar noises of the forest, than within the safety of the hidden village. Samuel wondered once again if Bruin's fears and prejudices about the outsiders had deprived him of experiencing some of the very best that the forest had to offer.

If only Willow and Fern could be with us.

Quicksilver picked up on his friend's emotions and turned to snuffle and nuzzle the top of Samuel's head. Samuel snuggled down, the warmth of his faithful companion at his back.

A gentle breeze blew through the forest. The trees nodded and talked to one another in hushed tones. Each type had their own distinctive voice and Samuel had come to know them all like close friends. The old and deeply rooted ancients spoke in a profound, dark manner, the spindly thinner trees, more flexible and easily manipulated by the faintest breath of wind were higher in pitch. Others rustled their dense leaves, quietly chatting over the day's events. Some swished or made long sighing sounds like sleepy yawns. The forest was alive and breathing all around them.

Lulled to sleep, Samuel and Quicksilver were totally unaware of the one that watched them from the arms of the old oak tree they had chosen to camp beneath. Even with their powerful skills, the two companions would not have been able to sense the presence of their watcher unless he himself allowed it. After all, it was the watcher who had been the very one to give them their skills in the first place. He was the centre of all life and growth in the forest. Nothing that happened there was a secret from him.

The Man In Green smiled down on them. They were doing well, these two special creatures, he had been right to guide them to one another. But then, he thought to himself with an impish grin, wasn't he always right? He wondered how strong they were, this pair, and whether they would stand up to what lay ahead of them. Alas it was not his place to lead but to guide – what they chose to do with the life given to them was their decision, but he felt confident as he looked down on their sleeping forms that they would do their best, and perhaps their best would be good enough. The boy was certainly a little overenthusiastic at times but that might work in his favour, time would tell.

Scratching his leafy chin, the Man In Green leapt down to the forest floor. His movements were cat-like, full of stealth and agility, his landing soundless. Gently he pulled Samuel's cloak over the boy and his dog companion before dancing off through the sighing trees, caressing each trunk lovingly as he went.

The sounds of woodpeckers drumming fat juicy grubs out of their hiding places in a nearby fallen tree roused Samuel and Quicksilver from their slumber early the next morning. After washing in the river and covering up the signs of where they had set their fire, the pair were ready to move on.

How far they had to travel, how long it would take them, Samuel didn't know, but he remembered roughly where the scorch-marks had been and that was where he and Quicksilver headed for after a quick breakfast.

They found the right area without difficulty. But the exact position of the markings was lost to Samuel, having been somewhat distracted the first time he had seen them. Boy and dog walked side by side covering the area methodically until Samuel discovered what he was looking for.

Quicksilver sniffed and pushed his nose along the forest floor from one scorch mark to the next. They certainly did look like footprints. Could the children's tale from the forest village be true? Perhaps it was true, in part, just like the tale in Crossways was true, in part, about himself and Quicksilver.

'We're going to follow these, all right? I don't know exactly why, I just feel it's something I need to do. Are you okay with this?' Samuel looked into the dog's silver eyes and waited for his answer.

Quicksilver gave Samuel a slobbery lick in the eye and then moved off in the direction that the markings seemed to lead; his tail held high, his eyes to the track.

'I guess that's a "yes" then.' Samuel followed, wiping his face.

Most of the way the 'footprints' were easy to follow but in deeper vegetation, or where their path wound between closely packed trees, the two friends floundered a little before picking up the trail again. There was no scent for Quicksilver to pick up; whatever had made these markings had passed this way a very long time ago.

All the way along, Samuel's mind mulled over what he was doing. Who or what would lie at the other end of this? Perhaps nothing would. Maybe whoever or whatever had made these tracks, were long-since gone; maybe not even within the boundaries of the forest anymore? There may be a completely different explanation for their existence, he realised, perhaps the tale had merely been made up to entertain.

But if that was so, then why had Bruin forbidden the telling of it?

Amiably the pair moved on, stopping only to gather food or to drink. On one such stop, the hairs on Samuel's neck tingled as he sensed that a friend was nearby. Shielding his eyes against the sun he looked up and saw a bird of prey circling high above the treetops.

'Hello, Swift,' Samuel called to him with his mind.

Although part of him wished Willow had not sent her companion on such an errand, Samuel was very pleased to see her hawk.

'Willow should be keeping you close, not send you off to find us two.' Samuel said as he watched the bird swoop down through the branches towards them. Alighting, with his own snack of a dormouse held in his talons, Swift spent a short while in their company. Samuel and Quicksilver sat in the shade and enjoyed the scent coming from a patch of nearby honeysuckle as Swift deftly devoured his meal.

'Give this to Willow for me?' Swift allowed Samuel to tie a tiny parcel of deerskin containing a chain of yellow flowers around his leg before lifting off into the air again and disappearing into the blue sky.

The rest of the day was uneventful, that night too. The two friends were soothed to sleep by an owl with huge orange eyes and a deep and velvety hoot.

On they went, the next day and the next. The footprints still leading on, Samuel's doubts still spinning in his mind.

Many days later, and when the sun was reaching its highest point, the companions came to a stop. The footprints had led them away from the river earlier in the morning but were now bringing them back to its bank. It seemed the river had taken a long curve through the forest and the one who had made these prints had continued on a straighter, more direct route. As the river came into sight between the trees, the twinkle of sunlight reflecting off the water, Samuel noticed that the footprints were fading. And then, they were gone altogether. Where there had been scorched dead earth now there were plants, flowers, and ferns, just the usual greenery and flora of the forest floor.

Sweeping around, neither Quicksilver nor Samuel was able to pick up the trail again. It had ended. It was over. Samuel sat on his backside on the ground and put his head in his hands.

'What a fool! Now what?' He looked up at Quicksilver, who was standing with his head on one side listening to the sounds of the river splashing over the rocks in its path. 'Do we go back for Willow and Fern and try to make a home of our own someplace? I thought we might find... I don't know. I hoped we might find some answers out here...'

Quicksilver glared at him and Samuel switched out of his self-pity to cast his senses around. Someone was nearby. By the edge of the river a short distance ahead, there was a figure. Samuel couldn't fix who it was, but there was something faintly familiar about him or her.

'Let's go and see who it is. We'll need to be careful, though – I've no idea if we'll be welcome around this part of the woods.' No sooner had he thought this to Quicksilver than he was on his feet again and moving alongside his friend through the trees

310

which bordered the river.

It was a while before the figure came into view. A boy, around nine or ten years old, was crouched by the edge of the river. He seemed to be washing something.

'Now hold still, silly! How can I get you smelling all nice if you wriggle so!' the boy giggled and a flash of something black and white squirmed in his hands and flicked water up over his head.

Getting a little closer Samuel caught a glimpse of what the lad was washing. It was a skunk!

'No, no! Not to be smelly tonight or you won't be allowed to sleep in with me.' The boy continued with the unwanted bath. The lad's shoulders hunched a little and his head tilted to one side as if he was trying to hear something, 'Is that you sneaking up on me, Fawn?' The boy called out. 'Naughty girly! I'll catch you and give you a bath with Pipit here!'

Samuel realised that it was his own presence that had been sensed by the youngster and so he stepped out from the cover of the trees to reveal himself. Still crouching, the boy turned on his heels and looking up, saw Samuel and Quicksilver standing there. His eyes grew large and the grip he'd had on his animal companion loosened, leaving the sneezing and bedraggled Pipit to scamper off into the forest for a dirt bath.

'Samwell! Is it really you, Samwell?'

It was Samuel's eyes that grew large in surprise next. Even Quicksilver was shocked. Leaping to his feet, hands and arms soaking with river water, the boy ran towards them.

'Big silver doggy too! Good to see you. *So* good to see you!'

The boy threw himself at Samuel and hugged him.

'You were always good to Beetle. I've missed you,' he said grinning up at Samuel with a smile that stretched almost ear to ear.

The boy was the same one whom Samuel had known in Crossways all that time ago. The boy whom everyone had turned their back on, even his parents.

'Beetle? That's your name now?' Samuel managed to say.

The boy danced around and around Samuel, looking him over. 'My new friends gave me it. Suits me doesn't it?' Beetle tickled Samuel, 'Beetle, beetle, tickle, tickle.'

'Yes,' Samuel laughed, 'it suits you very well.'

'You look different. You live in the lovely forest now too?' Beetle asked.

Samuel nodded.

'Good. You come and meet my new friends.' Beetle said and without waiting for a reply he linked his arm through Samuel's and led him away from the river.

'What about your skunk?' Samuel asked.

'Naughty Pipit, he'll just have to sleep out here tonight. I'm not allowed him in my bed if he won't take his bath. Stinky!' Beetle pinched his nose to demonstrate.

'Yes, I expect so.' Samuel agreed. Bath or not he couldn't imagine wanting to share sleeping space with that particular creature.

'It's *so* beautiful here isn't it?' said Beetle.

'It certainly is. How did you come to be here? I wondered what had become of you.' Samuel asked, as they walked along avoiding thorny bushes and winding their way between the trunks of a group of tall pines.

'I wasn't very happy in Crossways, the people there were mean to me. Except for you Samwell!' Beetle squeezed his arm affectionately. 'One day I decided to go into the trees to see if I could make a new home for myself, but the sun went down really quickly and I was all alone in the dark. It was scary, all the noises that the night animals make... I wasn't used to them.'

'It takes a bit of getting used to doesn't it?' Samuel agreed.

'Yes, but I love it now. Now I know most of the animals and the plants and trees. I know how to make my own fire and shelter and how to catch food. I know lots of things. But back then I knew none of these things. When the sun came up, after that first scary night alone in the woods, I was going to go back to Crossways. But when I tried, I couldn't figure out which way I'd come, I was lost. That's when Lichen found me.'

'Lichen?' Samuel asked.

'Yes, he took me home with him. I'm part of his family now. You'll see.' Beetle let go of Samuel's arm and skipped off between the trees. 'Come on! Follow me.' He laughed as he left ferns dancing and bobbing in his wake.

'Wait, Beetle... shouldn't you let your friends know we're coming first?' Samuel looked at Quicksilver. 'Shall we follow him?' Quicksilver gruffed his 'yes' and the pair ran after the boy.

The small group of tepees that they came to in the clearing up ahead looked similar to the ones back in the forest village they had left behind. There were around a dozen of them altogether, but this group did not hide away like a secret in the forest as Bruin's village did. Beetle's excited voice came from within one of the dwellings and next he was pulling someone by the hand out into the daylight.

'I hope they don't mind us arriving like this,' Samuel thought to Quicksilver.

Beetle brought the man towards them. The stranger was tall and lean, his bright yellow hair shining in the sun; the hair of a true forester. His dress was very similar to Samuel's own, his trousers and tunic of deerskin, his simple shoes of hide sole and uppers made of woven grass cord.

'Come and see!' Beetle was saying excitedly. 'This is him, this is the one I told you about.'

Samuel guessed that the tall man was older than himself by around ten years or so. There was no hint that he was displeased to see two strangers in his camp; in fact, his face was gentle and friendly.

'Welcome!' he called out to them. 'I'm Lichen.' The man reached them and took Samuel's hand in both of his own. 'Beetle tells me you're old friends from your time living in Crossways?'

314

'Yes, that's right, though I wasn't much use to him, I wish I had done more...' Samuel felt a little guilty.

Lichen lifted his hand to stop Samuel's self-recriminations and shook his head. 'He told me that you were kind to him and for that I'm grateful. Beetle is like a son to me now. Please, will you come and meet my family? We were about to eat, I'd be delighted if you and your companion would join us.'

Lichen's easy manner put both Samuel and Quicksilver at ease straight away. It would be good to spend time in the company of others, to catch up with Beetle and to meet new forest people. Perhaps this man, or someone in his group, would be able to help him find the markings in the woods again. Maybe they would know something about them; have a story of their own which might help him decide what to do next.

'We'd be honoured to meet your family,' Samuel answered politely.

'Very good,' Lichen grinned and squeezed Samuel's shoulder warmly. 'Come on in.'

After entering Lichen's tepee, it took a moment for Samuel's eyes to adjust from the bright sunshine outside before he could make out the three people who were already there.

'This is my wife, Hazel, and our daughters Pollen and Juniper. Pollen is the one on her mother's knee and the squirming one on the rug is Juniper.' Lichen introduced them, pride shining in his eyes.

Lichen's wife was very pretty, startlingly so. Her skin was

pale, her features delicate but the most striking thing about her was her hair... her jet-black, glossy hair that hung over her shoulders all the way to her waist.

'Pleased to meet you.' Samuel said as he sat down by the woman's side and smiled at Pollen.

'You've come a long way?' Lichen asked as he poured Samuel a cup of refreshing herbal tea and set down a bowl of water for Quicksilver.

'A few days travel through the forest, not too far.' Samuel answered, unsure whether it would be right to divulge exactly from where he had travelled. Although he was angry and confused about his uncle, he still felt drawn to keep the secret of the whereabouts of the forest village as he had been told to.

Lichen smiled at Samuel. 'You've come from the forest village of Bruin and his people?' he asked, but Samuel could tell by the tone of Lichen's voice that he already knew the answer to his question.

Samuel stopped drinking and looked over the brim of his cup at him.

'Don't worry, I recognised your cloak as soon as I saw it. Bluebell's handiwork. I have one myself, though it's too small for me now. I couldn't bear to get rid of it though; I'm keeping it for Pollen when she's big enough. I've tried to make myself another but I simply don't have the skill of that dear old cantankerous woman. Is she still going strong? I can't imagine how old she must be.' Lichen smiled.

'Yes, she's still well and still grumpy. You're also from Bruin's village?' Samuel asked, although he had already guessed that his dream of the woman with the ebony hair had been more than just a dream and that the woman in it, had been Lichen's wife Hazel. This could make Lichen the young man from his dream and as such, the outcast he had been looking for.

'Yes, I used to live there, a long time ago it seems.' Lichen looked over at his wife and they exchanged a sad smile. 'But we have a new little community here now. It's a story I'll tell you later. Let's eat first and then, after you've met the others, perhaps we could take a walk together?'

'Thank you, I'd like that.' Samuel agreed. He struggled to be still even though the excitement of having found this second settlement buzzed around inside him.

Beetle helped Hazel to prepare the plates of food for their meal whilst Lichen and Samuel played with Pollen and Juniper. Both girls had their father's golden hair but as Samuel played and tickled them he noticed that they had the same deep brown eyes of their mother. They were a mingling of both their parents; a coming together of forester and outsider.

After their meal was over Lichen and Samuel walked around the small camp, meeting the other inhabitants. All new faces to Samuel but each had the same blazing golden hair of the forest people. Lichen's mother Linnet, who seemed to live alone, had the tepee next to Lichen and his family. She was a striking woman, strong, tall and with piercing blue eyes like the sky on a brilliant and clear summer's day.

'I'm glad to meet you, Samuel.' Linnet said as she looked intently at him. 'May I?' she reached forward and put a hand on his shoulder. Leaning closer she stared into his eyes. Samuel felt something stirring in his mind as Linnet connected with him briefly. 'I thought so.' A gentle smile spread over her kind face. 'You're very like your mother, in both looks and spirit.'

Samuel was shocked. 'You knew her? My mother, Lily?'

Linnet nodded. 'She was a lovely little thing, like a shimmering butterfly. I'm sorry for your loss but I'm glad you've found your way back to the forest where you belong.'

Samuel longed to spend more time with Lichen's mother. He wanted to ask her questions, and not just about his mother, but he politely bid her goodbye as Lichen moved him on to meet the others.

When Samuel was later introduced to Willow's childhood friend Brook, the one who had been taken away from Bruin's village at such a young age, Samuel was further convinced that he had arrived at the right place. He felt sure that Lichen would hold some of the answers he so desperately wanted to learn.

Beetle and Pollen passed them by on their way back from washing the plates in the river. Lichen ruffled his adopted son's hair. 'Help your mother now and make sure you behave yourselves!' he called after them as they ran giggling towards home.

Lichen led the way between the trunks, Quicksilver and Lichen's animal companion, a grey-coated, amber-eyed wolf named Mist, following on behind.

'I'm so glad you found Beetle, he seems really happy here.' Samuel said.

'Yes, Beetle is a child of the forest, he was born to it. I'm sure it was the Man In Green that caused our paths to cross that day when I found him. He's a blessing on our family, on our whole group.' Lichen stopped and looked seriously at Samuel. 'But let's speak of you, Samuel. You're troubled. I feel that we have rather a lot to talk about, am I right?'

Samuel nodded. 'Yes, but I'm not sure where to start.'

'Well, how about telling me what you're doing so far from your new-found forest home? I sense you were looking for something, but what drove you to look? What did you hope to find? And what brought you here?'

They seemed like simple enough questions, but Samuel's head reeled at the thought of how to begin to answer any of them.

L i c h e n

Sitting with their backs against two broad trees, Lichen and Samuel faced each other. Lichen's eyes were intense as he gave Samuel his full attention. Samuel longed to trust this man. Everything he had seen of him so far showed him to be caring, loving and dependable; but hadn't he thought the same of Bruin not so long ago? How could he rely on his gut-instinct about Lichen after finding out how misguided he had been about Bruin for such a long time? And there were the stories, and his dreams; if this man Lichen was the one to whom the footprints led, the one who had created them, could he be trusted? Was he dangerous?

Unwilling to commit himself without first delving a little deeper, Samuel carefully brushed Lichen's mind with his own, looking for clues to his true personality. There seemed to be nothing deliberately hidden, no darkness or malice bubbling away below Lichen's friendly exterior.

Lichen looked into Samuel's eyes and smiled. 'Ah, you've been checking me out? Did I pass your test?'

Samuel reddened; 'I'm sorry, it's just that...' he was horribly embarrassed at having been found snooping. Usually when he did this, the person felt or sensed nothing. He had made no mistakes, had kept his contact brief and strictly reined in. The only explanation for his discovery was that Lichen must be far more in tune with the gift than anyone Samuel had come across before. Perhaps he was even more gifted than Samuel himself?

'That's all right. I understand. You don't know me and so want to discover if you can trust me. Really, I don't mind. I hope that you feel you can confide in me, but that's a decision for you to make.' Lichen continued to run his fingers through Mist's luxuriously long and thick fur. 'Your skills are very strong, Samuel. Bruin has taught you well,' Lichen added.

Samuel thought a moment before answering, 'Bruin taught me a great deal, but there are a few things I have picked up for myself.'

Lichen nodded, 'I thought so. Since leaving the forest village and coming to this place I've learned to develop my own gift too. There are many things I was never taught or shown back there that I've learned since, some of them quite powerful and surprising.'

Samuel sensed a snub against his uncle in Lichen's words. 'You feel that Bruin kept things from you?' he asked.

Lichen nodded. 'Yes. I think he keeps things from all of his people.'

'But why? Surely he would want us to be the best that we could be. To push our skills as far as they can go?'

Lichen shrugged. 'You would think so, but I'm not so sure, Samuel. I've wondered about it many times in the past. But perhaps I'm wrong, perhaps he simply didn't have some of the skills that you and I have discovered for ourselves. But...'

'Go on.' Samuel gently coaxed.

'Well, I can't help thinking that maybe he just needed to be sure none of his people would surpass him in skill.'

Samuel thought back and recalled the look on Bruin's face when he had won the last of The Tests. When his uncle had extinguished the flame that hovered in the air before him, Samuel had seen an expression that could have been one of satisfaction, which would have been understandable. But, if Samuel was more honest with himself the look his uncle had given the gathered people as they cheered all around him had held less honour than that; it had been more like smugness or even arrogance. Unable to put his finger on it at the time, Samuel had felt a little uncomfortable, as had Willow, he remembered.

Lichen could be right; to be the leader of his people it was possible that Bruin kept secret how to develop the more taxing skills linked to the gift so that he was the only one to hold that power. If that was true, then Samuel felt it was wrong. Knowledge, he believed, should be shared amongst all the people.

Mist and Quicksilver eyed one another with interest. Each animal had placed his head in the lap of their respective human

322

companion and was content to lie still and accept the affection being lavished on them.

Samuel made his decision to trust Lichen and began to speak.

Lichen listened, as Bruin had all that time ago, as Samuel told him about where he had lived, worked, about his mother, Quicksilver, and how he had become a member of the forest village. The next part of his story was harder as he had no way of knowing how Lichen would react to it; he told him the story that the children had been forbidden to tell of the young man who had cursed the village and left it with anger and hatred burning his way through the forest.

Lichen looked down at Mist then, and Samuel paused.

'Are you all right?' Samuel asked him.

'Yes, please go on. I'll wait until you've finished before I speak on that matter.' There was emotion in Lichen's voice but it sounded more like sadness than anger to Samuel, so he continued.

Next he gave an account of the story that had played out in his dream about the young lovers in the clearing; of the beautiful dark-haired woman and the young forest boy who had been dragged away from her. Samuel finished by telling what had gone on between himself and his uncle on the night he had decided to leave the village behind and follow the scorch-marks through the forest in the hope of finding some answers for himself.

Samuel's throat was dry by the end of all his talking and he watched Lichen around the side of his water-pouch as he took a long draw on it to quench his thirst. Lichen stayed quiet for a long while and Samuel let him be, sensing that he was thinking over all he had said and would respond to it in his own good time.

The air had cooled as the sun had curved her way back down through the sky. Tantalizing cooking smells gently wafted on the breeze. Back at Lichen's small settlement the evening meal was being prepared. Samuel had spoken for a long time; there had been much to tell. He watched as Lichen stretched his back against the tree and looked over at him.

'I am the one in both the story that the children tell and your dream. I think you guessed as much?' Lichen said.

Samuel nodded, though his heart fluttered like a startled bird in his chest as he waited for Lichen to continue.

'I was being trained by Bruin, as you were, to better my skills and learn how to become a good forester. I was good at hunting, connecting with the animal companion I had back then, and I could open the village archway. I enjoyed every moment of my training and never felt more proud than when Bruin would praise me for a hard day's work well done but then... I betrayed him. I did a terrible thing, going against his most important rule. To Bruin, what I did was so dreadful that when he found out about it he held me prisoner within my own home for many weeks. He wouldn't allow me to see or speak to anyone other than himself during all that time, not even my mother.'

'What was it that you did?' Samuel asked.

Lichen smiled sadly up at him, 'I think you know the answer to that too.'

Samuel thought back to his dream, the tender kisses and touches shared by the young forester and the girl. 'You fell in love... with an outsider,' he said.

'Yes. I was out in the forest hunting one day when I met Hazel. I had seen other outsiders before but they had only been hunters setting traps or men cutting down trees, people that had only confirmed all that I'd been told about the outsiders by Bruin. But Hazel was nothing like that. She wasn't doing anything wrong; she was enjoying the forest, the trees, the birdsong and the flowers. I tried to see the wickedness that I had been told about, the wickedness that was in each and every outsider, but when I looked into her mind I saw nothing there that was any less beautiful that her sweet face.'

Listening to Lichen talk of Hazel brought Willow to Samuel's mind.

Lichen continued. 'There was nothing I could do about how I felt. I knew how angry Bruin would be about what I did next. Bruin was both my leader and teacher and I respected him. I knew I should turn my back and walk away before I let things go any further but... I just couldn't.

'I watched her for a little while longer, but there was no

turning back. She had already captured my heart before I found the courage to step out from my hiding place into her sight and greet her for the first time. It didn't matter to me whether she had been born in the forest or outside of it, or whether she had fallen from the sky above, I knew that she was good, no one could ever tell me different. Thanks to the Man In Green, she felt the same way,' Lichen smiled, remembering. 'We met as often as we could, I told her about my life and of how my leader felt about her people. But the time came when our short meetings were no longer enough for us; we couldn't bear to be apart. We were going to go away together, leave both our families behind and start afresh somewhere in the forest... I don't know how he found out, but Bruin was the one in your dream who dragged me away from her that day. He kept me locked up in the forest village, took my animal friend away from me, spoke to me over and over about how I had been tricked; that Hazel was no good and that there were plenty of forester girls who would suit me better.

'There was no point in trying to make him understand. His hatred of the outsiders was too deep for him to believe that they weren't all bad, greedy and wicked. Eventually he could hold me no longer. What he was doing caused a rift in the village. Most of the families agreed with Bruin but there were a small number that believed that he was being unfair, that my love for Hazel was real and should be respected. They stood up against him and told him they were prepared to have her come live with us and accept her as my wife.'

Samuel imagined Bruin's anger at having his people, even if it was only a small group, rise up against his beliefs in that way. He had only seen a glimmer of the anger that his uncle felt for the outsiders, but to have his own people, people of the *forest*, who had been taught and nurtured by him, suggest that he allow Hazel into their very midst. To have a dark-haired outsider live in his village...

'He called the foresters together for a meeting,' Lichen continued. 'In front of them all he told me that I must give up this "outsider girl" or leave the village forever. I remember looking around at the faces of my friends; people I had known all my life and my heart ached at the thought of leaving them behind. But, in the end there was no real choice to make. I loved Hazel.'

'But you weren't the only one to leave that day, were you?' Samuel asked.

'No.' Lichen shook his head. 'All those who had stood up for me chose to leave too. The forest people that you met in our little camp are the ones that came away with me that day. Though our number has swelled a little since that time.' Lichen allowed himself a gentle smile at the thought of the children that had been born and were growing up in their new forest community.

'And what they said about the footprints through the forest...' Samuel ventured to ask but found himself unable to find the right words.

'I'm not proud of that.' Lichen's face darkened again. 'I would never have caused any damage to the woods on purpose, it was something that I couldn't control at the time.' Mist looked up at Lichen, their eyes locked and Samuel felt the connection between them like a buzz of energy in the air. Mist nudged Lichen's chin softly with the tip of his nose. 'We had gathered all our belongings together and said our goodbyes to the other foresters. I felt like my insides were being torn out. Bruin wouldn't hear another word from any of us, he even refused to watch us leave. He stood there, I remember it like it was only yesterday; he just stood there with his back to us as we left the forest village.

'We weren't even permitted to close the archway behind us – he said that he'd send one of his "own people" to do it, after we were gone.' Scratching Mist's snout Lichen took a deep breath before continuing. 'As we walked away through the trees all my emotions whirled through me. I felt like I was burning up inside. I did make those awful marks, but I didn't mean to and they didn't come from anger or hatred but from grief and sadness. I knew in my heart that Bruin was wrong about Hazel, and maybe about a whole lot of other things too, but I still loved and respected him and couldn't help feeling guilty for standing up against his teachings. Already I was mourning what I, and those who had joined me, was leaving behind. With every footfall further away from what had always been my home my anguish turned to heat, the heat to flames and every step I took flared and burned into the soil of the forest floor.'

Quietness fell between them. A lull filled only with the sounds of the river running nearby and the insects and birds of the forest.

'I don't know what to say, Lichen, I'm so sorry.' Samuel let go of Quicksilver's neck as the great dog got to his feet and shook himself vigorously.

'Thank you, Samuel, but you shouldn't feel sorry for me. What happened was a great sadness, I can't deny that, but what's come out of it has been both amazing and wonderful.' Lichen smiled over to Samuel and got to his feet.

'You mean your family?'

'My family, yes, but many more things too.'

They began to walk slowly back to camp, Mist and Quicksilver charged off together, anxious to get to the source of the delicious aromas first.

'We've come to live more closely with the forest, we're not hidden away for one thing, we live right in the midst of the Man In Green's land. Sometimes it can make things a little harder, but we all prefer it this way.'

'What about outsiders, do they bother you at all?'

'Occasionally some hunters pass our way but they've never troubled us. We're pretty far out here, too deep for most of them to take the time or effort to travel to.'

'You've never wanted to go back?' Samuel asked.

Lichen shook his head. 'We all miss the people we left behind but we're far more free here. Not just with where we live but also the *way* we live. Hazel became one of us straight away and we've learned things from her about the ways of the outsiders just as she's learned new things from us. That would never have been possible under Bruin's leadership. We're all the same deep inside, we all have the skills of the forest people no matter where we live, it's just that the outsiders have forgotten how to use them. Their gift is locked away inside them but it *is* still there, forgotten, but still there.'

'You mean anyone can learn to use the skills we have? Whether they're an outsider or forester?'

'Yes, of course.' Lichen replied.

'But how can that be? If the Man In Green is the master of the forest but the outsiders were born outside of the forest...'

'Yes Samuel, but think back. Where did life first begin?'

Samuel shrugged, 'In the forest?'

'Yes. We're taught that when this world began there was the forest and *only* the forest. It covered all the lands as far as you could see and further still, all the way to the great oceans. Every human creature alive is descended from the ones who lived in that time. Their existence was a simple one, as ours is now, and they were mostly content with their lives. But some of them chose to try a new way, they cleared vast areas of woodland, they built bigger and bigger homes and began to live in a very different way. They turned their backs on the old

330

customs and the skills that had been given to them by the Man In Green, but they were still "forest people" just living outside of the forest. In my opinion Samuel, there are no "outsiders" we are all "foresters" some of us have simply chosen to forget that fact.'

Samuel felt as if a thick blanket had been removed from his eyes. If everyone was in possession of the skills of the foresters then why couldn't they be taught how to use those skills? When his grandfather Alder had approached the villagers of Crossways he had told them what they should do, but he had never explained that they could learn how to be in harmony with the forest by rediscovering the skills that lay deep within themselves. This was the answer, the way forward. If Beetle and Hazel and Lichen's children... *and even me...* thought Samuel, if *we* can all learn to use our skills then we can teach those who live outside of the forest to do the same.

'I sense your mind is working hard, Samuel. You have plans to change the world, I think?' Lichen smiled and put his arm around Samuel's shoulder.

'I can only try. Surely it would be a better way than Bruin's? But if I must begin with the village of Crossways... Well, I'm not sure that they will listen to me on my own, what with my past, and the lies they've told about me. Will you help me, Lichen?' Samuel asked.

Lichen took a deep breath and lifted his face to the sky. 'Well now, there's a question. If I can... yes, I will.' He squeezed the back of Samuel's neck lightly before taking his hand away, 'Come, let's eat and we can discuss this with the others.'

The Plan

When the meal was over and the children were asleep in their beds, Lichen asked for the others to gather and listen to what Samuel had to say. Reluctantly Samuel had stood before them and given a brief outline of what he had told Lichen earlier in the day. He finished by asking if they would be willing to help him to talk to the people of Crossways.

'What makes you think they'll listen to us? You know what happened to your grandfather, why would it be any different this time?' came one voice.

'I don't believe the outsiders had any idea of what happened to my grandfather and his people. They killed wild animals that were approaching their village; they thought they were protecting themselves and their families. How could they have known the effect it would have on our people? They were never shown or told of our abilities, they were ignorant of our connection with the animals.' Samuel paused a moment whilst the small group discussed this quietly before he went on.

'And I can't promise that they'll listen to us this time, but we'll be approaching them in a completely different way: we'll be *offering* them something. My grandfather tried to bully them into changing, he never gave them the opportunity to witness our ways or understand fully the differences which they could make to their own lives, or that of the forest, by developing these skills for themselves.'

'But their ways bring them what they want quickly and easily,' said a young woman. 'They won't want to take the time to learn how to do things properly in a way that doesn't harm the forest.'

'That's what we've all been taught to believe, but what if it's not true? Bruin's hatred for the outsiders, because of what happened to his father, sister and friends, has tainted all our views about what the outsiders might be willing to learn. Look at Hazel, look at me, even young Beetle, you've accepted us into your homes with love and understanding and we've grown strong in our skills; in the gift, yet we came from the 'outside'.' A murmuring went around the people.

'That's different,' said an older man. 'You were all good-hearted, the Man In Green had given you a love of the forest which we could see in you. Hazel, Beetle and you were part-forester already.'

'And how many more people could there be in Crossways or the villages, towns and cities further away that may feel just as we do but need your guidance to realise the truth? Do we just ignore them and carry on as we are? How long will the forest last if we do that?' Samuel's heart was quickening pace, he glanced around the faces in front of him. 'Maybe the forest will remain much as it is now for the rest of your lifetime,' Samuel pointed to the oldest man in the gathering, 'or yours,' a woman around the same age as Lichen. 'Perhaps there will still be enough of the woods left for us to hide ourselves away in when you're an old man,' this time Samuel pointed to the youngest lad who sat by the fire, 'but what about your children or their children? What will be left for them? Will the Man In Green have a single tree to care for if the destruction goes on?'

Perspiration stood out on Samuel's forehead, he wiped it away with the back of his hand. Quicksilver got to his feet and padded over to stand by his friend's side.

Only the sounds of the logs crackling in the fire could be heard as Lichen and his friends thought over what Samuel had said.

'We are all the same deep down,' Samuel continued, more calmly this time. 'Maybe a bit of understanding and patience will bring us to a place where we can live in harmony together, and with the forest. Isn't it at least worth a try? I've told you what Bruin means to do, he will flatten the village of Crossways and anyone who gets in his way, I have to try to turn things around before he does that, but I need your help. Please.'

Linnet stared up at Samuel from where she sat nearby. Her piercing blue eyes tinged with the orange glow from the licking flames of the fire. As he returned her look, she got to her feet.

'I will stand with you, Samuel,' she said.

The gratitude he felt for her gesture made his head spin, his heart soared in anticipation.

Lichen was the next to stand. 'And I.'

One by one each and every member of the gathering got to their feet and pledged their help to Samuel in whatever way they could.

That night Samuel was given space to sleep in Lichen's home. By the dancing low flames of the fire in the centre of the tepee Samuel watched as Hazel got little Juniper ready for going back down to sleep after her late night feed. Lichen was still outside bidding goodnight to his friends.

'I hope you're not angry with me, Hazel,' said Samuel.

'Angry? Why would I be angry with you?' Hazel looked at him quizzically.

'You've got such a lovely place here and I've arrived and managed to turn everything upside down in one single day; getting your friends and family to come away with me to try to sort out this situation. I'm worried you might wish I'd never found your home.'

Hazel turned and placed a hand on his arm, 'Samuel, what you said at the fire about us all needing to do something to try to preserve our forest home for our children and our children's children was right. How could I be angry with you when you bring us the hope of that? I want the best for Pollen and

Juniper and, if the Man In Green wills it, their descendants when the time comes. I'll be proud to know my husband is standing up for what's right and good, and that you'll be with him.'

Samuel fell silent at her kind words and looked down at the sheepskin rug that Juniper lay on.

The thick fleece was turned to the ground to prevent any chill getting through to the baby as she slept. The skin-side of the rug was uppermost and silky smooth to the touch. Samuel ran his fingers over part of a faded pattern or picture that had been burned into the surface of it a long time before.

'What is this? Does it mean something?' he asked Hazel.

'It's a story rug.' Hazel answered. 'It was Linnet's. She brought it with her from her old home and gave it to me as a present when Pollen was born. If you don't mind holding her for me, I'll show it to you properly.' Hazel held out her youngest daughter to him, her chubby legs kicked at the air. Samuel accepted her carefully.

Hazel turned the rug so that they could both look at it straight on. 'Linnet told me that this rug tells the story of when Alder and the others went to meet the outsiders,' she ran her fingers over each picture as she explained it. 'This is them leaving the forest village.' Hazel pointed to the group of tiny stick figures with the archway of the forest village, easily recognisable to Samuel, visible in the background. 'This is their walk through the woods towards Crossways.' This picture had trees, animals and birds, all in harmony and looking peaceful in the forest.

Samuel studied this picture carefully. 'Who is this up here?' Samuel pointed out the head of an extra figure peeking down at the party of foresters through the leaves of a nearby tree.

'Well spotted, most people don't see him. I'm told that it's supposed to be the Man In Green watching over them on their journey.'

Samuel nodded. 'Did Linnet say if the Man In Green had sent them on this mission?'

'Not exactly, but she told me what *she* thought about that.' Hazel hesitated.

Samuel was anxious to hear the opinion of Lichen's mother, but didn't want to push Hazel into telling him if she was uncomfortable about it. 'Can you tell me?' he asked gently.

'Well, she believes that they went with his blessing but that the outcome was due more to how Alder handled the situation than what the Man In Green would have had them do.' Hazel looked curiously at Samuel. 'I guess she feels pretty much the same way as you do about it.'

Samuel hoped that was true. He was already grateful to Lichen's mother, for being the first one to support him after his speech at the gathering, but to have her even more firmly on his side was an encouraging thought. 'Please, do go on,' he told Hazel.

'This next picture shows the forest people talking to the

outsiders, and this one is when they were forced back into the forest. Here it shows them sitting in a circle and sending their animal companions into Crossways.'

There were no more pictures on the skin and Samuel was grateful for that, knowing that all that could be added was the sad and awful massacre that had followed.

'It used to be the tradition to make these story rugs to preserve important events from the past. I find this one terribly sad though; I'd much rather have one which celebrated something happy and joyful.' Hazel mused.

Hazel took Juniper from Samuel's arms and laid her back down on the story rug. The little girl, who was now sound asleep, raised her eyebrows as if trying to open her heavy eyelids but the weight of sleep kept them shut. She made small wet noises as she suckled her thumb a few times before falling deeply into dreams once more.

'What are these markings up here?' Samuel asked, noticing for the first time a number of lines and dots at the very top of the rug, well above Juniper's head.

'Linnet told me that was the sign Alder saw in the sky. He believed that it was telling him that it was time to prepare his people to go to the village of the outsiders.'

'The sign?' Samuel looked more closely at the markings.

'Yes, the star-shower. There was another one last year, didn't you see it?'

Samuel froze. *The star-shower.* He remembered back to

that night in the woods when he and Quicksilver had watched the wonderful streaming stars above them in the night's sky. It had been the very next day when they had met Ash and arrived at the forest village. Something his uncle had said when they first met had always puzzled Samuel, but now he felt sure what he had meant. Bruin had said that he had been 'expecting' Samuel. Samuel had put it down to some skill or perception that his uncle had, but now it made perfect sense; Bruin believed that Samuel's arrival had been foretold by the star-shower – a sign that the time had come again to prepare for action against the outsiders and that Samuel was to play a part in that. Hadn't Willow told him that Bruin had meant him to be the new leader of the forest people? Had Bruin thought that he might not return from the new assault on Crossways and was hoping to leave his people with a new and well-trained leader, one of his own line; his own blood?

'Are you all right, Samuel?' Hazel asked, her face lined with concern.

'Yes, I'm sorry. It's just that things are slipping into place now.' Samuel felt panicked; they were going to have to move faster than he'd thought.

After he had left Bruin and the forest village behind, there was no reason for his uncle to wait any longer before moving on Crossways. After their angry conversation the night before he left, Bruin must have been outraged that the very one whom he had been preparing to take his place had stood against him to protect the outsiders. Surely Bruin would now want to get to Crossways before Samuel could warn them of his intentions? The last thing his uncle would want would be for the outsiders to be prepared for his attack. That must have been why he had come into the forest to look for him with Finch and Rowan; to take him back before he could do anything to stop his plans.

Samuel got shakily to his feet, 'I think I'll take in a little fresh air before I turn in for the night, do you mind?'

'Not at all, I'll see you in the morning. Are you sure you're all right?'

'Yes... thank you.' Samuel lied.

'Well, if you're sure. Goodnight, then,' and she kissed him lightly on the cheek.

Lichen entered the tepee just at that moment. 'Hey! I know you for one day and you're trying to steal my beautiful wife!' he grinned.

'Lichen, behave yourself.' Hazel flicked her husband's arm with the back of her hand.

Lichen looked at Samuel and noticed that the colour had drained from his face. 'You all right there?'

'Yes, but... would you take a short walk with me?'

Lichen thought of protesting, it was fairly cool outside now, a light mist was settling and he was tired, but something in Samuel's eyes had him nodding in agreement instead.

Samuel rushed into his explanation as soon as they were clear of Lichen's home.

'So you see, I think that Bruin will move on Crossways any time now. We'll need to leave as soon as possible.'

'We can't all just up and walk out of camp tomorrow, Samuel. What about the children? Who's going to care for them?'

'We don't *all* need to go,' Samuel reasoned.

'No, but we do need time to prepare, to think out what we'll do once we get to Crossways, even time to pack what we need for the journey.'

'But there's no time! Don't you see? If we don't get there before Bruin and his group it could be too late to make a difference. After he carries out what he plans to do none of us will be safe. The outsiders will hunt us down like animals, they won't care that we had no hand in Bruin's plans. There'll be no turning back, the forest will be lost.'

Lichen placed a hand on Samuel's shoulder. 'All right, all right. I understand what you're saying. But we must get our rest tonight. There's nothing to be done right now. A good night's rest will help us more than careering off into the forest unprepared and without having slept properly. Tomorrow I'll choose those who are best suited to travel with us. We'll need the ones who are most blessed with the gift and who are fittest for a hard and fast trek. But Samuel,' he turned Samuel to face him, 'you *must* try to rest tonight. Calm your mind.'

Samuel nodded. 'Yes, you're right. Tomorrow then, thank you Lichen.'

Crossways

Something instinctive took over Samuel's mind and body that night. As he listened to Hazel's gentle voice humming the same lullaby his own mother used to sing to him, he managed to fall into a deep sleep despite his whirling thoughts. His mind stilled, his body relaxed, and the full benefit of the night's sleep was put to good use, recharging every part of him for what lay ahead.

Beetle desperately wanted to go along and Samuel had felt terrible when he'd overheard the young lad's sobs as Lichen explained to him the reasons why he couldn't. Immediately after waking, Lichen had gathered those members of his group whom he had chosen to take along on the journey. They had listened carefully to Lichen's explanation of why there was now such an urgency to approach Crossways. Samuel was immensely grateful to discover that each one of them had agreed to leave with them that same day.

Samuel had witnessed good organisation and quick action before, back in Bruin's village, but still he was impressed with how well Lichen's people worked together to organise themselves for the journey. Before the sun climbed to its full height in the sky, the party was assembled, equipped and ready for the off. Partners, friends and children were bidden farewell and, having eaten early, the group of six left Lichen's home in the forest at a good pace.

'Do you feel that our number will be enough?' Lichen asked Samuel as he plotted their direction by familiar landmarks and the position of the sun in the sky.

'I hope so, we can only do our best and try to get there first. In any case I'm very grateful to you all.' Samuel spoke loud enough for the other members of the moving party to hear him. He was answered with words of encouragement and support.

Their party consisted of Lichen, his mother Linnet, Samuel himself and three others; Shrew, Lark and Spruce. Shrew was a small woman with dark eyes full of quiet intelligence who'd had to gently prise the fingers of her young twins from her clothes as she had left them behind with their father. Lark, a young man older than Samuel by a few years, had proved himself deeply blessed with the gift and had been specially chosen to go along with them by Linnet. And then there was Spruce; an older and extremely fit forester, who had left his ailing wife in the care of Hazel back home. As there had been so little time to get acquainted and get moving, Samuel had only been briefly introduced to these people. They were strangers to him, as he was to them, and it filled him with a great sense of hope that these people would leave so much behind to join him.

Lichen said that the journey to Crossways could be done in three days if they moved swiftly, slept little and stopped seldom. It would be a hard trek to cover such an expanse of ground in this time, but they would if Samuel thought it necessary? Samuel did.

'I've no idea how many Bruin will take with him or when he'll leave, but if we have any chance of getting there first to warn the outsiders of his intentions, then we should do our best.' Samuel explained.

'You realise that even if we make it there first, they may not listen to us?' Lichen asked.

'Yes, I know. But we have to try.'

Lichen nodded.

The party moved on. Sweat flying from them as they made their speedy progress through the forest, walking as quickly as they could over rough ground, accelerating into a jog through the more flat or open areas. They were moving like one purposeful animal towards their goal, Samuel hoped that this togetherness would last and stand them in good stead for what was to come.

Setting a fire and putting together a camp each night was done quickly and efficiently, each member of the team knowing what they needed to do and getting on with it, no time was wasted. They were all up and on the move again long before the sun was more than a sliver through the great trees. Even though they were fit and healthy, they all still felt the strain building in their muscles, yet no one complained.

At last they grew close to Crossways in the velvety dark on the night of their third day of travelling; they had made good time. Samuel had hoped that he and Lichen's group could spend the night in the clearing where his mother was buried. But when he eventually found their special place, having had trouble recognising it as so many of the trees round about had been felled and dragged away, he saw that this would be impossible. The outsiders had destroyed so much of the woodland that separated his mother's clearing from the edge of Crossways that the light from their evening fire would easily be seen by anyone looking in their direction from the village.

Samuel put down his pack and walked to the great oak that stood over his mother's grave. Its huge broad trunk had suffered some horrible damage. Deep and ugly chop-marks covered one side at waist-height. The yawning gouges were just visible in the gloom, scarring its ancient beauty. It seemed that someone who knew little about how to handle an axe had tried to bring the massive tree down or, Samuel thought with horror, perhaps they had just been practicing their swing. Samuel traced the wounds on the tree's trunk with his fingers, remembering how his mother had danced around in the shadow afforded by the tree's vast branches in happier times.

'Samuel? Something's wrong?' Linnet's voice came from behind him.

'This was my mother's favourite tree,' he explained. 'This is where I laid her to rest.' He gestured to the ground beneath.

Thankfully his mother's grave remained undiscovered. Samuel was glad that he hadn't marked it in any way that might have caused the outsiders to wonder what or who lay there. Placing a hand on the dry earth at his feet he sensed that her remains were still there. Her soul had long since flown free to mingle with the new life of the forest animals and plants; Samuel could feel her presence all around him.

'I'd hoped we could stay here tonight and go into Crossways tomorrow, but I see now that we can't, Samuel said to the group. We'll need to backtrack a bit to a safer, more concealed spot.'

Samuel recalled how his mother and he had walked through the beautiful piece of woodland that had separated the place where their wooden hut had stood and where their special clearing lay. Many small forest animals had lived there; rabbits, squirrels, birds and there had been dozens of different types of grasses and flowers to see. Now it was all but gone. Destroyed and flattened. The area reduced to little more than a tree line; a band of around three or four trees in depth was all that now sheltered the clearing from the group of wooden huts that Samuel could make out in the near distance. How many trees had the outsiders cut down in the past year? A thousand? Ten thousand? If they had been felling this ferociously all the way around the edge of the great forest, it could be many more than that. Suddenly the problem facing the survival of the forest loomed in its horrendous magnitude. He closed his eyes and rubbed his eyelids with the heels of his hands.

'I don't think we'll be camping anywhere tonight, Samuel.' Lichen said.

Samuel stared up at his new friend then turned his face to look back towards the huts again.

And froze.

Quicksilver uttered a guttural groan by his side as he too sensed trouble.

A small fire had been lit between two of the huts. Standing beside it a group of shadowy figures were silhouetted by its glow. As Samuel and the others looked on, these figures moved apart, darting quickly between the huts. Another fire bloomed into life, then another and still another.

'Oh no, we're too late. They've started.' Samuel groaned. 'We must stop them!'

Samuel called out to the others to join him as he began to run towards the place where six fires were now beginning to blossom and heighten, jagging their yellow brilliance into the blue-black sky. Dropping all their belongings, Samuel's five companions ran after him through the trees and headed towards the wooden huts.

As they got closer, the sounds of people awakening to the danger in their midst, came to them on the smoky air. A few of the huts had now caught light and the figures of those who had started them, Samuel counted six in all, were standing with their arms outstretched before them. They seemed to be willing the flames on.

Samuel thought back to the final Test when Bruin had controlled the single flame. The six small fires had now grown together and combined their force to form a moving wall of flames. Was Bruin going to use his gift to push this wall right through the village of Crossways? Did he possess the strength of will for that?

The fire moved on, quickly eating its way through the huts, driving out the families who had been sleeping inside and sending them fleeing screaming through the night towards the main street of the village. Samuel's teeth juddered painfully in his jaw as he thundered on as fast as he could.

'Bruin! Bruin, stop!' he screamed, first at the top of his voice and then with his mind.

The tallest of the six figures turned for a moment and saw Samuel with the others as they ran to intercept them. Samuel caught hurried orders being passed from Bruin to his five companions and saw these others turning to face them, leaving their leader to concentrate his will and energy into the destruction of the village.

Each of the five foresters had the uppermost parts of their faces hidden by grotesque masks. Masks of bone, horn and animal-skin, daubed with what looked very like blood. Samuel's horror and confusion blurred his ability to identify them properly, but he sensed that he knew them all and tried desperately to communicate with them.

'Stop him! For the sake of the Man In Green you *must* stop Bruin. He's lost his way; the loss of his family has driven him to this. If you help him he may cause the death of many innocent people. You must know that this is wrong!' he pleaded with them to see sense.

But the five held their ground. As Samuel, Lichen and the others came within an arm's breadth of their opponents' line, they came up against a wall of resistance that stood invisibly in the air between themselves and the masked foresters.

'What is *this*?' Lichen asked, feeling the air in front of him.

'I don't know, it must be something that Bruin's taught them,' Samuel replied. 'I've never experienced it before. I don't know how to fight it, we'll have to persuade them to let us pass.' He turned again to face the five. 'If you won't stop him yourselves, then please, let us through.'

All five figures were blocking their minds to any intrusion and although Samuel felt sure he could break through their defences, the panic he could hear, that was now coursing through the village, was distracting him and dampening his gift.

'Please, this isn't right. You know it.' Samuel tried again. 'Bruin may be our leader but that doesn't mean we have to agree with this... If anyone dies this night it will be *murder*, pure and simple. There are old people and children in this village who won't be able to escape the flames. Please, stop this and help me find another way. There *has* to be another way.'

Samuel saw one of the five falter. Their arms, which had been held out in front to concentrate and combine their strength and gift with the others, now drooped a little. Then she allowed them to fall limply by her sides. The other four cast this deserter a glance. Their macabre ghoulish masks turned questioningly towards this one.

'He's right. You know he is,' this one said in a defeated and miserable voice. 'Bruin's our leader but on this... he's wrong.' And the forester reached up to remove her mask.

'Willow!' Samuel cried as he saw her face revealed.

Willow threw her mask down and turned to the others. 'We need to help Samuel to stop Bruin before anyone gets hurt.'

The four remaining foresters, who were still holding the barrier in place, now let their arms fall. One by one they threw off their masks and Samuel saw their identities; Rowan, Flint, Finch and Heather.

The strange resistance in the air disappeared and Samuel ran to hug Willow and greet the others. There was no time for introductions but Samuel could see from the look on Rowan's face that he, at least, recognised Linnet and Lichen well enough.

'Are you all right?' Samuel asked as he kissed Willow's face. There were tears on her cheeks.

'Yes, I'm fine. I'm sorry Samuel, I didn't know what to do, Bruin told us we had to follow him and do as he said. He's been like a father to me for so long...'

'Shh, it's all right, I understand. Let's go and see what we can do to help now, there'll be time to talk later.'

Willow nodded and the group of eleven ran through the wake of devastation caused by the advancing wall of fire.

The flames were unbelievably high now. They licked and tore at the sky; the sound of them devouring everything in their path both deafening and terrifying. Wood crackled and spat as the flames began to greedily eat their way through the shops on the main street.

Samuel could see Bruin up ahead. His figure was glowing with an inner-heat and energy as he walked slowly behind the wall of flames pushing it on with his every step. The soles of his boots had all but melted away, smoke twirled up from the remnants but he didn't seem to notice. The intense heat was enough to blister the skin on Samuel's face as he stood yelling at his uncle from ten or so paces behind him.

How can he bear to be so close to that heat?

Samuel couldn't understand it. His uncle seemed to be almost a part of it, that energy and power, that dreadful and insatiable hot beast. Together the eleven tried to communicate with Bruin, they sent him mind-messages begging him to stop. They pleaded with him to cease his attack, but it was no good.

On and on, slowly advancing, pushing, Bruin moved forward. Exasperated, Samuel lifted a heavy rock and threw it at his uncle's back to try to break the trance he was in. The rock hit Bruin hard between the shoulder blades but still he moved on, completely oblivious to it.

'It's like he's become part of the fire, I don't know how to stop him. What can I do?' Samuel screamed to Lichen over the noise of the flames.

'You have to take the power away from him, Samuel! Somehow, you must take control of the firewall.' Lichen shouted back.

Samuel looked into Lichen's eyes, 'But... I don't know how, I can't...'

'I think you *can*, Samuel. I think you're the only one of us who can.'

Willow looked in horror from Lichen to Samuel. 'It might kill him!' she screamed. 'Look what it's doing to Bruin, you can't ask him to try it, you can't!'

Samuel took her hands in his. 'I've got to try, Willow, it's what I came here to do. Keep hold of Quicksilver, don't let him follow me.'

Willow could see the determination in Samuel's eyes and knew there was no point arguing with him. She kissed him hard on the mouth and took hold of Quicksilver around the neck. Sensing that his human friend was going to put himself even closer to that scorching heat, Quicksilver pushed forward and Willow had to be joined by the rest of the group as she struggled to prevent the dog from going after Samuel.

Samuel did his best to shut out the sound of Quicksilver's terrible mournful bark as he left the others behind and forced himself to walk forward, closer to the inferno. He could feel his hair, eyebrows and eyelashes singe in the intensity of the heat, but still he moved onward.

The sweat that coated his skin from head to toe evaporated under the fierce temperature as he closed his eyes and became as one with the fire. He felt its hunger, its unquenchable desire to devour and destroy, and he felt his uncle's will pushing it on.

There was no point trying to connect with Bruin any longer, he was lost now, deep inside the power of the flames. Lichen was right; Samuel would have to take control of the fire from Bruin and then find a way to stop it destroying the village.

Samuel could see nothing of the street on the other side of the towering wall of flame but he could feel the fear and terror of the people running from it. He focussed on his will to help them survive this, as he slipped into the life force of the fiery beast.

The heat of the fire seemed to fall away almost immediately. The flames still burned as robustly before him but their effect on his body diminished as he joined with its energy. He felt its power, a sensual delicious power that was infectious and consuming.

Samuel felt bigger than himself, bigger than anything; he could do anything he wanted, he believed that he was in complete control. He could have the wall of fire turn right around and send it coursing through the forest instead, if he so desired. To be so powerful that he could burn down every last tree in the great forest, the forest that had stood since the beginning of time. Such power, such brilliance. He pictured the scene in his mind, saw the trees crackling and splintering under his mighty command.

No! The fire is trying to control me. I must fight it. I must!

Samuel turned his mind away from the strange impulses that rippled through him and sensed his uncle's control slipping as he tired. Bruin was losing his grip on the energy of the fire and Samuel was taking over, like accepting the reins of a stampeding horse from a weary rider.

Forcing himself deeper into the orange-yellow element that seemed to be all around him, Samuel came to the sudden realisation that he now truly had control over the flames. Somewhere outside of himself he sensed that Bruin had stumbled and fallen to the ground, unconscious and barely alive. Samuel could not allow his mind to be distracted; he could spare his uncle neither a look nor any help. He had to trust that his companions would pull Bruin away and take care of him. The anger and hunger of the fire continued to fight against Samuel's will. It bucked against the restraints that he now began to put on it. It jostled like a wilful child and tried to persuade him to let it continue on its fiery path.

You hate this village, Samuel. It never did you any good... why not let me wipe it from the face of the earth? The fire seemed to hiss in his ears in its lulling snakelike voice.

'*NO! You must stop now. You* will *stop now!*' Samuel shrieked back at the wanton creature that his uncle had ordered to be unleashed.

The fire struggled against Samuel's powers, against the full force of the human's gift but found itself to be no match for him. Wailing and cursing, the flames stopped their advance and, held stationary by the power of Samuel's mind, began to grow smaller, fraction by fraction, as the fuel in their immediate vicinity wore thin. Forcing his red and swollen eyes open, Samuel could see that the wall of flames was now only as high as his chest. On the other side of it he could see many of the villagers who had stopped to stare at the awe-inspiring sheets of flame as they dampened and grew smaller. Men, women and children stood open-mouthed, some crying, some laughing hysterically, as they looked at Samuel's badly blistered face through the dying heat-haze.

'It's all right. It's stopping now. You're all right.' Samuel managed to shout to them as he continued to force the fire to the ground.

Behind him, Bruin had been pulled clear and was now cradled in the arms of Linnet. Tears streaked her soot-covered cheeks, her brilliant blue eyes sparkling as she watched Samuel.

At last the flames were extinguished. The living flame-ridden beast that had been set loose on Crossways was dead. Smoke trailed up in winding plumes from the debris left in its wake and at last Samuel felt that he could let go, could allow his mind to fall quiet.

His legs gave way and he collapsed in a smouldering heap on the ground.

A man with a shotgun immediately stepped forward and aimed the twin barrels at Samuel where he lay looking weakly up at him.

'NO!' Willow screamed and ran to stand in front of Samuel sheltering him from harm.

'Get out of the way, girl, or I swear I'll shoot you first and do that freak right after.' The man's face was smeared with blood that oozed down from a head wound. He had sustained an injury during his escape from the flames.

'Father! Don't! I know him; he's the one I told you about, the one who helped me in the forest.'

Samuel's sight was blurred and doubled and he heard things only faintly, as if from a long way off, but he recognised the voice as Daniel's, the boy he had pulled out of the animal pit.

The young lad came forward through the crowd and pushed the muzzle of his father's gun away from Willow.

'Don't, lad, you don't know what you're doing! He tried to kill us, all of us!'

'Don't be a fool, Father! Can't you see he stopped it?' Daniel answered. 'Can't you all see that he stopped the flames?' Daniel called his question to the gathered villagers of Crossways.

The man looked down at his son who was leaning on the crutch that Samuel had made for him.

'But he's... not *right*. It isn't natural what he can do.'

'Is that any reason to kill him? I'm telling you he saved my life out there in the woods and he's saved a great many more here tonight. If you insist on shooting him then you'll need to kill me first.'

Daniel shuffled forward. His father made a grab for the boy's sleeve but the youngster shook him off and turned to face his father defiantly as he stood by Willow's side. His father stared at him for a moment longer before lowering his gun and letting it drop to his side.

Willow fell to her knees, 'Samuel, oh Samuel, how bad is it? How do you feel?' she asked gently. The sight of his poor burnt face hurt her heart.

'A bit crispy, but I'll live, I think.' Samuel tried to smile, but it hurt too much.

A voice whispered faintly inside his mind and it took all his concentration to make out the words through the fog of pain that was flooding through his body.

It was Bruin.

'Samuel, hear me, boy. I'm so sorry. I was wrong, forgive me... I...' Bruin's voice faded into silence.

'Willow, help me over to Bruin, quickly.'

'You shouldn't move, Samuel, you're not fit to be moved...' Willow protested.

'Now, Willow! He's dying, I need to touch him, help me!' Samuel struggled to find the energy to get up.

With fresh tears streaming down her filthy face, Willow

helped Samuel to stand and supported him as best she could as he shuffled his burnt and bloodied feet over to where Bruin lay.

Linnet looked up as Samuel let himself buckle at the knees and come to rest by his uncle's side.

'Is he... going?' Linnet asked him, seeming to know that Samuel could tell such a thing.

'Not if I can help it.' Samuel managed to reply, then placed his charred hands on his uncle's chest.

Bruin opened his eyes and saw Linnet's face above him.

'Lin... my Linnet. How good it is to see you.' Bruin hacked out an awful smoke-filled cough. 'Is Lichen well? Is my boy well?' he asked.

'I'm here, Father.' Lichen replied, and those of the gathering too young to know or to remember their leader's son, who had been banished from the secret forest village all those years before, looked on dumbstruck.

Samuel had guessed as much, somewhere along the way, but this confirmation of his belief only served to boost his gift and he hoped with all his soul that he would have enough energy to save his uncle.

Closing his eyes to the scene of the long overdue family reunion, Samuel forced himself to block out all else, and concentrate his mind on the life force held within both himself and his uncle. The red energy that weakly flickered within Bruin was frighteningly low, but his own was little better. He would be unable to do this alone.

Samuel looked around the group of foresters, 'I need you all to trust me. I don't have time to explain this to you but I need you to link hands.'

They exchanged puzzled looks but did as they were asked.

Many of the inhabitants of Crossways had edged closer and peered at this odd spectacle. Samuel paid them no heed and wasted no time in channelling the linked energy into his uncle's body. Taking only what he needed of the life force from each of them, Samuel watched as the energy within Bruin's body began to glow brighter and stronger.

Opening his eyes Samuel looked into the face of his uncle, the pair exchanged a weak smile before Samuel found himself slipping sideways into blackness.

Samuel had taken none of the energy to help himself.

The smoke, darkness and stench of burnt timber drifted away on a breath of sweetly scented forest air. The breeze ruffled through Samuel's hair as he sat up and found himself in his mother's special clearing, below her beloved old tree. The forest was full of life again, the trees as healthy and abundant as he remembered, and the ancient old oak tree showed no sign of having been harmed. Samuel could hear his mother singing, and sure enough there she was dancing through the flowers, hand-in-hand with the Man In Green.

'Isn't it beautiful, sweetheart?' she called to him as she floated by, her hair streaming out like liquid gold behind her.

'You've done well, Samuel.' The leaf-covered Man In Green called to him as he twirled Samuel's mother giddily, making her giggle. 'But there's still much for you to do. She'll be here for you when it's your time but you've a great many years left in you yet, young Samuel.' His vivid green eyes sparkled with mischief and hidden secrets. 'It won't be easy, but I think you'll manage. I've faith in you boy.' The Man In Green swung Samuel's mother gracefully over one of his arms so that the small of her back lay curved against it, her head tilted back, her hair splayed out over the grass.

'Go well, my love, and take care of that pretty girl of yours.' His mother said and blew him a kiss. Samuel spun off once more into the darkness.

When Samuel next awoke he found himself staring into another pair of vivid green eyes.

Guess it was *my time after all.* He thought. *For here's the Man In Green come back for me.*

But as his senses connected, he saw that it was Willow's eyes he was looking into. Pain shot through every part of him and his face and hands felt as though they had been plunged into lava.

But he was alive.

'I thought I'd lost you for sure.' Willow smiled down at him and gently stroked a lock of his hair between her fingers, afraid to touch any other part of him for fear of causing him pain.

'Quicksilver?' Samuel asked, his voice sounded scratchy and course. There was a *gruff* nearby, which satisfied him.

'He's fine, I'm afraid I've tied him up so that he can't lick the skin right off you. He's been terribly worried about you, we all have, but you need time to heal before you can take a good dose of his love.'

Samuel managed a feeble smile, how his face did sting.

Thanks to Samuel's actions Bruin made a speedy recovery. Samuel's recovery was far slower and a great deal more painful as his burnt skin flaked away and fresh healthy skin grew to replace it.

Daniel had persuaded his father to take Samuel into their home and with Willow's help they nursed him gradually back to health. When Samuel was fit enough to emerge into the afternoon sunlight many weeks later, the Crossways he discovered outside Daniel's front door was quite changed to the one he had known before.

'Samwell! Come see what we've been doing!' Beetle was there and gently pulled Samuel by the hand along the street.

As he walked through Crossways he saw many of the foresters mingling with the villagers there. Rowan and Flint both raised a hand in greeting as they stood chatting to a small group of young village lads, some of which Samuel recognised from having worked at the bakery in his time. Finch and Poppy, carrying baby Flake in her arms, were deep in conversation with Mr Cardell the butcher. They were pointing to the trays of meat in his window and seemed to be offering him their advice. Samuel even noticed the wizened old Bluebell who was seated outside the village clothes shop, drinking tea with the proprietor.

'Well I never!' Samuel exclaimed as Bluebell cracked her face into a grin and tossed a wink in his direction. 'Next they'll be selling her cloaks in Crossways!'

He felt like pinching himself to see if he was dreaming.

There were still signs of the destruction that had been caused the night of the fire, but it was obvious many hands had worked to clear most of it away. New homes were being built and Samuel noticed that a number of tepees had been erected to temporarily house those who had lost their homes that night.

'Where are we going, Beetle?' Samuel asked and squeezed the young lad's hand in his.

'Shhh! Samwell! Secret! You'll see soon. Close your eyes now Samwell.' Beetle sniggered.

'But how will I *see* if I have to close my eyes?' Samuel teased.

'Don't be naughty! I'll set Pipit on you!' Beetle scolded.

Samuel remembered Beetle's skunk friend well and held his tongue.

Leading him by the hand Beetle took him further down the street until they came at last to a halt.

Samuel had promised not to peek but his senses told him that there were many people assembled before him.

'Open now, Samwell! See what we've done for you.' Beetle stepped away and stood with the rest of the silent gathering.

Samuel found himself before a pretty little building. At first he didn't recognise it and thought it brand new, but there were signs that it had been there for some time when he looked closer. Ivy wound its way around the front of the building and twisted lushly above the windows. The newly cleared pathway that led from the gate to the front steps showed signs of wear where many feet had tracked up and down the old stones a long time ago. Casting a look over the gathered crowd Samuel once again was amazed to see the intermingling of familiar faces; foresters and Crossways people standing shoulder to shoulder, looked back at him. Willow was there; she stepped forward from the crowd and took hold of Samuel's hand.

It was the old village school. The same unused school that his mother had looked at so longingly as it had fallen further and further into disrepair.

'Go on inside Samuel, have a look around.' Beetle coaxed.

The sound of children's voices filtered out of the open windows as Samuel walked slowly up the path and took the three steps up to the newly hung front door and stepped inside.

'This room will be for the adults, those who want to learn about our ways.' Willow gestured to the empty room on the left. Tables and chairs were neatly laid out awaiting a class of students.

'And this is for the children.' Willow opened the door to the other room in the small school. As Samuel stepped in, the group of children who had been sounding out their ABC's turned around in their seats to look at him.

'Samuel! So, so, *so* good to see you!' Fern was standing up at the front of the class and Samuel realised that he had been the one leading the children in their lessons. Carefully, Fern laid the book he had been holding on the big table in front of him. He ran down the aisle between the school desks and threw himself into Samuel's arms, hugging him tightly.

'Steady, steady.' Samuel winced a little at the onslaught but couldn't have been happier to see him.

'I hope you don't mind Fern starting off with the little ones? I took real good care of your Mama's book.' Fern gestured to the book he had been reading from.

'I think it's wonderful, Fern; you're a teacher!' Samuel hugged him back.

'Only for a little while 'til Samuel got better, now it's your turn to teach and Fern's turn to learn, learn, learn!'

Samuel allowed himself to be pulled to the front of the class where Fern placed Lily's book in his hands before taking a seat of his own at an empty table. Beetle ran over to take the seat by Fern's side, the two youngsters grinned widely at each other; Samuel could sense that a bond had grown between the two of them during the time of his recovery.

There were many empty seats in the class, but it was a start, a wonderful and unexpected start. It was then that

Samuel spotted Bruin sitting at the very back of the class, his eldest granddaughter seated on his knee.

'Hope you don't mind me sitting in on your first lesson, lad, but I need to make sure you know what you're doing if you're going to be teaching my grandchildren.' Bruin sent the thought to Samuel and grinned, tears of gratitude standing in his eyes.

Samuel didn't trust himself to respond. He looked down at his mother's book and struggled to compose himself.

You're still here Mama; I know that now for sure. This is for you.

Samuel lifted his head, smiled at Willow, and began to teach.

Just the Beginning

The village of Crossways was a village split down the middle. Many chose to continue doing things in the way they always had, but there were enough listening to the foresters; enough sending their children to the school and attending it themselves to start making a difference.

The few who came with bad intentions to the newly refurbished school, to learn how to harness the gift for unworthy purposes, left again soon after, having neither the patience to learn nor the skills to control their potential. But there were others; good people, who wanted to learn better ways and whose hearts were purer. Their ears were unsullied by the stories of evil magic and the untruths told by those too lazy, jealous or afraid to try for themselves. Soon these 'outsiders' learned how to use their gift; hunting successfully and respectfully in the forest, replanting to replace the trees, which they took to build and heat their homes, helping the foresters to clear the filth from the river and learning how to keep it clean.

Samuel taught at the school and helped in Crossways to spread the word to those who would hear it. At first, there were many who would curse Samuel and the other foresters openly in the street, but as more listened and saw the benefits of employing the forest ways, these unwelcome encounters became unusual.

Bruin began to teach the adult outsiders who came along to learn about the different facets of the gift. He even led small parties of Crossways villagers, those whom he had learned to trust, deep into the forest in order to show them his hunting skills and teach them the secrets of the plants and animals. He showed them all he knew about surviving in the great forest and, through his enthusiasm, their respect for it grew and grew.

Samuel had come face to face with Mr Sanderson one day in the middle of Crossways Main Street. The pair had eyed one another, Mr Sanderson's face turning purple with rage. Slipping into his thoughts Samuel saw what Mr Sanderson would like to do to him. This insolent young 'freak' had burned down his business and now had the cheek to return and all but take over his village! Quicksilver must also have sensed the baker's intentions because he moved protectively between Samuel and his obese former employer.

'One day that creature won't be around to look after you!' Mr Sanderson had spat the words out whilst wagging a plump sausage of a finger in front of Samuel. 'I know what you did, even if I can't prove it, but mark my words you little creep; you'll pay for what you did! Oh yes, one day, you *will* pay.'

'Quicksilver and I are inseparable, Mr Sanderson, he's

always around to protect me. Perhaps you should get yourself an animal companion, the company would do you good and the exercise you'd get wouldn't do you any harm either.' Samuel grinned at the baker.

Mr Sanderson's eyes bulged dangerously, Samuel had struggled to hold in his laughter. The baker shuffled off in the opposite direction, as fast as his fat little legs would permit, muttering obscenities under his breath.

Word travelled. Stories of how the inhabitants of Crossways had become 'soft in the head' and gone all 'primitive' in their ways, soon reached the ears of other outsiders living in towns further away. Many travelled to see if the tales were true. Had wild folks come out of the forest to pass on their magic? What they found when they got to Crossways was a village that was healthier, more prosperous and cleaner than it had ever been before. In many cases a village that looked, smelled and worked better than their own. The school needed more seats, more desks, and more teachers as the demand to learn escalated steadily.

It's working, it's really working. Samuel thought to Quicksilver as he peeked through the door of Bruin's classroom one day.

The room was full; soon they would have to move to a larger building. Samuel saw many new faces, all intently listening to the lesson being taught; eyes wide in wonder as they watched

Bruin demonstrating the power of his gift as he rolled a pebble across his desk using only his mind. Samuel's eye rested on a man who was seated near the back of the class. His heart gave a sudden start as he recognised the line of the man's jaw, his dark eyes and that habit of pushing his hair back from his face. Samuel forced himself to breath more regularly as he gently brushed the man's mind with his own.

He was no longer the brash, opinionated, proud man he had once been. Samuel sensed a longing in him to be part of something, to be useful. Sifting through the man's memories Samuel came across regret and sadness. He saw in him the boy he had once been, the boy of whom so much had been expected. That boy had become a man who didn't like himself, but hadn't known how to change. But he was changing now. Samuel could sense that he was *very* different now. He was a broken man in the mending, Samuel felt; and a new man in the making.

It was his father, Samuel Cuthbert, Senior.

The time would come when Samuel would walk up to him and reveal his true identity, but not yet... not yet.

Willow appeared by his side just then.

'Everything all right?' she asked him gently with her mind and slid her hand into his.

Samuel pulled her into his arms and kissed her. 'It is now,' he replied as he took her by the hand and led her outside. 'Come on, Fern's looking after the little ones today, I need some fresh clean air and good company.'

He pulled her along as he ran, Quicksilver running alongside, his long pink tongue lolling out of the side of his mouth.

'Where are we going?' Willow called as she was swept along, laughing and waving to those they passed on their way towards the trees.

'To the special clearing, *our* special clearing of course! It's a beautiful day and the sky is blue.' Samuel laughed as he leapt over the tangled undergrowth and darted between the trees.

The Man In Green heard them coming. He was sitting high in the branches of Lily's old oak. He watched the young couple dancing and leaping around like newborn deer but when they fell into each other's arms and snuggled down into the lush green grass together he felt that it was time for him to move on to another part of the forest.

'Ah well, life goes on.' he smiled to himself, jumped down from his branch and with a nod of his leafy head, slipped silently into the woods.